A NEW DAWN

THE LION'S DEN SERIES BOOK 2

EOIN DEMPSEY

This book is for my sister, Orla.

1

Berlin: January 30, 1933

Bruno Kurth waited for the tram to pass, then shuffled across the street at the Hardenbergstrasse intersection. The winter rain had come suddenly, catching him unawares and making it a priority to find a spot beneath the tram overpass before it was too late. If his military-issue overcoat became soaked through, he had no way of getting dry. A drenching could lead to hypothermia and death in this icy wind, even during the daytime. Thankfully, January's rains hadn't yet turned to snow, but he knew there was worse to come, and many homeless would die of the cold before spring.

He reached the underpass just before the rain became a deluge.

A man he had a passing acquaintance with had already secured his own place on the sheltered pavement. A sign indicating his war service to the Reich was scrawled on cardboard and laid out in front of him. A bowl beside it held a few pfennigs. Enough for a meal, and perhaps a beer afterward.

The best begging spots were filling up, but Bruno found a

place at the edge and took his own sign and bowl out of his backpack. He wrote the sign a few months before, but it was still good. It had taken a while to learn to write with his remaining left hand, but he mastered it in the end—enough for his writing to be legible, anyway.

LOYAL VETERAN OF THE WESTERN FRONT.
PLEASE GIVE SO I CAN EAT TODAY.

He laid it down in front of him, along with the bowl, sat down, and waited. Out in the street, pedestrians were running for cover.

A young well-dressed couple with a child ducked in out of the downpour to stand in front of him, peering out at the traffic through the sheets of freezing rain. The child—a girl, perhaps eight years old or so—turned around to peek at him, still clutching to the safety of her father's hand. Bruno waved to her, smiling though his thick beard with his mouth closed, wary of the strong smell of whiskey off his breath. He drew comfort from the fact that the bottle, in his back pocket, was still half-full. He'd take a swig when the people left. It didn't look good to drink in front of them—they'd think that was all he spent the charity on.

The little girl vanished behind her father's leg, only to reappear a few seconds later. Bruno winked at her with his one eye. She was staring at his eye patch and the jutted, scarred skin that layered the side of his face. The kids always did. He put his one hand over his one eye and played peekaboo with her for a few seconds. She ducked behind her father's leg again with a smile. The jarring of his leg seemed to gain her father's attention, and he whirled around to glare at Bruno.

"I fought for this country. Gave my health and well-being for the Reich. Can you help me, please?"

The man, clean-shaven and dressed in an expensive coat,

shook his head. "You ought to be ashamed of yourself," he said. "Do you think I sit around asking for handouts? You think I want to go to work every day to support my family?"

"I was on the battlefield when you were still in short pants. I saw my best friends die in a pool of mud, gasping for air, calling out for their mothers. What right have you to call me a disgrace?"

Bruno forgot himself. He was usually able to resist rising to the barbs, but the look on this man's face set something off inside him. "All I ask of you is a few coins from your pocket—nothing you can't afford."

"How do I know you're not going to spend it on booze? You reek of it."

"I spend whatever I get on sustaining myself, on keeping myself alive for one more day. There's little help for me apart from what people like you give me."

The whole family was staring at him now; the man's wife nudged him, and her husband reached into his pocket. A few coins jingled in Bruno's bowl. Perhaps enough for a cup of coffee.

"Thank you," Bruno said.

That was it. The man took his wife and daughter down to the other end of the underpass to wait out the rain. Bruno took a dirty finger and pressed down on the coins in the bowl, swirling them around, knocking one against another. Some people thanked him for his service. Didn't he deserve as much? He thought back to the over-zealous idiot he'd been. The fresh-faced young man who joined the army on his eighteenth birthday to serve the Kaiser seemed as dead as those he left behind on the battlefield.

Another man, older than the last, stepped in front of him to escape the rain. Bruno rattled the bowl to attract his attention, but received nothing other than a sniff and a grimace. At only ten o'clock in the morning, a long day lay ahead.

Darkness descended on the city like a cloak before the clock in the store window across the street struck five. Bruno stood up, his tired joints screaming. He shouldered his backpack and set off. The other homeless veteran at the other end of the underpass was still there and greeted him with a nod as Bruno shuffled past. He didn't stop to talk.

There was a decision to make—a warm hostel for the night, or a bottle to comfort him as he lay down on a ratty old mattress in the freezing abandoned apartment he shared with a half-dozen other men? He let the coins drop from his hand into the pocket of his overcoat. The jingling sound they made reassured him as he headed toward the liquor store on the corner. The bottle he had at the start of the day was gone. He drank most of it with the sandwich he had for lunch.

The man behind the counter recognized him and turned to pick up a bottle of whiskey before Bruno had even to ask. "Good day today, Bruno?" he asked.

"Not bad. I would rather have spent it doing something else, but not the worst I've had."

He reached into his pocket for the coins and spilled them out on the counter. The shopkeeper waited as he counted them out.

"You want a sandwich too? I have some leftover from this morning. Should still be fresh." He put two white bread sandwiches in a paper bag and placed them on the glass counter. "Seems like you have some money left for breakfast tomorrow morning."

Bruno smiled. "Perhaps. Thank you."

He waited until he was around the corner from the grocery store to unscrew the cap from the bottle for a swig. The amber liquid burned his throat on the way down, warming his belly and reinvigorating his tired limbs. He couldn't stop at just one gulp—he paused a few steps later to take another. The bottle was half drunk by the time he reached the apartment building. Some of the upper floors still housed paying tenants, though they must have been some of the poorest in the city. The lower floors, with broken windows and kicked-down doors, were for him and his kind. Several men, all wearing their military coats, were lounging on filthy mattresses as he entered.

He trudged toward his spot in the corner, took the backpack off his shoulders and put it down beside his mattress. It felt good to sit down. He rested against the wall, reaching into the brown paper bags for one of the ham sandwiches. He finished it in seconds before going for the bottle once more. He fell into a trance, not moving for a few minutes, his only thoughts of the whiskey in his hand.

Twenty minutes of lying on the flea-bitten old mattress was enough for the cold to take hold of his body. He wrapped his one remaining arm around himself the best he could and curled into a ball. His teeth were chattering and sounded like a woodpecker inside his head.

"Here..." Ludwig, a veteran of the ill-fated attack on Verdun, reached across and handed him an old newspaper. "This'll keep you warm."

"Thanks," Kurth said. He spread some of the paper across himself, deciding to look through the rest. It was yellowed and covered in dirt. He wiped it off with his fingers, thankful for something to read.

The paper was from the middle of November—over two months old—and the big story was the aftermath of November's elections. Hitler was trying to jockey for position, asking to be made chancellor while refusing to compromise with the other elected parties. Bruno scanned the other pages for more interesting subjects. He liked a good story, though he never was the studious type. He left school at twelve to work on his father's farm, and then joined his three older brothers in the

Wehrmacht on his eighteenth birthday, back in '15. He was the only one who made it back, and his father never forgave him for that. With no family, no work, and nightmares of the war haunting his every waking moment, there seemed no other recourse but to join the other veterans on the street. The bottle was his only family now. His father was likely long dead.

A headline beneath the picture of a middle-aged man in an army uniform caught his eye. Kurth recognized him as the man who owned the building above the basement he slept in for a few months before he came here. They never spoke, but he saw him around enough times to recognize the picture.

The headline read: *Industrialist's son still missing.* He dropped his gaze to read the text below.

OTTO MILCH, THE FATHER OF ERNST MILCH, WHOSE DISAPPEARANCE HAS BAFFLED LOCAL POLICE, HAS VOWED NOT TO GIVE UP THE SEARCH UNTIL HIS SON IS FOUND. HERR MILCH, THE PRESIDENT OF MILCH INDUSTRIES, GAVE A PRESS CONFERENCE YESTERDAY, APPEALING FOR HELP IN FINDING HIS SON, WHO DISAPPEARED ON THE NIGHT OF NOVEMBER 16. ERNST MILCH'S WIFE AND TWO CHILDREN WERE ALSO PRESENT AT THE PRESS CONFERENCE AND PLEADED FOR ANY HELP THE PUBLIC COULD OFFER. THE MILCH FAMILY HAS OFFERED A SUBSTANTIAL REWARD FOR ANY INFORMATION LEADING TO THE DISCOVERY OF ERNST MILCH OR THE ARREST OF THOSE INVOLVED IN ANY FOUL PLAY. SOME SOURCES WITHIN THE NATIONAL SOCIALIST PARTY HAVE BLAMED HIS DISAPPEARANCE ON LOCAL COMMUNIST ELEMENTS, BUT HAVE NOT PRESENTED EVIDENCE TO BACK UP THEIR CLAIMS. ERNST MILCH, A DECORATED ARMY OFFICER AND AN ACTIVE MEMBER OF THE NAZI PARTY, WAS LAST SEEN LEAVING HIS FAMILY HOME ON THE EVENING OF NOVEMBER 16. IT IS UNCLEAR WHERE HE WAS HEADED, THOUGH THE POLICE HAVE SUGGESTED HE MAY HAVE MET AN UNKNOWN PARTY AT AN APARTMENT HE OWNED ON WÜRZBURGER STRASSE IN THE NOLLENDORFKIEZ AREA OF BERLIN.

A light flickered on in the dark recesses of Bruno's mind.

The basement. He'd been staying in that area then...in the basement of that empty building on Würzburger Strasse. It was hard to reach into his mind to separate one night from the other. He took another sip from the bottle of whiskey on the ground beside him.

He was there that night. Yes. It was hard to say what date it might have been, but he was there in the basement when the man in the suit—and the pretty girl he'd seen in the building before—came down the stairs carrying a rolled-up rug in the half-light. It wasn't hard to remember their faces. He might have been drunk, but he wasn't stupid and left with the dead man's money in his pocket.

He'd put it behind him. Another rich man murdered wasn't his problem—it was theirs, and their society, not his. He was locked out years ago. A hefty reward might be his ticket back in, and would certainly jog the memories he'd neglected these last few weeks. Would a man like Otto Milch take the word of a homeless man? He remembered the look the man carrying the rug had given him, and the panic in the woman's eyes. Things were becoming clearer in his mind now. The haze of memory was beginning to shift.

He brought the newspaper up to his eyes again. The words on the page were clear—there was a reward. The missing man's father was head of Milch Industries. A rush of adrenaline charged through Bruno's veins. *This could change my life!* It didn't say how much the reward would be, but surely enough to rent an apartment of his own. Enough to make a fresh start and put the past behind him.

Then a horrible thought emerged in his mind. Was the case solved? Was he too late? He cursed himself for not following the news. He raised himself to his feet and approached two men playing cards by candlelight, demanding an answer to the status of the case. They had no idea what he was talking about, and neither did the others at the end of the room. The men there were more concerned with staying alive than keeping up to date with current events. Citizens on the street had the luxury of focusing on things they could not.

Bruno still had the bottle in his hand. He knew he couldn't leave it there, so he stuffed it into the deep pocket of his coat and made for the door. His other stuff would be safe. No one in the squat would be concerned with his begging bowl and cardboard sign, but the whiskey would stay with him. The temperature outside had dropped several degrees, and his breath plumed out in front of him like tiny clouds in the darkness. The streetlight outside the crumbling residential block was broken, so he guided himself by the light coming from the apartments on either side of the street. The stars above were obscured by clouds; he never looked up at them anyway. His eyes were permanently fixed on the pavement. The stars may as well not have been there.

The newspaper stand on the corner was still open. Bruno waited a few seconds for a customer to leave, not wanting to anger the newsie behind the counter by scaring anyone away. The fear that he saw in others' eyes as they beheld him was real, even though he'd never hurt anyone except in service of the Kaiser. The mere sight of his scars, his missing arm, and eyepatch was enough to render most people disgusted. They talked about the smell too, but he didn't notice that anymore. The customer gone, he drifted over to the newsstand. The newsie was about fifteen and wearing a flat cap. A familiar look of fear distorted his face as he saw Bruno.

"Get out of here," the boy said.

"I don't mean you any harm."

"Then what do you want?"

There was no one else around. The newsie must have figured Bruno meant to rob the day's takings. But that was the furthest thing from his mind. "I want to see today's newspaper."

The young boy, most likely new, seemed to calm down. He

would soon get used to the neighborhood, and perhaps wouldn't be so nervous when one of the men from the squat approached him next time. He waited until Bruno pressed a coin down on the counter to reach back for a newspaper.

"You been doing this long?" the older man asked.

"A while. Only been on this block a few weeks."

Bruno thought to offer him some words of advice, but knew how he'd take it, so he decided not to bother. Instead, he stood back to read the paper as the young newsie cleaned up. His eyes skipped past the top stories of the tug-of-war between Hitler, Papen, and Hindenburg over who was to be the latest in a long line of chancellors. What difference did such things mean to the likes of him? None of them cared about his kind. Nothing on the front page. He expected as much. It took him a few minutes to leaf through all the pages. There was no mention of Ernst Milch anywhere. No upcoming trial, no suspects, nothing. Bruno folded the newspaper under his arm and approached the counter again.

"You remember a story from a few weeks ago about a gentleman by the name of Ernst Milch?"

"Yeah, sure," the boy said as he wiped down the counter. Bruno made sure to stand back so as not to dirty it again. "I read about that. He was a Nazi, the son of some rich guy."

"Did they ever find him?"

"No." The boy dropped out of sight below the counter.

"Do they think he was murdered?"

The boy's head appeared over the counter. "Why are you so interested?"

"The man was Wehrmacht, just like me," Bruno said, tapping on the insignia on his chest. "We look after our own."

The boy looked at him for a few seconds, seeming like he would question who exactly was concerned about Bruno and the other homeless veterans, but instead he said, "The Nazis blame the Communists for his disappearance."

"What about Milch's father, and the reward?"

The boy's eyes widened. "You know something?"

"No, I was just curious."

"If you saw something—"

"I didn't see anything. Why would I be asking six weeks after if I did?"

The newsie didn't seem to accept his logic. The quizzical look on his face remained. Bruno almost asked him if he knew how to get a hold of Herr Milch, but decided it was time to leave and walked away without another word.

"Hey, anytime," the kid said as Bruno walked away. "You come back and see me if you remember anything. Anything at all."

Bruno didn't answer, just pulled the lapels of his thick coat over his jaw one at a time in an attempt to stave off the night's biting cold. Waiting until he was around the corner, he reached into his pocket for the bottle and took a swig. It felt good. He was tired, but his curiosity got the better of him. Sleep could wait.

He reached the squat and continued past. It was about a fifteen-minute walk to Würzburger Strasse. The people he passed on the street gave him a wide berth, but it was nothing he wasn't used to. He kept on along Augsburger Strasse until the turn onto Würzburger Strasse came into view. The café on the corner was closed for the night, and the street was largely dead. Only a few lights on in the windows served to show any sign of life. It had been weeks since he was here. After the couple with the rolled carpet spooked him, he moved on. He used the money the man had given him to stay in a warm hostel for a few nights.

He made his way down the quiet street. A car's headlights shone from behind him. The driver pulled down his window and shouted something at him, but Bruno kept walking. He looked over his shoulder to make sure the car didn't stop, ready to run. He knew friends who'd been beaten within an inch of their lives for the crime of being homeless and in the wrong place at the wrong time. Men were killed for it. The car turned the corner and kept driving. He let out a sigh of relief and got back to the business of trying to earn that reward.

The alley at the end of the block came into view, and he glanced around before proceeding. He half-expected to see homeless people littering the pavement, but it was too cold to be outdoors at this time of year. Sleeping rough meant death in the January cold, so the alleyway was empty. He made his way around the back of the building, looking for the familiarity of the one black door he'd been able to open. It was difficult to make out in the dark. It would be easier in the daytime, but there might be prying eyes, and he didn't want anyone else to steal his reward money. Finally he came upon the door, feeling for the scratches around the lock with the tips of his fingers. There were no lights on in the building above it. The door was locked, but he remembered being able to get it open. He reached into his pocket for his knife and slid it under the lock. The door opened to reveal the darkness of the basement.

Bruno wondered if the family had rented the apartments out after Ernst Milch's disappearance, or if they intended to leave it empty in the hope that he might return.

He looked around one more time before pushing through the door. He felt around for a light switch. One bulb illuminated the room enough that he could make out the bike in the corner, the boxes against the wall, and the stairs leading up. The scene came into sharp focus in his mind.

"This is where they carried the body down the stairs," he said. He went to the stairwell, feeling scuff on the walls where the rug had left a mark. Had the police missed this, or just ignored it? He got down on his hands and knees, looking for anything—a clue as to the identity of the couple who carried the carpet. He found nothing.

He sat on the box in the corner, where he was when the man and the girl came down the stairs. He could see the man's face in his mind and thought he'd even be able to pick him out of a crowd. Someone in his line of business never forgot a person who gave them money—especially a lot of money. He and the pretty woman with brown hair murdered Ernst Milch and brought him down these stairs to the street to dispose of the body. He was sure of it. Bruno was the only witness, and the only person who could claim the reward Otto Milch was offering. He'd been waiting for some miracle to save him from the pit he'd fallen into. This was it.

Where did they take the body from here? Why had they killed him? *Irrelevant. All that matters is the reward money.* Ernst Milch was a Nazi, and Bruno had seen them goose-stepping along the street in their brown uniforms, toting those strange flags. But that didn't make any difference to him. Governments had come and gone almost with the seasons since the war, but nothing had changed for him and the other men on the street. He heard the Nazi talk about the veterans, but they never did anything for him. They never actually followed through on their promises to help those who served the Reich they cherished so much. They seemed more interested in using veterans as a talking point—a prop to get their message across. He and his homeless patriots knew they were alone. No one was coming to rescue them. Few would have the chance that he had now to make good after more than fourteen years living on the street.

He went back to the door and popped his head outside again to make sure he was alone. The alleyway was still deserted. The only sound was of an occasional car rumbling along in the distance. He returned to the basement, still looking around for anything he might have missed. Finding nothing, he climbed the stairs, which led up to a wine-colored door on the first floor.

This must have been where they killed him. Then, they wrapped him up in the rug and carried him down the steps to the car, and got rid of the body somewhere. Probably in the Grunewald or Spandauer forests. Plenty of places to choose from outside the city.

He knew it wasn't a good idea, but he took a pull from the bottle of whiskey. He tried to imagine who Milch was, and why two clean-cut people would kill him. He likely had it coming. Perhaps it was self-defense. That would be for the police to sort out. The face of the man he saw carrying the rug down the stairs drifted into his mind. He tried to hold onto the image of it, to stop it slipping away like water through his fingers. Who was that man? Would Bruno's testimony be enough for him to feel the executioner's blade? Why did he kill Milch? For money? He and the girl didn't look like gangsters—he almost felt bad for them. Yet the prospect of a reward, and the new life it would bring, was too much to pass up. No attack of conscience about being a rat was going to stop him from claiming what was his.

He walked back down the stairs, to the basement. Taking one last look around, he walked over to the exit. Once outside, he closed the door behind him, only then realizing the problem of locking it once more. He took the knife from his pocket and tried to pick the lock to turn the deadbolt. It didn't work, and two minutes later, he decided that being caught trying to lock the door was more dangerous than leaving the basement unlocked, and set off.

What to do next? Should he go to the police? What was the point? They'd never listen. He'd do well to get into the station house. It was a strange thing to be dismissed by society, to be stripped of the notion that you might be useful or trustworthy. It was almost like being a child again, albeit one no one cared for. How could he find Otto Milch? Perhaps Herr Milch would want to hear his account directly? He heard of rich men like him circumventing the regular paths of justice, and if the killers were going to face the axman anyway, what would be the difference? Going to Herr Milch could negate the need to testify in court—something he didn't relish. He wanted to stay out of it: Tell Milch what he saw, get his reward money, and go.

What would he do with the money? Stay in the city? No. He'd go back to Tauche and buy a little farmhouse. Perhaps get some chickens and eat fresh eggs every day. He probably still had cousins there. What would it be to have a place of his own —not to have to worry about where you'd rest your head at the end of the day? The dignity that the war had robbed him of could be restored. All he needed to find out was how and where to find Otto Milch. The hard part would be getting someone to listen to him, but that worry was for another time.

He left Würzburger Strasse behind and walked for a few minutes until he came upon a lively tavern. Loud jazz music boomed through the windows. He stopped to look inside and saw it packed with young men and women dancing and drinking beer. He took a sip from the now almost-empty bottle in his pocket. He stood there for a minute or two until several patrons emerged through the door, shouting at him to move on. He did as they asked without arguing and made his way back to the squat.

The eight men he shared it with were all asleep, and he tiptoed between them, trying not to wake anyone up. He settled down on his mattress and finished the rest of his whiskey. Images of the war flickered in his mind and he was back in the trenches again. The smell of cordite, of rotting sandbags, of stagnant mud and poison gas lingered in his nostrils, though the stench of where he was sleeping was far different. He could feel rats crawling across his body and hear artillery shells whistling overhead. He thought about the shell that landed in the trench beside him that took his arm and his eye and left him deformed. The same one that killed Eric and Julius as they sat eating their lunch beside him on a sunny afternoon in April. It took a few minutes to dismiss the memories that swirled around him. He had other things to focus on now. For the first time in as long as he could remember, hope swelled in his heart.

2

Saturday, February 11

Lisa Geisinger slipped into her wedding dress, marveling at the feel of silk against her skin. It was created of stunning white lace, embroidered with floral patterns all the way down to the long white train. Maureen Ritter, her would-be stepdaughter, smiled beside her. Lisa hugged the seventeen-year-old, Seamus's oldest child.

"You look so beautiful," the young girl said.

"So do you, but we're not quite done yet." Lisa brought her to the mirror. "I don't trust anyone else to do this."

The hairdresser had pinned flowers in her soft brown hair, but she sent the makeup woman away and now set to finish applying Maureen's lipstick and eyeliner. It was hard to comprehend standing in a dress this expensive when a few months ago, she and her mother were living in a hovel in Kreuzberg. Now they lived in a mansion in Charlottenburg, and her fiancée, Seamus Ritter, was able to spend six months' salary on a dress that would only be worn once. *And why not?* She reassured herself that she deserved this. Saying it over and over in her mind seemed to have some effect.

She threw Maureen a bright smile after she finished her makeup. "How do I look?"

"You're the most beautiful bride I've ever seen," Maureen replied seriously.

"Not as lovely as you. I know I'm officially going to be your stepmother now, but I can't see bossing you around. I was thinking... I never had a sister."

"That sounds perfect!"

They hugged again. Maureen broke away and sat on the bed as Lisa finished her makeup.

"Are you sure you want to marry my dad? You could just move in and be my sister anyway, couldn't you?"

Lisa didn't react to the joke, didn't even crack a smile. "I've never been surer of anything in my life. And besides, I think it'd be a little awkward if I moved into the house after leaving your father at the altar. I think he'd have something to say about that."

"I suppose so."

"Please try not to be angry at him. Just for today, at least. He's been trying so hard. I know we haven't seen him as much as we'd like these last few weeks, but the work he does at the factory is for the family, to make sure we have everything we need."

"It just seems like he's avoiding us again—just like he did back in America. We're over here living in this huge house, and he has this big important job now, but sometimes it seems like nothing's changed."

"Give him some time. He has to sort out the mess Uncle Helmut left. The old man was great, but his bookkeeping wasn't all it should have been. Be patient. We have a wonderful life. Be thankful." She came over to where Maureen was sitting on the bed. "And enjoy the wedding. This is the best day of my life,

apart from when Hannah was born. I want you to be happy
with me."

"I am happy. For you, for my dad, all of us. All of our new
family."

Lisa kissed her on the cheek before going back to the mirror
to pin on her veil.

Maureen excused herself to use the bathroom, leaving the
bride alone. Lisa's thoughts inevitably turned to Ernst Milch
and the secret that would bond her and Seamus forever. Every
day seemed like a bonus. Perhaps one morning, she'd wake and
not see Milch's dead face, but that day hadn't come yet. It
seemed like she'd never be free of him. The police investigation
seemed to have come up against a brick wall. They hadn't come
to call to the house in weeks, and Otto Milch had gone silent
too. No more press conferences or posters pinned up across
town, offering a reward for any information about his missing
son. She never found out who had talked to the police at the
club, or who had furnished them with the photograph of her
and Milch from when she first met him. What did it matter
now? Her time there was done. Her focus had to be on her
family now. Her mother was likely going to need some form of
care, and wouldn't be able to help with Hannah any longer.

Her nights of dancing on stage appeared to be behind her.
She'd miss the thrill of performing, the glamor of the makeup,
and the extravagant outfits, along with the music and the
feeling of being part of something extraordinary. She'd miss
the thrill of doing what she loved in front of an expectant
crowd. But she wasn't unhappy to lose the leering men and the
catcalls. No more being pulled onto strangers' laps, as if she
were a piece of meat, or being treated as less than human by
sexist, married managers who expected to be able to use her
and the other girls. She'd miss her friends, but she was to be
married now, and her priorities had changed.

Still, she felt marred—even on this day—by what happened

in that apartment on Würzburger Strasse back in November. They likely had Maureen to thank for their freedom. Had she told the truth, Lisa might have been behind bars, or awaiting the executioner's axe. Dragging the rest of the family into her mess was the last thing she wanted, but that's what it felt like happened.

Seamus had spoken little of Ernst Milch since, except to thank Maureen for telling the police he and Lisa had been home all evening.

After that day, he threw himself into his new position as head of the factory, undoubtedly to make a good impression on his new employees and to honor the promises he made to Uncle Helmut, who left it to him upon his death. But was there another reason? Was he trying to escape, to keep himself occupied so as not to get caught in the snares of his own mind? Whatever it was, he wasn't talking. Lisa had spent as much time with her future stepchildren as her future husband these last few months.

Maureen came back into the room. Lisa wanted to thank her again for what she did, but knew this wasn't the place or time.

A knock on the door interrupted her thoughts. Greta, one of her dancer friends from the nightclub, stuck her head around. "Are you ready? They're waiting for us. You've got a man to marry."

"Nearly there," Lisa replied, adjusting her veil one last time.

"Look who I have with me," Greta said. She pushed through the door to reveal Hannah, dressed in a white dress and carrying a basket of flowers. Lisa rushed over to pick up her three-year-old daughter. She was so different from her biological father, Ernst Milch, the man Lisa killed to defend herself less than three months before.

"Oh, you look so pretty,"

"So do you, Mama."

"I do? Well, thank you, my darling. As long as you think so, that's all that matters to me."

"Ready to go?" Maureen asked.

"It's time," Lisa said.

Greta clapped and jumped up and down. Her joy and excitement were infectious, and all four left with bright smiles on their faces.

Maureen was first into the church. Her father's fiancée had included her in every part of the wedding planning. With little interest, her father claimed to be too busy with the factory, but she reveled in helping the bride-to-be organize the church and the venue for the reception. For a while, it had even taken her mind off the strange times they were living in. And they were strange times. Dark times.

Less than two weeks ago, when she and Lisa were out picking up the dresses together, they saw a teary-eyed Adolf Hitler addressing a crowd of supporters outside the presidential palace. They stood and watched for a few minutes as he proclaimed his joy at being named chancellor of the republic he'd sworn to destroy.

It was hard to comprehend how it happened, but Lisa comforted Maureen with the fact that many chancellors and governments had come and gone since the war. Despite the proclamations of the small band of Nazis gathered to greet their leader, there was little reason to think this would prove any different than the many short-lived governments that went before them. The general populace seemed to greet the coming of these so-called *revolutionaries* with a shrug. Few of Maureen's classmates, or even her teachers, seemed to care. When Maureen broached the topic of the new chancellor with her favorite teacher, Herr Groening, the old man told her to ignore the ridiculous fantasies the Brownshirts espoused and wait for the next election, when sanity would surely be restored.

Still, Maureen remained unconvinced. Something about what was happening felt permanent. Perhaps it was because she was foreign and unused to snap elections and fragile coalitions that crumbled and were rebuilt with the seasons, but she wasn't able to shake the unease that gripped her all week. It was something similar to the disquiet that both Lisa and her father grappled with in the days and weeks before and after the visit from the police detective back in November.

Maureen's father was at the altar, dressed in a new suit, as she moved into the nave. Lisa's friends from the club were there in the church pews, glamorous and gorgeous in their fur coats. Many workers from the factory attended, along with the circle of Seamus's journalist friends. Still, Maeve and the girls hadn't been able to travel from America, and the occasion felt emptier for that. Her father's cousin and business partner, Helga, was the only family member present. She was sitting alone at the front, dressed in an expensive-looking black dress.

Her father held out a hand to Maureen as she reached the front of the church. "I'm so proud of you."

He took her hand in his. Her father wasn't perfect—far from it—but he deserved this. It wasn't any kind of betrayal to her dead mother. Lisa was a wonderful person, and Maureen was sure that whatever happened that night in November was innocent or justifiable, or both. She cursed herself for thinking about lying to that detective now, but she couldn't seem to scrub it from her brain.

Maureen's siblings—Michael, fourteen; Fiona, eleven; and Conor, eight; and her stepsister Hanna, three—looked resplendent in their new outfits. Lisa's mother Ingrid was looking after them for the day. She had her own room in the house Seamus inherited from Helmut, and seemed happy to look after the children as needed in return. Lisa wanted her mother with her, and Seamus grew to appreciate, and even love her. The children loved her too. Their joyous eyes reflected the hope that coming to Berlin had restored in them.

Their father had been forgiven for his past trespasses of leaving them in Aunt Maeve's house in Newark for two years, and reinstated in his previous position as their hero once more. *I just wish I shared their naïve trust in his strength*, she thought as she took her place at the side of the altar. Clayton Thomas, the young American journalist they met on the boat trip over, nodded to her from his position at her father's side. It was funny to have someone you'd only known a few months as best man, but that was the nature of being strangers here in their new adopted home, their roots not yet sunk into the soil. It was either a splendid unique opportunity to start over, or a soulless life with no one who knew them. It all depended on the day... and one's mood.

Greta ambled down the aisle as second bridesmaid and took her place beside Maureen. Then came the bride, and the whole crowd stood to greet her. She beamed as she made her way to the altar, never taking her eyes off Seamus Ritter, who looked happier than he'd ever been in Maureen's memory. Fiona was crying, with great big joyous tears running down her cheeks. The world outside might as well have been a million miles away. It seemed like years of pain had led to this, and nothing could check the joy of that moment.

It was hard to find even a minute to be alone, but Seamus took a few seconds on the balcony to examine the new wedding ring on his finger. His feelings for Lisa were so strong, he felt like a balloon, overstretched with love so he was about to burst. He never thought he'd find a woman again, let alone fall head over heels and get married.

The view from the balcony stretched over the city, the Reichstag bulging out from among the other smaller buildings. The sun was fading, the air darkening by the moment. He briefly thought about his late wife Marie. Today didn't feel like a betrayal, just a goodbye. He remembered the beautiful Irish girl he'd met when he was seventeen, and how he fell for her in moments. Now, he wanted to talk to her—to ask her for guidance, for approval, but the time for that was done. His life with Lisa was beginning. A bright new chapter with the most beautiful and determined woman he'd ever known. Marie would live on in his children, and their children, her influence never waning. He took one last look at the ring on his finger. It fit into the indentation the last one had left in its wake.

"Goodbye, Marie," he said and made his way back into the ballroom. He got a beer at the bar, stopping for a few seconds to talk to Gert Bernheim, his factory manager, and his wife Lil. They greeted him with warm smiles, but Seamus had little time to speak. He made his excuses, promising to talk to them later, before returning to his bride at the head table. A hundred guests sat below them. The employees from the factory, in their simple suits, drew a stark contrast to Lisa's glamorous friends from the nightclub. Two different worlds at his wedding. He walked past his wife and went to Hannah, took her hand, and bent down to kiss it.

"The prettiest girl in all Berlin," he said.

She giggled. He was just about to say something else when Ingrid reached over and put the little girl in her seat between Fiona and Ingrid. He took a minute to speak to his sons but was interrupted as dinner was about to be served. A small army of waiters descended on the tables carrying plates of schnitzel and sauerkraut. Seamus clinked glasses with Clayton beside him and took a sip of beer. The young journalist stood up and quieted the crowd.

"I'd like to say a few words," he said. The crowd looked up with expectant eyes. "I was there the night Seamus met Lisa," he began. "I thought I'd drag the old guy out to a nightclub on his first weekend in the country. We ended up in the Western bar, complete with cowboys twirling their lassoes. It was fitting, in a way, because I don't think Seamus had been anywhere fun like that since Jesse James was robbing banks." The crowd laughed. The young man looked down at him with a smile.

"Little did we know that he'd meet an angel that night. A beautiful young lady who'd change his life and wouldn't mind getting his cane and his pipe and slippers for him." The crowd laughed.

"I'm only eight years older than her," Seamus complained loudly, so the crowd could hear.

"Oh, my old man," Lisa said and kissed him.

The crowd reacted with cheers and raised glasses. Seamus was glad to see that Maureen and the other children were in convulsions of laughter. Fiona especially looked like she was about to burst.

Clayton waited for the crowd to settle before continuing.

"I want to thank Seamus for making me his best man today. It's been my privilege to get to know these two wonderful people. And to Lisa, the beautiful bride you see before you today, I give the highest compliment of which I am capable: Lisa, you deserve him. You deserve someone as loyal, brave, hardworking, and loving as the man you now call your husband. Seamus, you've endured war, upheaval, tragic loss. You've seen the hardest times, and yet, you sit here today among these splendid people, married to this wonderful woman. Your children are thriving, and your family has grown to include little Hannah, whose eyes swell with love every time she sees you. This day is the culmination of your triumph over adversity, my friend, and it's my sincere honor to share it with you."

Seamus stood up to embrace his friend as the crowd erupted into applause. Lisa gave him a bear hug and the children were on their feet. Maureen winked and gave him a thumbs-up. He basked in the adoration of the wedding guests for a few seconds before he took his seat once more. Then the crowd turned their collective attention to the food. Lisa put a hand on Seamus's leg, and he kissed her.

The band, made up of some of Lisa's musician friends from the Haus Vaterland, was ready to begin once dinner was over. Seamus and his new wife made their way out onto the dance floor as the rest of the crowd looked on. Maureen and Michael and the other children could only resist for so long and were soon out dancing with them. Even Helga was on the dance floor, with Hannah in her arms, tossing flower petals in the air. And then the rest of the crowd came.

Seamus watched Maureen spin around only a few feet from him. *How many years has it been since I saw her like this?* The joy in her eyes brought him back to a time before he and the world had let her down so badly. The moment seemed like a gift from time. He swore to never let anything he did extinguish the fire he saw in her.

He felt exhausted but elated as he went to the bar after almost an hour on the dance floor and ordered a beer. His jacket and tie were gone, and he took a handkerchief from his pocket to dab his forehead. Clayton was standing nearby with Hans Litten, the lawyer famous for grilling Hitler on the stand back in '31. It was said the Nazi leader was so incensed by him that he couldn't bear to hear his name brought up in his presence. The others drinking with them were journalists Clayton had introduced him to when he first arrived. Linda Murphy, Berlin correspondent for the *Chicago Daily News*, held her glass of wine up as Seamus approached with his beer.

"You throw one heck of a party, my friend," she said.

"I'm glad you're enjoying yourselves."

Arnold Muller of the *New York Post* was sipping bourbon. "We were just discussing the recent political developments. What do you make of our new chancellor, Seamus?"

"About the same as you, I imagine. I'm not a fan."

"I don't see it lasting," Arnold said. "He'll crumble like a sandcastle in a storm at the first sign of trouble."

"I don't know," Linda said. "Something feels different this time."

"Germany has become a madhouse these last two or three years," Hans Litten said. "I just hope a little patience will bring back a sense of normality once more. The Nazis are the iteration of all the insanity of recent times. The people's anger has made them blind enough to vote against their own interests."

Tom Lewis, who worked for the *Baltimore Sun*, returned from the bar with his own beer. "That's because they're desperate enough to believe the tripe the Nazis spew," he said. "I'm astonished that Hindenburg and Papen can be so naïve to think they can censure Hitler by giving him what he wants. I wish my parents treated me that way when I was a child. I could have kicked up a fuss every day and still had all the toys and candy I could ever want."

"They're counting on him to go down in flames, and for the people to come to their senses," Linda said. "I don't see it as a sound strategy. God only knows the damage that madman will do with power."

"He might not even get the chance," Arnold said, stroking his long beard. "Rumor has it that President Hindenburg won't even receive him without Papen."

"Papen's a powerful vice-chancellor?" Seamus asked.

Arnold took another sip of his drink. "Perhaps the most powerful vice-chancellor ever."

"Hitler has no interest in sharing power," Clayton said.

"Papen and the other conservatives have made a serious miscalculation."

Seamus frowned. "You don't think they'll be able to handle Hitler?"

"I think that people have underestimated him at every turn, and he's always proved them wrong."

"I tend to agree." Hans nodded. "I thought he was finished when his niece—"

"The niece he was likely sleeping with," Arnold said.

"Yes. I thought he was finished when she was found dead. I never thought he could rebound from that, but he did. Who could have predicted he'd be here after the putsch back in '23, and then going to jail? The violence he promotes? The things he says about the Jews? How can this man now be our chancellor? It defies belief."

Tom set his beer down with a bang. "This piece of political maneuvering will end so quickly that people aren't even going to remember it happened. Papen is a wily operator. Three months ago, Hindenburg was still referring to Hitler as 'the Austrian corporal,' for God's sake. There's no way he'll stand for Hitler assuming any kind of lasting power."

"They're already doing damage," Linda said. "They started cracking down on the Communists hours after Hitler took power."

"What are the odds of a civil war between the right and left?"

"I don't see it, because the Communists are braggarts," Linda said. "They talk a good game, but when it comes down it, they'll scatter. They don't have the organization or appetite for the violence the Nazis thrive on."

"This will all end soon. Hindenburg won't let Hitler carry out any of his insane policies. This could all be over by the end of Seamus's honeymoon."

"If I was going on one," Seamus said.

"No honeymoon?" Linda asked. "What happened to the spirit of romance?"

"I can't get away for long, and a weekend at Wannsee isn't as appealing at this time of year. We'll wait until summer."

"I wish I had your confidence about Hitler." Clayton lit a cigarette. "I've been investigating the background to all this, and it's no coincidence that Hitler was appointed as chancellor. The most influential forces in this country—the business interests—contrived to make it happen. They put pressure on Hindenburg and the powers that be because they thought it'd be most profitable for themselves, collectively and individually. But what if they've all underestimated Hitler too?"

"Impossible," Arnold said. "This is their country. No one knows it like they do."

"I wouldn't be so sure," Hans said.

Seamus asked, "Why do they think it'll be so profitable for them?"

"For one thing, Hitler's appointment will resolve—temporarily, at least—the Cabinet crisis paralyzing the country. For another, they figure he's a handy expedient. If he doesn't work out, they'll get rid of him. The political, industrial, and military powers are confident they can keep him and his Nazis under control and, if not, they'll dispose of him as required," Clayton said.

"Sounds easy." Linda's heavy sarcasm was clear.

"You don't think these powerful men know how to protect their own interests?" Arnold asked. "At any rate, Hitler can't really mean what he says in his speeches about the Jews, or his intention to destroy the republic, and gaining revenge for the last war."

"Why not?" Hans asked.

"It's all insane. The British and the French would destroy him," Arnold said.

"I don't know." Clayton shook his head slightly. "I spoke to a

Nazi Party spokesman on Thursday. He was so giddy with excitement, he could hardly contain himself. He told me that people don't realize what just happened. He said what's going on in Germany is no ordinary change, and parliamentary and democratic times are past. He said a new dawn has begun."

Hans took a sip of his beer. "The best thing we can do when people talk is listen to what they're saying. Their intentions are explicit. They're telling us what they intend to do."

Seamus admired the man's courage, but wasn't sure how prudent it was. "Where does that leave you?"

"What do you mean?" asked the young lawyer.

"Apparently Hitler hates you. Do you think it's time to get the next train to Paris, or anywhere out of Germany?"

"Not at all. The millions of workers in this country can't leave. So, I must stay too. If half of what that Austrian lunatic says turns out to be true, they're going to need all the legal defense they can get."

In the center of the circle, Seamus held up his glass. Now wasn't the time to question the young lawyer's incredible gallantry. "Here's to you, Hans—the bravest man I know." The other journalists joined him in the toast.

Lisa, red-faced from dancing, appeared at Seamus's shoulder. "I was wondering where you'd gotten to. I should have known you were talking politics with this crowd. Can we forget about those brown-shirted fools for one night? Hans, I haven't seen you on the dance floor all night, or you, Arnold, or any of you."

"I'd be more inclined to go out there if the floor wasn't filled with professional *artistes*," Hans said with a smile.

"You don't have to be good. You just have to enjoy it." She reached over and grabbed the young lawyer by the hand, dragging him out to dance. Clayton and Tom followed in their wake, undoubtedly lured out by the array of beautiful women. Seamus stood a few seconds, watching his new wife waltzing with Hans, who might have been the stiffest person in the room. It was impossible not to smile.

Helga was sitting with Gert and Lil Bernheim. Seamus hoped she was keeping her triumphant feelings about the ascendancy of the Nazis to herself. He decided to check in with them to make sure, moving an empty chair from a nearby table in front of them. They were talking about sales figures. Lil stood to hug him before he had the chance to sit down.

"Oh, Seamus, rescue me from this dull conversation," she said, white wine sloshing around in her glass like a raging sea. She took a sip. "They've been talking about the factory for the last hour."

"You should have come out dancing," he said.

"Tell that to Gert!"

"I danced the Ländler with you earlier," Bernheim protested.

"For about ten minutes."

"Wasn't that enough for you?"

"That's more than me," Helga said. "I never was much of a dancer."

Seamus considered responding to Helga the way his wife had earlier to Hans, but thought better of it. Some people were meant to dance to jazz music, and some were meant to sit by the floor talking about sales figures.

"Are you having a good time?" he asked.

"Very much. It seems like a long time since I've been out this late," Helga said.

Seamus marveled how his Uncle Helmut's only child was the polar opposite of the person he'd been. "Your father would have been out in the middle of the dance floor."

"Oh, yes," she replied. "He would have been out there as soon as he saw all the pretty plumage on display."

"You couldn't have dragged him off," Bernheim said.

"Can I drag you back on?" begged his wife.

"I'm talking to Helga now."

"How about me? Will I do?" Seamus asked her. "Would you trip the light fantastic with me?"

"With pleasure." She beamed.

It felt strange to leave his Jewish manager talking to his Nazi-supporting cousin, but such was the country they lived in now. Helga wasn't the only person here who voted for Hitler in the last election, and there were several who identified as Communist—the sworn enemies of the National Socialist German Workers' Party (NSDAP), or the Nazi Party. Hostilities at the wedding were confined to some slant-eyed looks or misplaced comments. If only the streets of the city were the same.

Lil was a small woman with brown curly hair. She dragged him into the center of the dance floor, right beside where Lisa and her friends were. She grabbed Seamus by the hand and he twirled her around. Her husband wasn't watching, still deep in conversation with Helga. When the song finished, Seamus escorted Lil to the bar. He ordered her another glass of wine and handed it to her while he waited for his beer. "Do you mind if I ask you something?"

"It depends on the question. Don't forget, you're married now!"

He laughed, clinked glasses with her, then became serious again. "Does it surprise you that your husband and Helga are able to work together?"

"Because she's a Nazi voter? Not really. Gert's always been good at compartmentalizing his feelings. We Jews do what we have to do to get along. What would be the use in confronting Helga for supporting someone who refers to our people as *traitors*, and *a disease on society*? You think he'd change her mind?"

"I don't understand her perspective," Seamus said as he took the beer. "How can she be so friendly with him and support a group who advocates the removal of all Jews from German society?"

"You've heard people saying that Hitler doesn't mean what he says, haven't you?"

"Let's hope he doesn't."

"Thirty years ago, my father was whipped in the streets of Kishinev during a pogrom against the Jews there. My uncle died that day, beaten to death by his neighbors. Father brought us here to escape the prejudices we faced, and I thought we had —to some degree, anyway. The years since the war might have been tumultuous for some, but for others they were a time to stop looking over our shoulders and to live with a sense of true freedom for the first time in our lives. That period could be over. Hitler means every word he says about the Jews, and if he has his way, a great whirlwind is coming toward us. Those who deny his words are denying the history of the Jewish people in Europe. Helga is trying to separate Hitler's economic policies, and his talk about returning Germany to its rightful place among the nations of Europe, from his intentions regarding the Jews. But it's like a great Irish poet once said: 'How can we know the dancer from the dance?'"

"They're one and the same," Seamus replied.

"That's not what Helga and her kind see. By ignoring the parts of Nazi rhetoric they don't support, they enable all of it, and we'll pay the price for it one day."

"And what about Gert?"

"He wants to keep his job. At the risk of sounding trite, he cares about the factory and the workers, and he trusts you. Helmut spoke to him before he died. He knows you won't fire anyone because of their religion or their political beliefs. Getting along with Helga is one of the tightropes that my husband walks on a daily basis. We Jews have always had to kowtow to those who would destroy us, or else quicken our fate. It's been our lot for centuries. Little has changed."

"I'll stand by my people, no matter what."

"We know that." She said and took a sip of her wine. "We have two teenage boys, sixteen and seventeen—not babies anymore. They read the papers. It's hard to know what to say to them now. As a parent, you always try to frame things for your children that things are going to be ok. 'Life is fair. Good behavior will be rewarded. Bad things aren't going to happen.' I don't know how to frame Hitler becoming chancellor to them. How can I tell them that what's going on is just or right? How can I tell them that those who would destroy them are now making decisions that could change their lives?"

"I had a conversation with the journalists about the Nazis. Half of them are convinced they'll be gone in a few months, and that Hitler is a pawn of the ruling classes."

"Even if they're right, the undercurrent will remain. Something terrible has been born." She downed the rest of her wine. "You weren't counting on this conversation when you brought me out dancing, were you?"

"I'm always happy to talk to you, Lil."

"And to dance with me?"

"Every time." The clock on the wall reminded him that it was almost time for the little kids to go home to bed. "Excuse me. I have to go say good night to the children. Lisa's mother will be taking them home soon."

"That woman is a saint," said Lil.

"She is indeed."

Hannah was sitting on her grandmother's lap with her head tilted backward, drowsing. As he walked toward them, Ingrid made an effort to get up, but failed.

"I think it's time I got this little one home now. She's had a big day. So have Fiona and Conor, so I'll take them too."

"Thank you, Ingrid…" He stopped as a sharp feeling of concern came over him. Ingrid's complexion was pale, and the whites of her eyes tinged yellow. "Are you feeling unwell?"

"I'm fine, just tired. Can you take Hannah for a moment so I can get up? She's getting heavier by the day."

"Are you sure you're up to bringing the three little kids home? I could come with you."

"Heavens, no! What would all this be without the groom? You stay here and enjoy yourself with everyone else."

Seamus lifted Hannah off her lap. The little girl clung to him, wrapping her arms around his neck. Anxious about Ingrid, he looked for Lisa. She was still on the dance floor, showing Hans some moves. Ingrid seemed to read his thoughts.

"Don't worry her about me, Seamus. All I need is a good night's rest."

Linda appeared beside them. "Do you need any help with the children, Ingrid? I can help you bring them home. I was going to leave soon anyway. I have a deadline to meet tomorrow."

Ingrid tried to argue, but the veteran journalist cut her off. "I insist—it's the least I can do. Seamus, give that darling child to me."

Hannah was already asleep on his shoulder. He thought he was past the children-falling-asleep-in-his-arms stage, but life had other plans, and it didn't give advance notice of what they happened to be. He passed her over to Linda and held out his hand to Ingrid. She seemed to be finding it hard to get to her feet by herself, as if she were much older than her fifty-nine years.

"Perhaps I had too much to drink tonight," she said as he pulled her up. And then her legs gave way and she crashed to the carpet.

"Ingrid!" He crouched over her in horror. Her eyes were half open, and the whites seemed even yellower now. The skin on her face was clammy. He felt her wrist, and her pulse was weak. "Someone call a doctor! An ambulance!"

A small crowd was gathering around the stricken woman;

the next moment, Lisa came bursting through. "Mother!" she screamed, falling to her knees and cradling Ingrid's head in her arms. The music, the laughter, all other noise in the crowded ballroom faded until the only sound was left was the sound of Lisa crying, bent over her beloved mother with her beautiful wedding dress spread out around her and tears streaking down her face.

3

Monday, February 13

Seamus was thinking about his mother-in-law as he arrived at work the Monday morning after his wedding. They found out on Saturday night—still drunk, Lisa in her wedding dress and he in his tuxedo—that Ingrid's cancer had returned. It spread to her liver and she had only weeks to live. Lisa spent their wedding night crying in his arms, and the entire next day in the hospital with her mother. It seemed so unfair, after all those years of living in that rat-infested hellhole. This should have been the time for her mother to finally relax, surrounded by the people she loved. She deserved that. But who got what they truly deserved? Lisa blamed herself, of course, and asked how could she have been so blind as not to see that her own mother was dying? All Seamus could do was hold her and remind her of everyone who loved Ingrid during her life.

There was nothing more to do than make Ingrid's passing as comfortable as possible. The doctors would send her home in a day or two.

Seamus walked into the factory. Several workers shook his hand and patted him on the back as he strolled around the floor. Being with them felt like home. Helga was at the top of the stairs and waved to him before disappearing into her office. Martina, his secretary, a woman of twenty-two with dark-blond hair and piercing blue eyes, beckoned from across the floor.

"Herr Ritter," she said.

"Yes, Martina."

"Welcome back and congratulations."

"Thank you."

"You have a meeting on your schedule this morning that I wanted to tell you about. Frau Ritter accepted it for you on Friday morning, when you were out preparing for your wedding. It's with a Herr Milch, of Milch Industries."

Seamus's heart dropped in his chest. "This morning?"

"Yes, at ten."

The look on Martina's face expressed that she knew how important this man was. But she could never know the tumult within Seamus at that moment.

"Thank you," Seamus said and sped up the stairs, taking two steps at a time.

Helga was at her desk. "Yes?"

Seamus closed the door to her office behind him. "You set up a meeting for me with Otto Milch this morning?"

"Yes, you don't turn down the likes of him."

"Why didn't you take the appointment?"

"He asked to speak to you. I suppose he couldn't square the fact of sitting down and talking business with a woman."

I certainly hope that's it. "Any idea what it's about?"

"None. His secretary called on Friday morning—said he wanted to speak to you."

Any residual joy in his heart extinguished, Seamus excused himself and went back to his office. Why would Milch come here? Surely if he knew something, the police would be the ones coming. Ernst was still listed as missing, so the Nazis had their martyr. The mystery of his disappearance had faded from the newspapers, but not from his father's mind. No, this was a business meeting. Otto Milch was a competitor. Ten times bigger, but a competitor nonetheless. It was imperative that Seamus keep his head and ride this out.

A ridiculous instinct to run reared up inside him. He controlled it by taking deep breaths, focusing on pushing them out. No one was coming to arrest him or Lisa. Milch just wanted to talk. Seamus had met several of his fellow factory owners even in the short time he'd been here—just none as powerful as Otto Milch. He was sure this was nothing more insidious than any of those meetings.

Being alone in his office wasn't conducive to calming himself down, so he spent the hour before the meeting with Milch walking the floor, talking to his workers. Even so, the time drew out like razor wire on bare flesh.

Ten o'clock came and he heard Martina's voice—his guest was here. Seamus's heart froze. He followed the secretary back to the waiting area at the front of the factory where she introduced him to Otto Milch. He was a small but stout man, in his sixties, dressed in a gray double-breasted suit with a matching bowler hat. He looked the same as he had in the newspapers when he appealed for information about his son. His black hair didn't show a single gray strand and his long dark beard was twirled into a point beneath his chin.

"Yes. Seamus Ritter. Pleased to meet you."

Milch offered a bone-crushing handshake. "Pleased to meet you. Fine operation you have here."

"Thank you. We're working to make it even better. Follow me up to my office."

He led the older man up the stairs to his office and offered him a chair. "Drink?" Seamus asked. A decanter of whiskey sat on a table in the corner.

"It's a little early, even for a business meeting. Your uncle was a fine man. The life and soul of many of those stuffy dinners we attended together."

"We miss him every day."

"Yes, he was quite the force of nature. His personality opened many doors. But let's not speak of him. How have your first few months in our city been?"

"Most enjoyable. It's a remarkable place. I'm from America originally."

"I know that." Milch picked up a framed photograph of Lisa on his desk. "This is your new wife?"

"Yes, just on Saturday."

"Congratulations. I heard she was an old acquaintance of my son."

He knows I married Lisa, and that she was in that photograph with Ernst. "I think they met once or twice in the club she worked in at the time. But years ago." *Stay calm. He's got nothing.*

"Is she still working there?" He put the photograph back down and reached into his pocket for a silver cigarette case. He offered one to Seamus, who refused. Milch lit his own.

"Those days are behind her now," Seamus said.

"Of course. Not the best environment for a newlywed to be working in. All those men, leering at her every night. Just how well did your wife know my son?"

"Not well. She did mention the case after we saw it in the newspaper. They met a couple of times years ago. She and the other girls from the club were distraught when they heard about what happened. He was a gentleman of the old school, apparently. I hope you see him safe and sound soon."

"You're sure she has no idea where he might be?"

"Herr Milch, I feel for you and your wife, and wish I could help. But Lisa has already told the police all she knows. I'm sorry about your son, but I can assure you that my wife didn't know him at all well, and she has no idea where he might be now."

The older man took a drag from his cigarette. "You understand I mean no offense. Wouldn't you be asking questions if it were your child who was missing?"

"Of course," Seamus said. "And I'm sorry I have nothing to tell you."

"He was my son, and I won't rest until whoever brought this long nightmare to bear on our family is brought to justice. Someone out there knows what happened to Ernst, and where he is."

"I understand." It struck him that this man was Hannah's grandfather. There was a beautiful, sweet little girl who loved dolls and books and dressing up that he'd never meet, that he could never know. "Was there something else you wished to speak to me about?"

"So, you're happy with your new wife in Berlin? No desire to return home?"

"Home isn't quite what it once was. We've settled here in the city. The children are doing well in school, and the business is flourishing."

He wasn't exactly convinced of the veracity of his words, but it was surely easier to present this front here and now, particularly facing this man.

"I'll get to the point," Milch said.

"Something I always appreciate."

"I'd like to buy your business."

Seamus shook his head. "Not for sale, sir."

"You haven't heard my offer yet."

He wasn't here to make Helga's fortune. The promise he made to his uncle to look after his business and the employees echoed through his mind. Selling wasn't an option, for many reasons. "I don't need to."

"How about my legal team pays you a visit tomorrow morning? I hope you won't consider the fact that I've already prepared an offer impertinent."

"Not impertinent so much as unnecessary. I'm sorry you wasted your time, but I can assure you the factory is not for sale."

Milch shook his head, looking like he tasted something sour. "You're making a mistake, Herr Ritter."

"I don't think so, Herr Milch."

A knock on the door interrupted the flow of conversation. Seamus excused himself. When he saw Helga's face, he waved her into the room.

"I'd like you to meet my business partner, Helga Ritter."

Milch stood to shake Helga's hand. He didn't match her level of enthusiasm.

She pulled up a seat and joined them. "I hope you don't mind my invading your meeting."

"No, it's right that you're here," Seamus said.

Milch agreed with a nod of his head. "We were just discussing the notion of my buying your business."

Helga sat up in her chair. "Were you?"

"I thanked Herr Milch for his offer, but told him Ritter Industries wasn't for sale."

"You have a lot of foreign workers here, Russians and Jews. Do you find them as reliable as the German workers I insist on in my factories?"

"I don't know how reliable your workers are, but—"

Helga jumped in. "I couldn't agree more, Herr Milch. We're proud to provide jobs in these difficult economic times, but shouldn't we put our own people first? With so many unemployed German workers on the streets, it's my opinion that we should focus on helping them—and not the Communists and Jews who would happily tear this country apart at the seams if they had their way."

"I see we are of the same mind, Frau Ritter."

"I'm proud to support the revolution occurring in our country. It's time we put the disaster of the last fifteen years behind us once and for all."

Milch stubbed out his cigarette and stood up. "I won't take up any more of your precious time." All three were on their feet now, and Milch shook both of their hands again.

"It was a pleasure to meet you today," Seamus said.

"And you. One last thing... Join us at the Industrial Chamber of Commerce dinner next week at the Kaiserhof. Just you, Seamus. Your uncle was a mainstay of the event for years. I'm sure he mentioned it to you."

"He did. I'd be delighted to attend."

"Excellent. I'll have your name added to the list. Nice to meet you, Frau Ritter."

Seamus walked the older man out to his car, where his chauffer was waiting. Milch shook his hand one last time. "Think about my offer. Don't dismiss it."

"I'll see you at the dinner next week," Seamus said and stood to watch the old industrialist leave.

Tuesday, February 14

Bruno spent two weeks searching the streets of Berlin for the man with the rolled-up carpet. The pretty girl's face was a blur. She'd been too far away to make out in the dim light of the basement, and he never really looked at her the other times he saw her around the apartment building. Years on the streets had trained him to keep his eyes down, and not to look people in the face. All he remembered was her brown hair and a general air of attractiveness about her. But the man she'd been with—his face was ingrained on Bruno's mind now. He obsessed over it every day, searching the city for him, walking around different spots, asking other homeless men he knew if they saw anyone like him. Of course, they all had, but he realized after a few days of questioning that they thought every man in the city looked like the one he was searching for. Men like him were everywhere.

After two weeks of fruitless searching, Bruno decided to track Herr Milch down at the corporate offices of Milch Industries. He made sure to wash his hands and face before he went to the office building on Rüdersdorfer Strasse. He knew that he had to create an excellent impression to even get in the door, let alone gain an audience with Herr Milch. But his efforts were for naught. The security guard at the front door refused to let him in. When Bruno shouted that he had information about Herr Milch's missing son, the man turned his head away.

Bruno didn't give up easily. He knew what he'd seen was real, and also that Milch would pay handsomely for what he knew. It was just a matter of getting to the old man. He stood there for half an hour, trying to reason with the burly doorman, but it was no use. The security man acted as if he were invisible; he may as well have been speaking Chinese. In the end, defeated, he traipsed back to the squat, the bottle of whiskey in his pocket his only comfort.

How can I get Herr Milch's attention?

He decided to go to the police. If giving evidence in court was the price he had to pay for a new life, then so be it. Perhaps the man behind the front desk would be a fellow veteran too, and sympathetic.

It was hard not to feel intimidated by the drab gray frontage of the police station on Friedrichstrasse, which was dyed even darker by the morning rain. He peered into one of the long rectangular windows; inside, a young secretary was tapping away on a typewriter. She glanced up, meeting his eyes for half a second. The look on her face was scared and hostile, and he retreated. Why were people so terrified of him and his kind when all they wanted was to survive?

At last he summoned up the courage to push through the heavy wooden doors and approach the front desk. A young policeman with glasses and a thick mustache was sitting behind the counter, and his face flushed darkly as Bruno walked up.

"Get out!" he cried angrily.

Shaken, Bruno stammered, "I... I have information about the disappearance of Ernst Milch, son of Otto Milch."

But the police officer was now shaking his fist. "Are you deaf?"

The thought of getting arrested on purpose and getting a meal, a dry place to sleep, and the opportunity to share what he had to say crossed his mind. "I just need to talk to someone for a moment."

The young man wasn't listening. "Out the door right now, before you feel my baton."

Bruno could see the young secretary pointing at him through the glass. The young officer with the mustache was on his feet now, and looked like he might carry through on his threats.

"I have important information about a missing person," he said more loudly. Again, no one was listening. They weren't interested in what he had to say. He understood that he wasn't a part of their society, but this was as if he'd stopped existing as a member of the human race.

"I fought for this country," he heard himself say, immediately recognizing his mistake. They could dismiss him as crazy now. They could say he was rambling about the war and take his words as a threat. He had to be perfect to have them hear him out, and the façade slipped when he mentioned the war. There was nothing else to do now but leave.

The flame of frustration burned through him as he turned

around to depart. The policeman at the window was still shouting abuse at him, but Bruno wasn't listening anymore. The secretary would go home that night and tell her husband how dangerous her job could be, and how lucky she was that day. He wished he had something to drink as he walked outside. He'd wasted his entire morning on this.

Should I go to another police station? Is there any point? Who would treat me differently? A mother and a young boy of about eight passed him on the street. The boy's eyes were on him like glue as the mother dragged him past.

He made his way down the pavement and back toward one of his regular spots on the river. The station, and the idea of going to the police, receded into the background. He wrapped the tatty, moth-eaten scarf he wore around his neck over his jaw, both to protect his exposed, scarred skin from the cold and to hide it from the world.

It was hard not to feel defeated. *What good is the information I have if no one will listen?* It took him about ten minutes to make his way to his spot. His stomach rumbled, but he had no food. It gave him the motivation he otherwise would have been lacking to ask strangers for money on the street.

He made enough that day for a sandwich and a bottle of whiskey. He shuffled home as darkness fell, with food in his stomach and drinking from the bottle in his hand. His vision was blurry as he passed by the newsstand. He kept on, eager to lie down and finish the Scotch. A voice came from behind him.

"Hey, mister."

He didn't turn.

The voice came again, and footsteps. "Mister!" It was the young newsie. "I've been looking out for you! We were never properly introduced. The name's Wilhelm, but most people call me Willi."

Bruno glanced at the boy before continuing on his way. The

lad came after him again. "Hey, wait! Stop a moment. Can't you just give me a few seconds?"

Bruno paused, impatiently—the whiskey was calling to him. "What? What is it?"

"I've been asking around a little about our friend Ernst Milch." The kid glanced around as if to make sure no one else was listening. "I found out about the reward. Have you told anyone what you know?"

"Good night, Willi." He started walking again.

"Wait! I might be able to help you out if you haven't!"

Bruno came to a halt again. Willi caught up with him. "You haven't been able to get anyone to listen to you, have you?"

"Who says I've got anything to tell anyone?"

"It's obvious. I bet you went to his office and got turned away. And, of course, no one will tell you where he lives."

"You've got it all figured out, don't you, kid?"

"I'm just trying to piece things together. And to help you—"

"Out of the goodness of your heart?"

"Of course. And 500 Reichsmarks."

"Forget it," said Bruno, walking on. The boy kept pace with him.

"No one's listening to you because they look at you and see a crazy old drunk."

Bruno felt his anger rising—not at the kid so much as at the society that marginalized him, that refused him, that didn't even value a word he might say. "Get lost."

"I know where Otto Milch is going to be next Saturday night."

"I'm not interested."

"What about the reward? It's 5,000 Reichsmarks. After you pay me, you'll still have 4,500. Just imagine what you could do with all that money. Buy a house in the country, or even an apartment in the city. You wouldn't have to sit on the side of the street begging for money ever again. But what use is that infor-

mation spinning around inside your head if you've got no one
to share it with?"

Bruno's feet slowed again. He stopped. "Fine. Where is
Milch going to be?"

Grinning, Willi pushed back the flat cap he was wearing,
then held out his hand. "Are we partners?"

Bruno looked at the hand. "Where can I find Milch?"

"Shake. I'm giving you top-secret information that might get
me into trouble." After a long hesitation, Bruno shook; his own
hand was filthy, but the newsie didn't seem to mind. A bigger
grin spread across his face. "He's going to be at the Kaiserhof
Hotel next Saturday night."

"How did you find this out?"

"How you think? I read it in the paper. It's the annual Industrial Chamber of Commerce dinner, and all the bigwigs in business are going to be there."

Bruno didn't know whether to be angry or laugh: the
cheeky kid had traded him public information for 500 Reichsmarks! But it was useless anyway. No way was he going to get
inside that splendid hotel. He started to walk again. "Fine, I'll
let you know what happens."

"What you mean, 'You'll let me know?'" Willi called after
him. "Nothing's going to happen unless I help you. You can't
just stroll up to a man like Otto Milch looking like you do.
You're going to have to lose that beard for one thing, and take a
bath. You're not going to get near him smelling like that. Come
to the newsstand tomorrow night at nine, when I get off work,
and I'll get you sorted."

Again, Bruno stopped and turned. "Don't your parents
expect you home after work?"

"I'm the third of twelve kids. They'd barely notice if I didn't
come back for a week. What's your name, anyway?"

"Bruno."

Willi walked backward, pointing at the older man. "Don't

forget to come. We're gonna do this!" Then he winked and swiveled on his heels to jog back to the newsstand.

Bruno walked down to the apartment and curled up on his soiled mattress with the hope of something better burning in his heart.

4

Ingrid came home five days after the wedding. Lisa held in her tears as they pulled into the driveway, knowing her mother wouldn't appreciate them. The doctors couldn't do any more for her, and she wanted to see the children and spend her last weeks on her terms.

"I don't want to be stowed upstairs like some luggage," she said. "Let me enjoy as much time as possible with the children before I go upstairs to die. Lisa, I forbid you to cry. This is going to be a celebration. You can mourn me after I'm gone, not before."

The kids were waiting. Maureen and Michael had made a banner that said "Welcome Home, Oma," and had hung it above the door. Ingrid wept a little when she saw it, her eyes dewy. The younger children spilled out of the house with the cards they made for her in their hands. Seamus offered to carry Ingrid in, but she shooed him away.

"I'm not that bad! Maureen, give me your hand..." As she limped into the house and sat in her favorite chair, she beamed at them all. "Turn on the radio, Michael. Seamus, get me a beer, and some decent food. A rat would turn its nose up at those hospital meals."

A few seconds later, the sound of Duke Ellington cascaded through the air around them. Seamus returned with beer and handed it to his mother-in-law. She sat back, watching the children dance. Hannah ran to her and climbed onto her lap. She wrapped one arm around her granddaughter as she drank from the tall glass.

Ingrid remained in the living room with the children as Lisa prepared the stew for dinner. Seamus stayed with her, helping her chop the vegetables.

"Anything happen in work this week?" she asked after a few seconds of silence.

"I was invited to the Industrialists Chamber of Commerce dinner next week. It's on in the Kaiserhof Hotel. Do you know it?"

"Every Berliner knows the Kaiserhof. It seems like you're going up in the world. Don't forget about us."

Her words were meant to come as a joke, but she realized the lack of mirth in her tone. Seamus came up from behind her and wrapped his arms around her chest.

"Are you ok?"

"No, I'm not, but thank you."

The entire family sat down to dinner thirty minutes later. Her mother struggled with the food, more excited by the idea of eating it than anything else.

"Don't force yourself," Lisa said to her.

After a few minutes of stubbornness, she agreed to retreat to the living room once more with a beer and a pack of cigarettes.

"When did you take up smoking?" Lisa asked.

"When it didn't matter anymore," her mother replied.

Lisa left her in the armchair, drinking and smoking to the

sound of American jazz. She was still sitting in the same place when Lisa and Maureen joined her once the rest of the kids were in bed. Seamus was upstairs, reading to Conor, as the three women talked.

"I'd like to visit where I grew up in Rostock, and see my cousin, Liesl."

Lisa reached into the recesses of her mind for the last time her mother saw Liesl. It was ten years or more—back when Father was still alive. Liesl's husband was the reason she and Lisa's mother lost touch. Ingrid didn't approve of his manners, but more particularly, his habit of taking his drunken moods out on Liesl with his fists. His death five years ago had been a release for Liesl in more ways than one, and opened the door for her to resume her relationship with Lisa's mother once more. It wasn't Ingrid's intention to desert her cousin in her hour of need during the tumult of her marriage to Gunther. She'd been trying to exact pressure on her to leave him—something her cousin never did. Their correspondence after Gunther's death had all been by letter. Ingrid even refused to attend his funeral.

"I wrote to her a few weeks ago to tell her about your wedding. She couldn't come," Ingrid said.

"You never mentioned anything."

"You were so busy. I didn't want to bother you."

"What else happened during that time that you didn't want to bother me about?"

Her mother picked up her beer and took a sip. "Liesl asked if we wanted to come and stay with her. I accepted."

"So we don't need to find a hotel?"

Her mother shook her head. "There'll be plenty of room for all. Her husband's gone, and her daughters are in Munich. I'd like to go to my old house first. Then we can make our way to Liesl's house for dinner."

"Are you sure you're up to it? It's a three-hour drive."

"It's what I want to do, with just you and Hannah. It'll be the last time I leave Berlin."

Her mother's words struck her dumb for a few seconds. She nodded her head. "Ok, Mother. We'll go in the next few days."

"How long did you live in Rostock, Ingrid?" Maureen asked.

"From the day I was born until I was fifteen," she answered. "My parents moved to Berlin when my father lost his job on the docks."

"Do you still have family there?"

"Just Liesl. My parents died twenty years ago, and my brother died in the war, along with my two boys."

Lisa's heart constricted. She wanted to ask about her brothers, even though they never spoke of them anymore. She had to take a deep breath before continuing. "Do you think about Henning and Ingo much?"

"A lot more these last few weeks. I didn't want to mention it to you, with the wedding and all."

"The wedding's over now."

"That it is."

She waited for her mother to continue, but she didn't. Soon, the only other person who knew her brothers well would be gone, and the memories of them would live on only within her. "What do you think of?"

"What?"

"When you think of the boys."

The answer was a few seconds coming. "Just the sheer waste of it all. I imagine what they would have been. I try and relate those thoughts to who they were as children, as if I can build a picture of what they might have become that way."

"Do you have any idea?"

"They were still boys when they died. Heaven only knows where life would have led them."

Something stopped Lisa from saying more, and her mother

offered nothing further. Perhaps it was too much grief to handle.

Friday, February 17

They waited two days to go. It seemed logical to give her mother some time to rest, even though she insisted she was ok. Lisa knew her mother's words were bluster. She could see pain in her movements and hear it in her voice, even when she insisted she felt as good as ever.

It had been twenty years or more since they went back to her mother's childhood home. She remembered the old house outside the town, and running her fingers along the chipped paint on the doorframe as her brothers played in the yard. Father was with them then, and in a particularly foul mood that day. He kicked through the dirt outside the old house like a child and went to play with the boys in the field out back.

This would be the first time Hannah had ever been out of Berlin. Lisa hoped she would remember this day. Her grandmother was so important in her life, but she was only three. What memories would she carry with her? Perhaps going to see Lisa's childhood home? There was only so much Lisa could do. Frustration and anger rampaged through her. Just when they had the means to avert the struggle their daily lives had been these past few years, the cancer came back. She tried not to think about it. Those feelings could only spoil the little time she had left with her mother.

Seamus had already gone to work, and the children were in school when they left. It was a gray morning, cold and damp. They brought raincoats with them and loaded the car with the suitcases they'd need for the weekend away. Hannah sat in the back, holding hands with her Oma.

It was lunchtime when they arrived in Rostock. Ingrid directed Lisa through the city, and they arrived at the Warnemünde Lighthouse as the gray clouds above their heads shifted to reveal a limp sun. Hannah had never seen the sea before, and Lisa let her mother have the moment with her. She held her Oma's hand as they walked to the water's edge. The little girl marveled at the massive expanse of leaden-colored water, which stretched out as far as they could see.

"It's so big," she said.

"More water than you could ever imagine," her grandmother replied.

"Who put it there?"

They looked at each other for the answer to that question.

Lisa burst out laughing. "No one put it there. It's just there."

The calm weather lasted a few minutes before a squall blew up over the water, sending cold, wet air their way. They drove back into the city. It was impossible not to notice that, just like in Berlin, the flags of the republic were gone, replaced by the old imperial flag, and even that of the swastika. Lisa wondered what this country would be like as she raised a three-year-old there.

"There's another of those flags," said her mother, pointing to the Nazi swastika above what seemed to be the town hall.

"Another election will be along before you know it," Lisa reassured her. "The people will come to their senses."

She pulled up on the street and parked the car. The three got out and made for a café. Five minutes later, they were sitting down to lunch. The food was on the table when Lisa's mother spoke again.

"I don't feel the connection with this place that I once did."

"Berlin must feel like home," Lisa said.

The house was smaller than Lisa remembered. It was about the size of the living room in the house they lived in now. It had been deserted for ten years or more, and the grass was overgrown in the front yard. The wooden fencing around it was rotten and falling apart, and they had to force the gate open. The porch leading to the front door had been stripped clean by the wind and rain, so that the wood was almost silver in color. Her mother pushed the door. It came free of the lock at her touch and hung open, inviting them inside.

Lisa wondered how safe it was and insisted on going inside first to check things out. What she found was an empty wreck of a house. Nothing remained—no reason to feel attached. She led the others inside, making sure to keep a tight grip on her daughter's hand. Her mother didn't speak as they walked around, just looked at each room and doorway for a few seconds before moving on. They were inside the place less than a minute when she gave the word to leave.

"Let's go and see Liesl," she said.

Lisa didn't argue, and they made their way back to the car in silence. Lisa was wondering why they came at all.

Liesl's house stood at the end of a meadow that led down to the beach, where the sun was setting as they arrived. The air was thick and gritty, and without the bright lights of the city to stave off the darkness, night seemed to fall like a cloak. The door to the house opened as they pulled up. A small woman, about five years older than Ingrid, held up her hand to wave to them before approaching the car. Hannah cowered in her grandmother's arms.

"Oh, no, my sweet, it's just Cousin Liesl."

Ingrid pushed the door open and went to her cousin. They embraced before she introduced her to the others.

"How long has it been, Lisa? Since you were a young girl?"

"I was probably about seventeen."

"Well, let's not stand out here in the cold."

She turned and led them inside the neat cottage. A pile of logs blazed in the fireplace, lending warmth and a golden glow to the simple interior. Lisa followed her mother to an old threadbare couch facing the fireplace. Their host went into the kitchen without another word and emerged with wine and cheese on a tray. The aroma of fish stew drifted out in her wake.

"I'm so pleased you're here, although I wish it were under happier circumstances." She turned to Lisa. "I'm sorry I wasn't able to make the wedding last week. I was recovering from pneumonia."

"It was a wonderful day."

"I ruined it," her mother said.

"Nonsense!" Lisa said.

She reached forward for a glass of wine as Hannah found a children's book on the shelf to look through. An old photograph of Liesl, her husband Gunther, and their two daughters sat on the shelf above the fireplace.

"How have you been?" Liesl asked.

"In some pain, but the pills the doctor gave me are having some effect."

"How long have you and Mother been back in touch?" Lisa asked.

"A few years ago. From around the time of her operation. She mentioned the cancer coming back in a letter she sent at Christmas."

Ingrid moved her hand onto Lisa's. It was best to leave her anger behind, but it was hard. The desire to scream at her reared up inside her like a wild horse, "You knew then and you didn't tell me?!" She repressed her natural instincts and reached forward for her glass of wine, taking a generous gulp.

The women sat there for a few minutes before they went to the kitchen table. Liesl served the fish stew. Hannah got up on Lisa's lap as she helped her with her food. Rain started outside, covering the windows in silver rivulets. A storm was rolling in from the sea.

~

Lisa woke in what seemed like a strange place. Her eyes flashed open, her heart racing. The nightmare was dissipating—the images of whoever had been chasing her through those dark woods fading like ripples in water. For some reason, she tried to cling to them, until she realized it was best to let them go. The room was dark and it was raining outside. She was in a double bed with Hannah beside her, who was asleep.

Lisa's throat was dry, but she didn't want to get out of bed. She tried to ignore it as Liesl's and Ingrid's voices drifted up through the floorboards. It was impossible to make out what they were saying, just that they were still talking. It must have been well after midnight, since it was past eleven when she went to bed. She rolled over, trying to block out the noise and the thirst burning in her throat. Five minutes went by before she realized she wasn't going to be able to sleep without getting a glass of water. She pushed off the covers. Her feet were cold on the thin carpet, and she searched for her socks in the darkness. Once they were on, she stepped onto the floor, trying not to wake Hannah as she made for the door.

Each creak seemed magnified 100 times, but somehow, the child didn't stir as she twisted the doorknob. She eased her way around the door, the downstairs voices growing louder. She was able to make out a few words now—something about her and Seamus. The two ladies were in the living room in front of the fire. Something inside Lisa, an instinct, told her to stop. The women's voices came into sharp focus.

"Don't you think Lisa deserves to know?" Liesl asked.

"I don't see what good that will do now," Ingrid answered. "Perhaps there was a time to tell her—after her father died, maybe. But now? She's newly married. She's happier than she's ever been. Well, at least she was until this damned cancer came back."

"It's better that you tell her. If she finds out after you die—"

"Who would tell her then? You?"

Lisa's heart froze in her chest. What were they talking about? A flood of guilt washed through her. She shouldn't have been standing here listening in. But she was trapped now, and she heard what she heard.

"I have no idea if he's dead or alive." Ingrid continued. "It's best to let the past be just that—past."

"It's a huge part of who she is. Everyone deserves to know who their real father is."

"I don't know if it would make any difference."

"Don't be ridiculous. Of course it would! What if he's still alive? What if she's missing out on that relationship because you're too afraid to tell her?"

"I can't do that. I made a mistake thirty years ago. I need to leave it behind."

"Why did you really come here?" Lisa heard Liesl stand up. "Did you come here to see me, or did you come for affirmation? Did you come to talk about the past or make sure it stays buried?"

"I only have a few weeks left. I came to see you, but also to ask you what I should do. I've no one else to turn to."

"I think she should know who she is. I think you've kept this from her long enough."

"I don't know if I can."

"You have my advice. Rest assured that she won't hear it from me. I'll respect your wishes, even after you're gone."

"Thank you," Ingrid said.

Lisa stood frozen at the top of the stairs. The women stopped talking. Her thirst was driving her down to the kitchen, to the cool glass of water that would quench it. She longed to go back into the bedroom and to forget—somehow—what she just heard, but her body wouldn't allow it.

She tiptoed back to the bedroom and opened and closed the door as loudly as she dared without waking Hannah. She then turned around toward the staircase and made her way down again, not taking any care to mute her footsteps. Ingrid and Liesl both greeted her as she came into the living room.

"I wanted a glass of water," she said. "I hope I'm not disturbing you."

"Of course not," Liesl said. "Let me get that water for you." She disappeared into the kitchen, leaving her alone with her mother. Lisa didn't know what to say to her. The urge to talk about what she heard was like a wild dog snapping inside her, but somehow the words wouldn't form in her throat. An awkward silence hung heavily in the air for a couple of seconds before Ingrid broke it with words that signified little.

"It's so late. I can't believe I'm still up."

Liesl appeared with a tall glass of water and handed it to Lisa. It felt heavenly cascading down her throat. The older woman waited until she was finished to take it from her. Ingrid stood as Liesl returned to the kitchen.

"It's time I was in bed." She went to her daughter and stood in front of her as if searching her eyes. "I'll see you in the morning, young lady."

Her heart was thumping as she followed her mother upstairs. Ingrid shut the bedroom door behind her without another word. Lisa went back to bed alone. Hannah was still asleep. She stared at her daughter's beautiful face. The weight of what she heard kept her awake until almost dawn.

5

Saturday, February 18

S eamus stood in front of the mirror, fixing his bowtie. He used a brush from the dresser beside him to smooth the shoulder of his tuxedo, wishing Lisa was here to give her opinion on how he looked. He wanted her reassurance that he wasn't out of his depth. Helmut had attended the Industrial Chamber of Commerce annual dinner every year for the previous twenty, and now he was expected to take Helmut's place. Seamus knew he'd never get a better chance to make contacts in the world of big business, but it was hard not to feel like a fraud. Six months ago he was digging dirt in Ohio, and now he was to rub shoulders with some of the most influential businessmen in Germany. They'd see through him in seconds.

Helga had urged him to go. She would have gone in his place, but they didn't take kindly to women at events like these. He had little choice. He knew he could do this, but it just would be so much easier with Lisa here to encourage him and to talk to him about the darkness in his heart.

And, of course, Otto Milch would be there tonight. A paranoid part of him imagined that this was some elaborate ruse to trap him for the murder of his son, but that wasn't true. Milch knew nothing. As long as Seamus didn't do anything stupid, Milch would remain none the wiser.

Michael poked his head around the door. "The taxi's here."

"Tell him I'll be out in a minute."

His oldest son disappeared. Fiona and Conor came up and stood by his side. "You look handsome, Dad," Fiona said.

He put his arms around them and looked at their reflection in the mirror. "You really think I'll do well?"

"Go get them, Dad," Conor said.

He directed the taxi driver to take him to the Kaiserhof Hotel, which was around the Wilhelmplatz.

The driver was chatty. "You know, that's where Röhm and Goebbels were the night Hitler was sworn in as chancellor."

"I hadn't heard."

"Hitler went there to tell them in person, and they stayed on to celebrate, although word is that the Führer doesn't drink or smoke, so heaven only knows how."

"Make a speech, perhaps, or have someone beat up a bunch of Jews in front of him?"

The taxi driver didn't answer and remained silent for the duration of the ride to the hotel. Seamus tipped him as he got out. The driver took the money and left without another word.

"They're everywhere," Seamus said under his breath and made his way up the stairs and past the doorman into the plushly decorated lobby. A sign directed him toward the ballroom, where he presented his ticket at the door and made his way inside. It was ten minutes past eight—the dinner was set to begin at eight, although he knew it would be some time after that. The room was already full. A hundred men in tuxedos stood talking to one another.

He took a few seconds to look around. It was impossible to pick Otto Milch out of the group. It seemed hard to discern one captain of industry from another. Almost all were twenty years or more older than he. Nearly all had a beard or a mustache. He ran his hand over his clean-shaven face and made for the bar, where a young man took his order for a beer. It would be easy to lurk in the corner, but what would that do for the factory and the workers? What would that do for him and his family?

Four men were talking together near the bar, and Seamus made his way over to the group. They shifted to let him into their circle, and he introduced himself. Two were from the chemical company IG Farben, one was a mining magnate, and the other was Gustav Krupp. Seamus shook Krupp's hand last. He had heard of Krupp—the latest in a long line of oligarchs, famous for their production of armaments and ammunition, among many other things. Seamus wondered how many of his friends had died at the hands of Krupp steel in 1918.

"You're American?" Krupp asked as he lit a pipe he drew from his pocket.

"Yes. I've only been in the country a few months. My Uncle Helmut left me his factory here in the city."

"We all knew Helmut," Carl Borzig from Farben said. "He was quite the character. We were all sorry to hear about his passing."

"Thank you. He was a great man."

"Good location for that factory, as far as I remember." Krupp puffed on his pipe. "In Nollendorfkiez?"

Seamus nodded and took a sip from his beer. "Yes. We've about 300 employees."

The old man's thin white mustache shifted as a broad smile

came across his face. "You might be a popular man here tonight if you're looking to sell."

"Gustav, let the kid enjoy his beer. He doesn't want to go back to America quite yet, do you?" Borzig said.

Seamus thought to explain that he wouldn't be able to sell if he wanted to—not without ceding all the profits to Helga, anyway—but instead returned Krupp's grin.

"I think I'll hang around the city for a while. The beer is so good, why would I leave?"

"Why would anyone want to leave with all the exciting goings-on?" Krupp asked. "The new chancellor promises to be great for business."

"Yes. It'll be a relief to leave behind the ridiculous trappings of democracy." Borzig said *democracy* like it was a swear word.

Krupp agreed. "Yes, the sooner we get back to the days of the Kaiser, the better off we'll all be."

"You think the National Socialists want the old ways back?" Seamus asked.

"I think they can be persuaded that the ways of their forefathers were the most efficient, and at least we might have a strong government at last," answered Krupp.

"Let's ask our foreign friend here," said Fritz Thyssen, a mining and steelmaking magnate. "Do you think democracy has served the United States well? We had our own little experiment with it here after the war, as you know. I'd be fascinated to hear what you think."

Seamus knew what they wanted to hear and what angle he should take in answering Thyssen's question.

"You're all, perhaps for the want of a better word, *capitalists*, the same as every man in this room. Everyone who came tonight is here for the same reasons—the betterment of their companies to build their personal fortunes."

"And to get drunk," Borzig said.

"And don't forget that girl you have waiting for you in the suite upstairs," Thyssen said to Borzig.

"Let the American speak," said Krupp, who seemed interested.

Seamus turned to him. "America was one of the first democracies, and one of the first countries to establish a free market where capitalism could prosper. America is a place where big business thrives, but where the people also get their say in who makes the decisions that affect their lives. It seems like a fair balance to me."

"And where the market crashes and takes the rest of the world down with it," Krupp said. "Stability is what we need—not insane rushes."

"Gustav wants to bring back the feudal system," Thyssen said.

"No, not at all. I want a robust economy where the decisions are made by the type of person bred to take on such responsibilities. The average person on the street has neither the mental capacity nor the instinct for the likes of what we deal with every day. Democracy has torn this country apart," Krupp said.

"It hasn't done America any harm," Seamus said.

"An economy based on slavery and an abundance of natural resources we could only dream of? It's my opinion that America could be nothing other than rich and would benefit from having its own monarchy," Krupp said.

"That's what we fought against back in our war of independence."

"Yours is a country with no tradition—a new world based on new ways of thinking. Germany was built on different principals. The old ways worked very nicely until the advent of democracy, and it's time we got back to what we do best," Krupp said and took a puff on his pipe.

No longer interested.

It was apparent Seamus wasn't going to change this man's—

or any other man's—mind here. He wondered what the average person on the street would think of these rich old men making decisions on their behalf. But then, with thirteen million Nazi voters in the country, perhaps many would approve. The dinner bell came not a moment too soon.

He found himself seated between Roland Eidinger, a shipping magnate from Hamburg, and Frank Helle, the head of a mining conglomerate. The slant of the conversation over dinner was much the same as he had with Krupp and the other men before it—the Nazis were a positive development. Eidinger was the only other dissenting voice among those at the table. Helle had something else to say as he lit a cigarette, having just finished the exquisite steak they'd been served.

"Communism is the real enemy of commerce and progress. The Nazis are best placed to defend us from the radical ideas that have spread here from the East. There's no doubt that limited government control of production, and privatization of banking and transportation, would be effective means of preventing the spread of full-fledged Communism to the country."

"And will thus save us from the rabid Eastern hordes?" Seamus asked.

"Quite," Helle answered.

"We'll find out more when the special guest speaker arrives in a few moments," Eidinger said.

A lectern had been set up while they were eating dinner, and a Nazi flag was pinned to the wall behind it. Seamus was sick of that emblem already, but had the feeling he'd be seeing a lot more of it in the coming weeks and months.

"Why, who are we expecting?"

"You didn't hear? One of Helle's new friends from the Nazi Party is going to come and enlighten us with their vision of the New World," Eidinger said.

"And promise us the world in exchange for a few million Reichsmarks," a fellow said from across the table.

"Give him a chance to speak before you make judgment," Helle replied.

A small man dressed in a brown suit with a swastika armband entered the ballroom. He walked with a noticeable limp, had slicked-back hair and a clean-shaven face, and was flanked by two SA men in their familiar brown uniforms.

The sound of chattering stilled and the crowd settled back in their chairs to listen. Most of the men had cigarettes or pipes in their hands now, and Seamus had to peer through a haze of gray smoke hanging in the air to make out the man at the podium.

"Good evening, gentlemen," he began. "My name is Joseph Goebbels. The Führer has personally dispatched me here this evening to address you."

He was probably the only man in the room younger than Seamus.

"I am humbled to be in this room full of luminaries such as yourselves. I come to you in a time of great need, yet also of great opportunity for a magnificent new era for the Reich. Not three weeks ago, our country swirled in a maelstrom of uncertainty and chaos caused by the curse of democracy and all it entails. In the midst of this turmoil, our president saw fit, in his infinite wisdom, to install our Führer, Adolf Hitler, as the first ever National Socialist Chancellor in the history of our state. A glorious new day has dawned on our beloved country, a day in which all our dreams are once more within our grasp. But myriad forces are operating within our country right now who want to derail this new opportunity before it even begins. The Bolsheviks, if they get their way, will drain all that is good and pure in our country, destroying all our institutions and everything great men such as yourselves have spent a lifetime building. And make no mistake—they are here in this very city, on this very night, plotting heinous crimes against our society that would render all we strive for irrelevant and bring us back into a new dark age such as we haven't endured in 1,000 years." Goebbels paused a few seconds. Seamus was sitting thirty yards back from the lectern, but could feel his energy. He was sure every man in the room could.

"But fear not," Goebbels continued. "Each epoch has been dominated by men whose obsessions have shaped our lives and handed down a better, more secure future for our children. Our Führer, Adolf Hitler, is that man for our time, just as Frederick the Great, or even Bismarck, was for his. Our well-being and the advancement of the German Reich is his lifetime obsession. This great man will lead us forward into the modern age, and will direct toward a country where the great industrial powers can prosper, but only if we support him now."

Several men in the audience began to clap, but Goebbels spoke again before it turned into a round of applause. "We have much in common, gentlemen. Our enemies are the same. Every man in this room knows that private enterprise cannot be maintained within a democracy. Look at what these liberal ideas brought to our country—nothing more than shame and ruin. It is up to the likes of us to drag this country back to greatness. The common man on the street will benefit from our progress, but we cannot allow him to hold us back."

The applause came in earnest now, and Goebbels stood back a few seconds to bask in it. The other men at Seamus's table were entranced. Seamus finished his beer. He thought back to the rally he attended with Helga in Potsdam before the November election. The people that heard Hitler speak that day were the unwanted, marginalized members of German society. Here, in this room, sat the elite—the men the poor people at the rally had railed at. But somehow, both strata of German society were drawn to the same Nazi ideals, just for vastly different reasons.

"The National Socialists are your party. We are the party of big business and industry," Goebbels declared. "Who else is going to keep the Communists and the working man in their place? The Center Party? The Social Democrats?"

Goebbels almost laughed at the idea. "We have been working for years behind the scenes on a vast plan to revamp the national economy, and we are ready to implement it. We will embark on an unprecedented period of rebuilding for both the military and our country's infrastructure. This rebuilding will create millions of jobs and will provide vast contracts for your companies to play their part in dragging this country back to its rightful place among the greatest on Earth. The stock market will come roaring back. We will keep the inflation that has crippled us all these years down, and by crushing the trade unions, we will keep wages down. We can leave the nightmare of the last fifteen years behind us. We can avenge the national humiliation that the November criminals inflicted upon us, but we need you now. This is the time to invest in the future of the Reich. Big business is at the forefront of our plans to revitalize the economy. The Führer cannot achieve these lofty goals without your help. With yet another useless election almost upon us, we, the National Socialist Party, ask for your help. We need you, as the leading lights in the bright constellation that is the German industrial core, to help us vanquish the enemies in our society, and help us lead the country back to glory."

"The Nazis need us," Eidinger whispered to Seamus. "They're bankrupt. They don't have enough money to contest the election in March."

"So, this is the big chance to restore sanity in the country," Seamus said quietly. "Leave the Nazis out to dry and return the regular order to power."

"I don't think many here would agree with your plan." Eidinger pointed across the table at Krupp, who was on his feet.

"I'd like to address the room if I may," the industrialist said.

Goebbels ceded the floor to him. Someone heckled Krupp, but was shouted down.

"I, like the rest of you, have long wondered what had become of the country that we were raised in. I have feared for what I might be able to leave to my sons because of the chaos of the last fifteen years, but I know now we have a chance to right the wrongs of the Weimar experiment. The National Socialists have offered us a concise view of a future where we are returned to our rightful place at the head of our society, and where our nation ranks among the greatest in the world once more. With this in mind, I've decided to donate one million marks to the National Socialist cause. I urge you to join me, this very night, in strengthening and confirming this young man's party in power."

Krupp motioned toward Goebbels, who bowed to him. The applause began again.

"Thank you, Herr Krupp. You are a true patriot, and Herr Hitler will not forget your generosity. And that goes for each man in this room who supports our noble cause tonight. Know that we will never forget this favor, and you will be repaid a hundredfold."

Most of the old men in the room were on their feet now as rapturous clapping echoed through the ballroom. Several at Seamus's table were writing checks. Helle didn't hide the fact that his was for a 150,000 marks and waved it in the air, seemingly to attract attention and encourage others.

Goebbels went from table to table with the SA men, making it all too apparent who was donating and who kept their pocketbook closed. It took him about fifteen minutes to reach Helle and the other men at Seamus's table who were donating. Seamus and Eidinger, not reaching for their pocketbooks, were in the minority. Goebbels passed them by without acknowledging their presence.

Bruno looked at himself in the mirror. If it weren't for the eyepatch and the mess of scarred skin across his face and neck, he looked almost normal. Almost. Shaving off his beard had revealed thick, wrinkled skin he hadn't seen in years...not since the war. The mosaic of lines on his weather-beaten face seemed to tell the story of every night he spent sleeping on the street.

He looked much older than his thirty-six years—easily double that. He tried to recall his birthday, or the last time celebrating it had meant something. Hazy recollections of a time before the war appeared in his mind. He remembered long hours in the linen factory and a father who beat him for coming home early or late, or for even coming home at all. He was always the runt of the litter, the brother who'd never amount to much. What would his mother think if she could see him today? He smoothed down the lapels on the suit the kid had procured for him.

"What do you think, Ma?"

Bruno flashed a yellow-toothed smile at the futility of trying to engage in conversation with his dead mother. But he felt sure she'd approve. Life on the streets had beaten him down, but tonight was his chance to rise from the flames that engulfed his life.

"Hey, Clark Gable, you ready yet?" Willi asked through the bathroom door. No way they were getting into the Kaiserhof Hotel, so they had to settle for getting ready in a seedier version a few blocks away.

Bruno took one last look at himself in the mirror. It was as good as he was going to look. Willi had forced him to the barbershop and helped him scrounge enough money together for a secondhand suit from a thrift store, which had cost them both several days' takings. He reached into the jacket pocket for the half of whiskey he snuck in there. The kid wouldn't like him drinking, but what did he know? He was going to need all the courage he could get to confront Milch. This was his ticket off the streets. This mattered.

"I'm coming out now," he called.

Willi was waiting anxiously as Bruno emerged. "Were you drinking? He's not going to see you if you're drunk, don't you realize that?"

Bruno ignored him.

Out on the street, it was dark and cold. He made toward the Kaiserhof Hotel, the kid scuttling along beside him.

"We're only going to get one shot at this. You know who we're looking for?" Willi held up a picture he cut from the newspaper.

"I know who I need to talk to."

"Just don't mess this up. You remember the plan?"

"I'm not stupid."

"Prove it."

He stopped walking, wanting to clip this young pup around the ear for talking to him like that. The boy was looking up at him, waiting for him to speak.

"I get him on the way out. The drivers pull up on the street in front of the hotel. He'll pause a few seconds to get in the car, and that's when I go to him."

"Remember to stay calm. He's not going to listen to the ravings of some lunatic."

"We've been over this 100 times." Bruno began walking again.

"Well, then, why don't I feel like you get it?"

Bruno calmed the ire rising within him. He longed to reach for the whiskey, but knew how the kid would react. He'd find a quiet time, a private moment, to steel his courage. He'd need it to speak to Milch.

They reached the hotel just after midnight. The street was

quiet, as no one had come out yet. They stayed around the corner, stamping their feet to ward off the bitter cold.

An hour passed before the men began emerging. Rich men with butlers to put coats around their shoulders walked down the long steps of the hotel to the cars waiting for them on the street. Bruno had his hand on the whiskey bottle in his pocket, and he drew it out and took a generous swig as the kid watched for Milch.

"That's him." The kid poked him, then saw the bottle. "What are you doing?"

"I'm cold. I need this."

Willi shook his head but turned back to point out an older man with a long dark beard who was walking down the steps. Bruno squinted to make him out. He was walking beside a younger man, who was also wearing a tuxedo. A taxi pulled up behind the car parked on the street.

"There he is," Willi said. "This is our big chance. Go!"

Bruno raised himself to his feet and wiped his mouth, seeing the car was about thirty yards away. He crossed the street as Milch was nearing the bottom of the steps. He had rehearsed what he would say a dozen times or more, and went over it in his mind as he made his way over: *Herr Milch, I was in your son's apartment building the night he disappeared. I saw two people acting suspiciously.*

The reward would be his.

The conversation in the ballroom was getting sloppy. The men were talking about their summer homes, their mistresses, the judges and politicians they had in their pockets. Seamus stood away from the group of industrialists he had been talking to and put his empty beer glass on the bar. He spotted Roland Eidinger across the room and walked across to him. The gray-haired man from Hamburg turned to him and held out a huge hand. Seamus took it.

"Time for me to get back to the wife and kids," he said.

"It was a pleasure," Eidinger said. "If you ever need anything from me, you call."

"Thanks, Roland," the younger man said.

"Don't let the Nazis get you down." Eidinger spoke so only Seamus could hear. "Without the say-so of the men in this room, they'll be gone in weeks. We'll keep them under control."

"I hope so."

"And don't let any of these old fools push you around. Most of them are nothing more than bootlickers. They don't know what it is to build something, just to get it handed to them. You show them what it's like."

"I appreciate that."

"Whatever you need. Remember that." Eidinger turned to rejoin the conversation.

The doorway was a few steps away when Seamus heard a voice in his ear.

"Leaving so soon?"

He turned around to see Otto Milch with his coat and hat on behind him.

"I figured it was time I got home to the wife. I'm only married a couple of weeks."

"I've had enough too. Let's walk out together."

Seamus knew there was nothing he could say and just nodded.

"I'm betting you came here in a taxi," Milch said.

"Intuitive of you."

"Let my driver take you home."

"No, I'm fine getting a cab."

"Have you had an opportunity to consider my offer?"

"The answer is the same."

"How can it be when you never even heard me out? Four hundred thousand Reichsmarks is a lot of money."

It was, but as part of Helmut's will, Seamus would have to forfeit it all to Helga in the event of a quick sale. His uncle had guarded against this. It wasn't his place to inform Otto Milch of the intricacies of his uncle's will, however. He just had to say no.

"It's a generous offer, but again, I need to respectfully decline."

They were through the lobby now and the splash of cold night air struck them as they walked outside. Seamus saw Milch's driver holding his hand up at the bottom of the steps that led up to the hotel.

"I'd be careful if I were you," Milch said.

"What do you mean?"

"I'm not a man you want to cross. I've made you a more than generous offer—"

"And I've respectfully turned it down. Now, if there's nothing else, Herr Milch, I'd like to get a cab home to my wife and family."

"There are many ways to make a man sell, you know."

They were at the bottom of the steps and Milch's chauffer was holding the door open. The older man got in.

"We'll speak again soon, Herr Ritter," he said. The chauffer closed the door.

Seamus stood a few seconds, watching the car drive off, aware of someone beside him. A man in an old suit was standing a few feet away. Seamus put his head down and started to walk away before something inside him dragged him back. The man was staring at him—with a patch over his eye and his face covered in scar tissue from a deep burn. One of the sleeves of his blazer hung lank by his side. Seamus felt his blood turn to ice as realization struck him like a hammer. It was him—the hobo from the basement. He was clean-shaven and wearing a suit, but it was him.

The homeless man seemed frozen to the spot. Seamus backed away, maintaining eye contact as he went. A taxi pulled up on the street and Seamus strode toward it and got in the back seat. He blurted out his address and the driver stepped on the gas. He turned around to see the man watching him as the car drove away.

Bruno didn't move for several seconds after the taxi left. Milch was long gone, but perhaps they'd unearthed someone better. He never even said a word to either of them, having frozen the second he recognized the man from the basement.

He was walking down the steps with Milch. What's going on? Did Milch hire him to get rid of his own son? If so, why did he offer a reward for his capture? Is the man going after Milch's family to get to the father?

Who knew how these fat cats lived their lives? None of it really mattered. All that did matter was that he took advantage of the new development.

Willi arrived beside him, red-faced and panting. "Did you even get to talk to him?"

"No. He bolted as soon as I opened my mouth."

"What happened? I knew you'd mess it up."

"Well, then, why did you ever partner up with me?"

He waited a minute or so for the kid to stop cursing and throwing his hands. "Why didn't you say anything to him?" The kid was talking too loudly. They were drawing the eyes of passersby.

"I saw someone even better. Let me explain."

Bruno walked away from the sidewalk and across the street. He turned to see Willi wasn't following him. "Come on," he said.

The young newsie ran after him, dodging a car which

honked at him as he crossed Mohrenstrasse. Bruno was down
an alleyway, out of sight, when Willi caught up to him.

"Now, are you going to tell me what happened? Did you
even say one word to him?"

Bruno wasn't going to admit any fallibility to this kid, but he
still needed his help. "I saw the man walking down the steps
with Milch."

"You saw what man? I don't have any idea what you're
talking about. Tell me what happened the night Ernst
disappeared."

The kid stared at him a few seconds, waiting for him to talk.
Was it better to share the secret with him, to fully enlist his
help? Would he steal the knowledge of what he saw that night
and claim the reward himself?

"Can I trust you?"

"Of course you can. You're the witness. I didn't see a thing. I
was in the bed I share with my three brothers that night."

"I'm trusting you now."

"Come on—spill. We're getting nowhere."

"I was in the basement of the building Ernst Milch owned
the night he disappeared. I saw a man and a woman carrying a
rolled-up rug down the stairs at four in the morning."

"Wow—they killed him? Did you get a good look at their
faces?"

"It was dark, and I'd been drinking—"

"Big surprise there."

Bruno didn't rise to the comment, though he felt like clip-
ping the newsie around the ear. "I didn't get a good look at the
woman, although I've definitely seen her around the building
before. I'm not sure of her face, but the man—I could pick him
out of a lineup."

"Why him and not her?"

"He gave me money. A beggar never forgets the face of

someone who gives them money, particularly when it's as much as he did."

"Why didn't you report it at the time?"

"I didn't care to. I figured it was their business, and I knew how the police would treat me. I try not to interfere in their world."

"So, who was the man you saw tonight walking with Milch?"

"The same man from the basement that night. I'm sure of it."

"He came out of the hotel with Otto Milch?" Bruno nodded. "Who was he?"

"I don't know. I heard him speaking—he had an unusual accent, definitely not from here."

"He must have been at the dinner in the hotel. God only knows why they left together. Maybe he's trying to take over Milch's company or something, but I'll bet the old man is none the wiser that he knocked off his kid. Are you thinking what I'm thinking?"

"We need to find this guy."

"What you think the chances are that the police listen to you, or that Milch cons us out of handing over the reward money?"

"High."

"Me too," Willi said. "We might be better off going directly to the source. These guys are all rich. It's not like he wouldn't be able to afford it. Five thousand is pocket change to these pigs."

"I don't know his name, and we can't get to Milch."

"You got a wallet?"

Bruno held up the tattered old leather wallet he found years before. It was coming apart at the seams. Willi took it and examined it before handing it back.

"Ok, it'll have to do. Here's what you do—go back up to the

hotel and tell the guy you found the fat cat's wallet. Tell him you need his name to return it."

"Got it."

Bruno crossed the street and ascended the stairs toward the hotel. The doorman looked at him with suspicious eyes.

"That man, the one who just got into the taxi, dropped this." Bruno reached into his pocket for his wallet, keeping it in his hand to disguise how beaten up it was. "Do you know his name? I'd like to return it to him."

"You can leave it at reception."

"I'd rather return it myself."

"I don't know his name, but give me a minute." He disappeared inside. He emerged two minutes later. "The younger man, was it?"

"Yes."

"Seamus Ritter."

"Ritter?"

"Yes. Of Ritter Industries, I believe."

"Thank you."

Bruno turned and walked down the stairs. They had a name: Ritter, from Ritter Industries. Finding a man with a name wouldn't be hard, and knowing the company name would make it even easier.

6

Sunday, February 19

Lisa and her daughter were still wrapped up in one another like a mother deer and its fawn when the little girl woke her up. The weight of what Lisa heard the night before came down on her consciousness like a hammer. It was the first thing she felt. Part of her wanted to march downstairs and confront her mother about it, all consequences be damned. But she was sick, and dying. They wouldn't have traveled here if telling Lisa the truth wasn't on her mother's mind. Why else would she come to see the only other person who knew, just before she died? Her mother didn't care about her old house, or even the town she grew up in. The reason they came here was for the conversation Ingrid had with Liesl the night before. She closed her eyes, as if the answer would come to her. Hannah moved her arms, stretching out like a flower opening its petals to the sun.

"Did you sleep well, my sweet?"

"Oh, yes."

Lisa got out of bed, the floor cold beneath her stockinged

feet, and threw the curtains open. The sky was slate-gray. The North Sea was boiling and booming against the rocks at the end of the meadow that led up to the house. She stood there a few seconds, staring out, afraid to see anyone else in the house. The thought occurred to her that if she were to find her real father, she needed her mother's help. *Have a little faith in her,* she thought. *Would she have come all this way if she intends to keep it to herself?*

Her mother pushed the door open and came inside. Hannah jumped out of the bed and ran to her. Lisa's heart felt like it was stuck in a vise.

"How did you sleep?" Ingrid asked.

Lisa took a few seconds to find the words. "Well. I slept well." She wished it were true. The instinct to ask her about what she heard the night before was almost too much to fight back.

"I think Liesl is preparing breakfast for us, if you'd like to come downstairs. I think we might just have time for a walk down to the beach afterward before the rains come in."

Lisa nodded, hoping that she was able to hide the storm raging within her. Lisa lifted Hannah in her arms and pointed down toward the sea. They watched the waves battering the coast for a minute or two before she returned Hannah to the floor to get her dressed. Her mother waited, not saying a word or acting any differently than she would have if the conversation last night had never taken place.

Ingrid took Hannah down for breakfast after the little girl was dressed. Lisa took refuge in the washroom, deciding to see what happened with Ingrid and Liesl today before confronting her mother about what she heard.

A breakfast of fresh bread, sardines, boiled eggs, and cheese was on the table as Lisa arrived downstairs. All the others were waiting for her, the food untouched.

The two women greeted her with warm smiles, though her

mother's complexion was gray and her skin dull. Lisa sat at the table, waiting for a moment that never came. The other ladies sat and ate, talking about the weather, the sea, and the prospects for a good walk along the shore.

The rain held off, and Liesl led them outside to stroll along the coast. There was no acknowledgment from Ingrid or Liesl, even through a look or a gesture, as to what Lisa might have heard. They had no idea. What if she never mentioned it? Things might go on as they always had.

Lisa pulled her raincoat lapels up over the sides of her face. She was lagging behind the group, even with Ingrid's slow pace. Liesl appeared beside her.

"Are you all right? You seem a little...off."

Lisa flashed a smile. "I'm fine—just a little tired, maybe. I'm having a good time. It's beautiful here."

Liesl didn't look convinced. "It's time we got back to the house. Your mother is getting tired, and is too stubborn to admit it. I don't want to get stuck out here in the rain, either." She gestured toward a foreboding black cloud over the sea.

"Mother, we need to go back."

"Not yet," Ingrid said.

"Don't be ridiculous, Mother," Lisa said. "You need to save your strength."

"For what? This will be the last time I'll ever see this place. I'll be dead soon enough."

Hannah's fingers curled tighter around Lisa's hand and a tear fled down her cheek. Lisa saw her daughter's reaction. She let go of her hand for a moment and went to her mother.

"Can you stop talking about dying in front of the child? You're upsetting her."

Her mother looked at her for a few seconds before nodding. "I'm sorry. I've never had to deal with anything like this before."

It was hard to know how to respond to that, so she gave her mother a hug before returning to her daughter.

They lingered a few more hours in the house. The secret tearing her insides apart never left her consciousness for more than a few seconds at a time. She began to resent Ingrid and Liesl, or at least being around them at that moment, and it was with some relief that she greeted the decision to leave after lunch. It was time to get her mother home anyway. She was getting tired, and the pain etched on her face was growing more apparent as the day wore on. Liesl stood at the door and hugged each of them in turn. Lisa took the opportunity to search her eyes for some hidden truth, but found none. Disappointed, she turned and walked back toward the car. She watched as her mother said goodbye to her cousin for what would surely be the last time. Neither woman shed a tear, instead greeting the moment with stoic resolve. They spoke to each other as if they'd see each other again in weeks or months.

Lisa sat in the driver's seat of the car and waved out the window as she pulled out onto the dirt track that led back toward the sea. Perhaps Ingrid was waiting for them to get back on the road to tell her what she was talking about with her cousin the night before, or perhaps for when they got home. She seemed distant in the car, barely speaking as they made their way back to the highway toward Berlin. They were almost halfway into the three-hour drive when she asked the question.

"What was my father like?"

Ingrid was looking out the window and turned her head back. Hannah was asleep on the back seat beside her grandmother. This was the time. She just hoped the little girl wasn't listening. Children were always listening.

"He was a good man until he succumbed. You witnessed it all. He wasn't always that way."

"I remember it well."

Silence. The sound of wheels on the road. She searched for the next words. They would be some of the most important she ever uttered.

"I barely slept last night."

"I'm sorry to hear that."

"I had a lot on my mind." Her heart was thundering in her chest. "I heard the conversation you had with Liesl."

"What conversation?" Her mother's tone was sharp.

"The one about who my real father was."

"Oh, Lisa. You must have been sleepwalking or something—"

"I heard what you said. What you both said."

"Don't be ridiculous."

"Tell me the truth!" Lisa said. She flicked her eyes up to the rearview mirror and saw shock on her mother's face. Hannah was still asleep. "I heard it all. Liesl told you I deserved to know who my real father is. So who is he?"

Lisa tried to fight back the tears, but wasn't able. Cars flashed past her on the road, hedges and green fields on either side.

Her mother seemed to be struck dumb. A few babbles came from her lips, but nothing more.

"Please, Mother. It's been tearing me apart since I heard."

"I told Liesl that the past is best left where it lies—in the past."

"How could you keep this from me all these years? Please don't leave me like this. I have to know."

Her mother closed her eyes and brought the hand she was resting on Hannah's side up to her face. "I never should have said a word."

"But you did, and I heard you. Who was my father?"

"It doesn't matter who he was—he's dead now."

"He died? When?"

"Years ago. What does it matter? Dead is dead."

"Who was he? What was his name?"

"I never meant to fall for him. It was all a mistake."

"Did my father..." She had to correct herself. "Did your husband know?"

"In the end, yes. He knew, but he stood by me and raised you as his own. We put it behind us and never spoke of it again."

"Who was my father?"

"What does it matter?"

"It matters!" Lisa shouted. Hannah stirred a little, but went back to sleep.

Ingrid looked out the window as she spoke. "He was a good man. A doctor. I was working as a nurse at the time. We never meant to fall for one another—it just happened. Volker and I had hit on hard times in our marriage, and J was kind and ready to listen."

"His first initial was J? What was his full name?"

"What does it matter? He's dead. We broke up before you were born, and he never even laid eyes on you. Volker raised you. He's your real father."

"He's dead? How do you know?"

"I saw the notice in the newspaper a few years ago."

It felt ridiculous to mourn a man she never met, but that's what she felt in that moment.

"Did you love him?"

"For a time, but like many things, it faded. It would've been too difficult for me to get divorced. His parents wouldn't have tolerated that. We were doomed from the start and went our separate ways."

"Did he even know you were with child?"

"I didn't see the point in telling him that."

Lisa took a moment to compose herself. She was wary of pushing her mother, even though the questions were piling up inside her mind like bricks in a massive house.

Just as the older woman was about to speak again, a grimace of pain came across her face. She closed her eyes.

"Are you all right, Mother?" Lisa asked from the driver's seat.

"It comes and goes."

"Do you have any of those painkillers I gave you?"

"I ran out this morning."

"And you didn't tell me?"

"I didn't want to trouble anyone."

It was difficult to keep from screaming at her. The urge to make her passing as peaceful as possible seemed to rule every conversation they had, but she was boiling inside. Not knowing the man's name was killing her, but she couldn't press her mother now. Lisa took a few deep breaths, composing herself before she answered.

"Don't do that again, Mother. Your pain is not an inconvenience to us. Your comfort is the most important thing."

"I'm sorry."

"How bad is it?"

"Getting worse."

"There's a town a few minutes up the road. I'm stopping off there to get you something for the pain."

A harsh silence descended in the car. Lisa flicked her eyes back at her mother, who was struggling to keep the agonies within her unseen. Lisa pulled off the highway and into a town called Neuruppin, which was covered in Nazi flags. The National Socialist revolution was well underway here.

A local policeman was happy to give them directions to the local pharmacist, and Lisa parked and ran in. She emerged a couple of minutes later with a bottle of pills in her hand. She took a flask of water that she filled at Liesl's house for Hannah and gave it to her mother. She watched her as she took the pill.

"It's morphine," she said. "The man behind the counter recommended heroin, but I wasn't sure."

"I don't like taking pills."

"Better to take some pills than live in agony," Lisa replied.

"The pharmacist said it'd take a few minutes to take effect. Just try to relax until then." Lisa cupped her mother's cheek before kissing her. She shut the door and got back in the driver's seat. Ingrid closed her eyes and fell asleep as the drug cast its spell on her. Lisa's questions would have to wait. They stayed parked outside the pharmacist's until Lisa was satisfied her mother was comfortable. She pulled out of the parking spot to make for Berlin once more. Thoughts of her father and who he might have been assailed her mind all the way home.

Maureen was in the living room reading *The Magic Mountain* by Thomas Mann. The radio was on, playing the American jazz they all loved. Her father was sitting across from her, reading the newspaper. It was still hard to believe they lived here. They'd come so far, and her father had kept his word about something. *At last.* So much had changed in such a short space of time, and with Ingrid's illness, more change was coming. The wounds from her own mother's sickness and death were still open, and now she and her siblings were to be witnesses to it again.

"I was at the dinner last night with all the bigwigs."

"How did it go?"

"It was an interesting night. Herr Goebbels made an appearance."

"Herr who?" Maureen asked.

"One of Hitler's best pals. He's in charge of messaging for the Nazis. He came with cup in hand to beg for money. It seems the National Socialist revolution is in trouble."

"They didn't get any, did they?"

Her father's face dropped. "Most of the business moguls there figured it was in their best interests to prop up the party. They gave a lot of money."

"Did you?"

"Of course not. I'd never lower myself, or Ritter Industries, to support those lunatics."

"I don't understand it. How can anyone support that madman?"

"Goebbels told the industrialists what they wanted to hear."

"And what was that?" Maureen asked.

"That the Nazis would crush the unions that threaten the owners' power. He promised they'd revamp the military and the country's infrastructure. The fat cats in the room all purred in unison when they heard that."

"Is that who we are now? Fat cats? We're taking advantage of the working people?" Maureen asked, anger rising in her.

Her father laughed, but she wasn't joking. Why did he agree to come here? They could have been home in Newark. They would have been poor, but at least not among the madness here. Was it better here in this mansion in Berlin when the entire country seemed to be falling apart around their ears?

"Of course not," her father answered. "We're who we've always been. I have a responsibility to my workers, and to the rest of you under this roof."

Maureen stared at him for a few seconds before she went back to her book. A honking sound came from the front of the house.

"They're back," Maureen said.

She went the front door to help bring Hannah in the house. Lisa emerged first. She looked exhausted—her eyes were ringed red and the light makeup on her face was ruined from crying. Maureen never saw her look anything like that before, and it shocked her.

"How was it? Is everything ok?" Maureen asked.

"The trip was good," came the lukewarm reply. "Mother took a turn for the worse on the way home, though."

Lisa opened the back door and checked on her mother, who

was groggy as she woke up. Maureen got Hannah and carried her to the house. The door opened before they got to it, but her father's wide smile melted as he saw Ingrid. He ran out to help her inside. The other three children appeared around the door too. Fiona went to hug Lisa, but stopped short upon seeing Ingrid.

"Let's get you up to bed," Maureen's father said.

"I'm fine," Ingrid murmured.

"This again?" Lisa said. "You need to rest. No arguments."

Maureen watched as they helped Ingrid up the stairs to her room. The children knew what was going on. Seeing someone as sick as Ingrid was in their home was all too familiar. The joy on their faces drained away, and they made their way back to the living room to play with the toys strewn all over the floor.

"Is she going to die?" Conor asked as Maureen sat down.

She had no idea how to answer the question other than by telling the truth. Conor knew what death was. They all did. "I think so. Lisa and Father are trying to make her as comfortable as they can."

"Tonight?" Conor added.

"No, not tonight," Michael said. "Keep your stupid questions to yourself."

Lisa's mother was semiconscious as Seamus carried her upstairs. He laid her in bed and she was asleep in seconds. Lisa thought to change her out of her clothes, but decided to let her rest. Her new husband was standing beside her as she shut the door behind her.

"What happened?"

"She was in too much pain on the way home. I had to stop off and get her something. You can see the effect it had on her."

He took her in his arms. It felt like medicine. "I'm sorry," he said.

"I need to talk to you. Alone."

"Of course. Hannah's with Maureen and Michael downstairs."

She led him into the bedroom and shut the door. She sat on the bed, barely able to speak. Seamus probably thought it was all about her mother's health. It took thirty seconds or more before she regained her composure enough to tell him.

"I couldn't sleep last night when we were in Liesl's house. I got up and heard her talking to Mother. Liesl was questioning her about something Mother never told me growing up, telling her it was time to speak to me about it. Mother argued with her. I didn't know what they were on about until Liesl said that it was time Mother told me *who my real father is*."

"What? Are you sure?"

"I gave her the chance to tell me when we woke up in the morning, but she acted like everything was normal. It was only when I confronted her on the way home that she finally admitted it."

"That the man who raised you wasn't your real father?"

"She had an affair with a doctor when she was working as a nurse. She never told him she was pregnant and they broke up. Her husband took her back and she never spoke of it again. She hasn't told me his name yet."

"What happened to this man?"

"He's dead. She read the notice in the paper a few years ago. I didn't want to press her about it because of her condition, but I could hardly help myself."

"I understand. Do you know how long they saw each other for? Was it serious?"

"I think it was. She said divorcing her husband wasn't an option, but it seemed like she and my real father discussed it. I just can't believe it. It seems like my whole life was a smoke-screen. She tried to dismiss it...as if it didn't matter anymore."

"I'm so sorry." Seamus sat next to her on the bed and held her for ten minutes. They went over what she heard again, but didn't find any answers. He didn't seem to know what to say, but the truth was, neither did she.

"Give me some time," she said as he broke away.

"Ok. We'll be downstairs when you're ready."

Alone on the bed, the same questions swirled around in her head like a whirlpool. She tried to imagine who her father was, but couldn't.

She came downstairs two hours later. Maureen and Seamus were in the kitchen. "Is anyone going to get dinner started around here?" she asked.

"I'll help you," Maureen said. "We can do it together."

"You can go, Seamus. We're fine."

Her husband nodded and walked out to the living room, where Hannah and Conor were playing with her new dollhouse.

Maureen obviously could see how upset she still was and put an arm around her. They separated as they got to the sideboard and Lisa reached into the cupboard for the carrots. She took a knife from a drawer and peeled them over the sink, letting the orange shards of skin fall on the plates left there. She knew Maureen was behind her, but didn't speak. They worked in silence a few seconds before her she addressed her.

"It must be hard—seeing my mother like this."

"I'm just sad for you, and for Hannah. I know how much her grandmother loves her."

Lisa still didn't turn around, just moved the carrots onto the cutting board to slice them. The *clack* of the knife hitting the wooden cutting board rang through the kitchen over and over.

"It's hard on her, and on me, too. I don't know what we'd do if we didn't have your father and the rest of you. It's as if my mother was waiting to leave us until Hannah and I had enough support in place. It feels like she held on just long enough to make sure we were taken care of."

Conor wandered in, unaware, and asked what they were making. Embarrassed about the tears on her cheeks, Lisa kept her back turned and continued chopping the carrots as Maureen answered his question. The little boy didn't seem to notice the tension and ran out, excited at the prospect of chicken and potatoes for dinner.

Lisa waited until the little boy was gone before she began talking again.

"It must be hard for you to be around someone sick again. Does it bring back memories of your own mother?"

Maureen didn't seem to know quite how to answer. *It must be. It should be, but knowing her, she hasn't been thinking of herself all this time.*

"I'm just sad for you and Hannah. Being here, away from home, makes the memories of my mother seem all the more distant. I don't know if that's good or bad."

"I just don't want to upset you or any of the other children. No kid should have to live through this twice."

"We're here for you and Hannah. At least we had Father when Mother died—for a while, anyway."

"Thank you. I appreciate that so much," Lisa said and finished the carrots. She pushed them into a pot to place on the stove.

"It must be even harder for you because your father is already gone. You've never talked much about him."

You mean the man who raised me, or the one I just found out about? Lisa didn't want to show how much her stepdaughter had unknowingly upset her by mentioning the man she thought was her father her entire life. *Best just to act as normal.*

"What do you want to know? He was a hotelier. He died back in '24."

"What was he like?"

Lisa put down the chicken she was in the act of pulling apart. She went to the kitchen sink and rinsed her hands under the water.

"He was a good man for much of my life. I try to remember the man he was when I was a child, rather than the drunken gambler he turned into later in life."

"I'm sorry."

"I say he died in '24, but the reality is, he was murdered. The police found him floating in the Spree with a bullet in the back of his head." She shut off the water and reached for a tea towel to dry her hands.

"That's awful. Did they ever find who did it?"

"The police? No. They knew, but couldn't make anything stick. He'd gambled everything away at that point. All our money...the hotel. Everything. And when he had nothing left to risk on a game of cards, they took his life. It was the last thing he had."

Maureen kept quiet, waiting for Lisa to speak again. "He fell apart after my brothers died in the war. I don't suppose he was ever as close to me as he was to them. That's what set him off."

"You were never close with him?"

"Not like he was with my brothers. I always felt left out, somehow, like the cat lover at a dog show. It's hard to explain at the time, but I think I realize why now."

"Why?"

Lisa shook her head and gave her the line she would have given if she asked the question the day before.

"I was born so long after my brothers. Henning was twelve

when I was born, and Ingo was just a year younger. I always wondered about that..."

Finishing the sentence was too hard.

"You didn't plan to have Hannah and you don't love her any less." Maureen said.

"I love her so much I feel like I'm going to explode sometimes."

Lisa took a breath. Their conversation returned to what it would have been if this were a typical night in the house, though they both knew it was far from that. They talked about school and fashion and movies and books and prepared the dinner side by side.

7

Wednesday, February 22

Three days passed, and Ingrid was fading fast. The woman in the bed bore little more than a passing resemblance to the mother Lisa grew up with. The determined, stubborn dynamo who had run her husband's failing hotel those last few years was gone, and all that remained was a wizened old woman whose sole mission in life seemed to be concealing her pain. The only thing worse than being by her mother's side was not being with her, so Lisa had taken to sleeping on the floor in the bedroom and only left to use the bathroom or to prepare the food that her mother almost invariably failed to keep down.

Time was punctuated by more pain. Her mother spoke little, trapped inside her eyelids much of the time. Dr. Scherzinger came after lunch. Lisa took a few seconds to do her hair before he arrived, making sure to look respectable before answering the door. He arrived with a grim expression that expressed the weight of the situation. Hannah was downstairs with the nanny, and Lisa took a few moments to be with her daughter as the doctor examined her mother. She bounced up when she heard his footsteps coming downstairs.

Dr. Scherzinger was only a few years older than her, with a well-trimmed brown beard and gray eyes. He kept his voice low.

"Your mother is in a lot of discomfort. More than you probably know."

"Can you help her?"

"Only to ease her passing. It's time to give her this." He handed her a bottle of morphine. "Place one drop on her tongue as her pain comes. It'll numb it the best we can."

"Now?"

"Just be aware that when you give her this drug, her pain will be reduced, but so will her senses. The lucid person you know, talking and interacting with others, will cease to be. This is far stronger than the medication she's been on to this point, but she needs it."

Lisa felt her eyes bulge and her vision blur, but wiped the tears away before they broke down her cheeks.

"Perhaps you should first ask her what she wants," Dr. Scherzinger said.

"She'll only say no. I can't let her live in agony. I'll let the children talk to her one last time first. I'll give it to her this evening, after they get back from school."

"I think that would be best," he said. "Say your goodbyes before you give the drug to her. It could be the last time."

The doctor shook her hand and told her to call him should she need anything else. Hannah ran to her once again as the door shut, and Lisa could not hold back the tears. She picked up her daughter and sobbed for several minutes. Then, when she was ready, she went back up to her mother and sat in the bed beside her.

"What did Scherzinger say?" Her mother asked through gritted teeth.

"He said you were in more pain than I knew, and also that you were hiding it from me."

"It's no use being a burden."

Lisa thought, *This is the last time I'll have with my mother. What questions do I have? What do I say to someone I've been through everything with, when I know I'll never speak to her in the same way again?*

"Is there anything else you can tell me about my real father? Did he have other children?"

"There's no one else. Forget about him. I understand you must be curious, but try not to look back. You have so much in your life now. The past will only hold you back."

"You've been a good mother to me," Lisa said and put her head on Ingrid's shoulder.

Perhaps her mother was right and they should put the past behind them. Her real father and the man who raised her were both gone, and soon the woman who concealed the truth from her all these years would be too.

The time had come to say their goodbyes. She wasn't going to fight with her mother now. Seamus wouldn't be home until after five o'clock. It seemed like an eternity.

A few minutes passed before her mother submitted to the escape of sleep, and Lisa sat alone, watching her until the kids came home.

Maureen, Michael, Fiona, and Conor were back for only five minutes when she made the telephone call to Seamus to come home. The thought of her mother suffering for any longer was too much.

Ingrid was awake when Seamus arrived. He was only half an hour earlier than he was meant to be, but Lisa was grateful.

"I wanted to bring you flowers," he said as he met her at the front door.

"Next year, or any of the dozens of years we'll have together after that," she said as she led him up the stairs. The children congregated in the bedroom. They knew something was wrong. Her mother couldn't get more than a few sentences out without grimacing in pain. Her conversation with the children about their day in school was punctuated with gasps, groans, and long pauses. It was time to tell them. Lisa left Seamus in the room with Hannah and took the other children aside. They looked at her with wide, innocent eyes.

"My mother has gotten worse," Lisa said.

"I'm so sorry," Fiona said.

"Thank you, my sweet," Lisa said and hugged the young girl. "My mother is in a lot of pain." The children were stone-faced and silent. Doing this to them tore at her heart.

"The doctor came earlier today and gave me some strong medicine to take her discomfort away, but it'll mean she won't be able to talk to us anymore. She'll sleep most of the time."

"Until she dies?" Conor asked. Michael shoved him.

"Yes. I don't know when that will be, but it won't be long. I think it's best that we take a minute with her to say goodbye before I give her the medicine. Before she...goes."

The children stood still for a few seconds before nudging each other back into the bedroom.

Seamus was sitting in Lisa's chair, holding his mother-in-law's hand. Hannah was on the bed, playing with her grand-mother, who was awake once more.

"The children want to say goodbye to you, Mother," Lisa said. "Your pain has gotten so bad that we're going to have to up your medicine and you might not be awake a lot of the time from now on."

"No need to say goodbye. I'm not going yet." She coughed after she spoke, so much so that Lisa reached out to her. It took her a full minute to regain herself.

Maureen stepped forward. "This isn't goodbye, then—just a reminder that we love you. Isn't that right, children?" They all replied in unison and then stepped forward to hug her. A smile

spread across Ingrid's gaunt face as the children came to her.
They didn't handle her too roughly. It seemed she might break.
The kids stood back when Conor finished.

"Thanks," Seamus said. "Go on downstairs now."

The children left as Lisa brought her focus back to her
mother again. She sat on the bed beside her and reached over
to hug her. The embrace seemed to cause her more discomfort,
so she drew back and kissed her on the cheek. It was like
kissing paper left out in the cold. Hannah got up on the bed
and put her arms around her Oma again. All the girl knew was
that she was sick and needed extra love. That was enough.

"You never were one for speeches or outpourings of
emotion," Lisa said with tears in her eyes. Her mother shook
her head, ready. "I can't stand to see you in pain like this." What
about her father? Could she ask what his name was? Just a
name?

"I need that now," her mother said, gesturing to the
morphine.

Lisa wiped away her own selfish thoughts and drew the
dropper from the small brown bottle. She had to wipe the tears
away with her other hand.

"I love you, Mother. Thank you for everything you've done
for Hannah and me."

"Thank you, Lisa. I know you're in safe hands now."

Seamus didn't speak, just stood up and took Hannah in his
arms. Lisa held the dropper in her mother's mouth and let the
liquid run down her throat. Ingrid settled back on the propped-
up pillows and let her eyes droop shut. She was asleep in
seconds. Lisa took Hannah in her arms and felt Seamus
embracing them both. She bawled like a child.

Thursday, February 23

Maureen and the children trudged out of the front door on their way to school. The bikes were around the side of the house, underneath an awning. Michael took the lead, as always, with Maureen at the back of their little convoy. They'd only been in the city a few months, but the changes they observed in that time were hard to miss. The Nazis had been in power a few weeks, and had seemingly spent most of their time hanging flags in every building they could. The swastika, a symbol she'd never seen before journeying here, was ubiquitous. The next government, which every sensible person assured her would come soon, was going to have a difficult time erasing the memory of the National Socialists.

Conor and Fiona viewed the flags as nothing more than interesting sideshows, unusual decorations for a strange new city. Michael was fifteen and read the papers. The last few weeks were dominated by stories of the new government. The sooner this Nazi fad collapsed, the better. Normal life could resume after the next election. In the meantime, the flags would remain, and the Stormtroopers would march. Hitler would make his speeches, and the crowds who worshipped him would cheer.

Maureen and Michael dropped the two younger children off at the Volksschule before carrying on. They parked the bikes, wished each other well, and carried on inside alone.

Maureen was on time for class. She knew a few of the other kids, but sat alone. She took her books out and laid them on the desk. A gentle rain began falling outside, and she peered out the window at it until the teacher ambled in. Herr Schultz was in his late fifties and had a gray beard and fuzzy hair that reminded her of Uncle Helmut. Perhaps that's why Maureen had taken to him so quickly. The students stood as he put his bag down on his desk. He bade them good morning and went to the board to begin the math lesson.

Herr Schultz was writing the morning's problems on the blackboard when a knock interrupted him. He went to answer it. Maureen didn't pay any attention to who the old teacher was talking to, thinking about Lisa and her mother. The door closed, and a new boy walked in. The girls in class fixed their eyes on him like limpets on the side of a fishing trawler.

"This is... What's your name?" Herr Schultz asked.

"Thomas Reus."

He was tall, with short brown hair and blue eyes. His broad shoulders pushed against his white shirt.

"Thomas will be joining our class, just as Maureen did. You're not all the way from the United States, though, are you?" the teacher asked with a smile.

"From Cologne," Thomas said.

"Go down and sit next to Maureen. You two should get acquainted."

Thomas walked through the lines of students and took the desk beside Maureen. "Hello," he whispered.

She didn't know where to look or whether to answer. A thin smile was the best she could manage as her pencil rolled off the desk. She reached down to get it at the same time as Thomas, and they bumped heads.

"I'm so sorry," he said.

"Watch where you're going." She swiped the pencil out of his hand. He rubbed the top of his head with a smile on his face she couldn't help mirroring.

"What's going on down there?" Herr Schultz asked. "I haven't heard a word out of you in all the time you've been here, Maureen. Good to see you're making friends."

The old teacher turned back to face the blackboard.

"You see? We're making friends," Thomas said.

Maureen tried to focus on the lesson and not to laugh, but it was hard.

It was still raining as Maureen arrived home with the other children from school later that day. They left their bikes and took the tram, but still got soaked. They ran for the door, bursting inside. Maureen went to fetch towels, throwing one to each of her siblings before tending to herself.

Margarete, the new nanny her father hired, was sitting on an armchair reading a book as Hannah played with some building blocks on the floor. The little girl ran to her and Maureen took her in her arms.

"I'll take her upstairs to see the others," she said to Margarete. The old nanny didn't argue, or even say a word.

Lisa was at her mother's bedside. Ingrid looked at peace. She was fast asleep. Maureen pulled up a chair beside her stepmother. "How is she?"

"The same," Lisa answered.

"Why don't you go downstairs and take a break? I'll sit with your mother for a while. It'll do you good."

"Don't you have homework?"

"I'll get to it later. Now, go and see your daughter."

Lisa gave her a watery smile and stood up. She kissed her mother on the forehead before leaving the room.

Maureen settled into the seat. Five minutes passed, and she was wishing she brought a book when her stepmother came back.

"I need a bath. It's been a few days. Do you mind staying a little while longer?"

"Not at all," Maureen replied. "Go ahead. We'll be right here."

She took a moment to go and get *The Magic Mountain* by Thomas Mann from her room and was back in less than a minute. The room was deathly quiet, just as it had been when her own mother was almost gone. She tried to focus on the words on the pages in front of her face, but found it difficult. She had only gotten through a paragraph when she heard Ingrid.

"Lisa?" she said in a tone just above a whisper.

Maureen threw down her book. "No, she's in the bath. Shall I go and fetch her?"

"I'm sorry, Lisa," she gasped. "I should have told you."

"No, it's Maureen," she said, but the words didn't seem to register.

"I lied to you. About your father."

Maureen looked around, not knowing what to do. Father wasn't home yet, and she could hear Lisa in the bathtub. "Let me get your daughter."

"I lied to protect you."

Maureen was just about to run to get Lisa when she felt Ingrid's hand on her wrist like an iron clamp. The woman's eyes opened. "Don't try to find him." Each word she spoke seemed like a monumental effort. "It's too dangerous. Too dangerous. He didn't marry me because we're Jews. Don't go to him," she whispered. The grip on Maureen's wrist relented and the older woman's eyes closed.

Maureen sat panting for a few seconds, desperately trying to work out what Ingrid said. Unable to make any sense of it, she got up and ran into the bathroom.

Lisa was in the bath and turned, startled, as Maureen burst in. "It's your mother. She was awake and talking."

"I'm coming," Lisa said and jumped out of the water.

Maureen was back in the bedroom when her stepmother joined her a minute later in a bathrobe, her hair still wet from the tub.

Ingrid was fast asleep, as if nothing ever happened.

"She was just awake."

"What did she say?"

"I don't know—something about your father?"

"What?"

"She said she lied to you. She lied to protect you?"

Maureen stopped there. The full truth seemed like a precipice she couldn't approach in that moment. Ingrid needed to be the one to tell her. It was between them. If Ingrid said it once she'd say it again. Lisa could hear it from her. The thought of telling her new stepmother everything she heard terrified her.

Lisa went to her mother, inches from her face. "Mother, are you awake? What did you tell Maureen? I'm here now. It's me —Lisa."

But the woman in the bed didn't stir.

Lisa waited in her bathrobe a few minutes until it became clear that Ingrid wasn't going to say anything more. Maureen sat alone as her stepmother got changed. She came back within five minutes.

"She said that about my father?"

Maureen nodded. "She must be hysterical."

"She must be," Lisa said and stood up.

"I should go and get my homework done."

"Yes, of course," Lisa said. "Thank you."

Maureen stood up and left Lisa alone, staring at her mother asleep in the bed as if searching for answers on her blank, sleeping face.

8

Friday, February 24

Morning came. The sound of the children coming into their room woke Lisa. She tried to mirror their sympathetic smiling faces, but it was beyond her. Even sitting with Hannah seemed like a distraction. Seamus seemed to quickly realize she needed to be alone and took Hannah downstairs with the others for breakfast.

The time came for her mother's medicine, but what if she didn't give it? Would she wake up and be more coherent? Would she be able to tell her what she was talking about last night? Did anyone else know what she was talking about?

The bottle was shaking in her hand. How could she be this selfish? Her mother was in agonizing pain. Maureen was right about her delirium the night before—she was dreaming or seeing things. But she needed her medicine, and it was time. She opened the bottle and took the dropper in her hand. Squeezing the rubber ball at the top of the glass tube, she readied the morphine. Her mother's eyes flicked open and then shut again.

A lightning bolt of pain seemed to flow through her, and her body stiffened. Lisa held the morphine in her hand, ready.

Her mother's eyes flicked open again in a rare moment of lucidity. Lisa couldn't resist asking questions.

"Who is my father? Why did you say you lied to protect me?"

"I don't know what I was saying. I wasn't myself."

Her mother grimaced. She clamped her eyes shut, trying to fight off the agony she was in. Lisa dropped the medicine onto her tongue, and her body relaxed. She was asleep again in seconds. Lisa sat alone for several minutes, staring into nothing. A strange mix of love, regret, sadness, and anger was infesting her every cell.

She stood up and went downstairs. Seamus was with the children at the breakfast table. He must have seen something in her face.

"What's wrong?" he asked.

He stood up—they all did. Hannah looked like she was about to cry. Lisa took her daughter in her arms. "Everything's fine. I just need to speak to you."

She and Seamus put on coats and went outside. It seemed the only place to get away from the children.

"She woke up for a few seconds," Lisa said. "I had to ask her about my father."

"Did she answer?"

"She denied it. She said she wasn't herself."

"I'm sure it's nothing—the drugs have taken a huge toll on her. Now, you should get back to her. She might start up again."

"Come with me for a few minutes."

"Of course."

Lisa took his hand, and they hurried back into the house. It took a few seconds to hang up their coats before they ascended the stairs, hand in hand.

Her mother was asleep when they entered the bedroom,

but a spear of panic struck her when she saw her pallid complexion. Something was wrong. The sound of her breath was gone. She let go of her husband and ran to the bed, holding a finger to her pulse. Seamus was beside her in a second and holding her. The same feelings of love and anger swirled around inside her. Tears flowed down her cheeks like rain on a pane of glass. Lisa was just able to make out Maureen at the door holding Hannah. Soon all the other children were in the room too.

Maureen had a strange, almost knowing look on her face. She had seen death before.

~

Saturday February 25

The memories of his mother came back to haunt Michael. Ingrid's death brought back memories he'd long suppressed. The people in the adventure books he read died in plane crashes, or saving native tribes from vicious prides of lions, but the death he knew was nothing like that. It was slow, and soul-crushing. It overtook all else until it subsumed everything around it, sucking everyone into its vortex. It happened again. Lisa was a good person and he didn't want to do anything to upset her, but it was becoming all too much to take. It was hard to know if anyone noticed how he felt. Even Conor and Fiona were tiptoeing through the house, afraid to wake or upset Lisa. It was all too familiar.

He had begun seeing his mother in his dreams again. This wasn't unusual in of itself, but the images were all of her on her deathbed, faded and drawn, her hair graying at the edges and her skin lined. The worst dreams were the ones where she returned alive. She'd lost her memory and forgotten she had children. She was in New York living without them, and suddenly remembered she had a family. The dreams seemed so real that he could almost feel her against him.

Waking up was like grieving her all over again, for it was as if he had lost her anew. That was how he woke up the last three mornings in a row—sweating and short of breath and almost in tears for the lack of his mother. It wasn't Ingrid's fault, or Lisa's, or even his father's. It was just something to bear, like so many other things. Like living with Maeve for those two years in Newark without his father. It was a burden they had to carry.

The things he expected to be hard—moving to Germany and settling in—had been easy. It was everything else that was difficult. School was fine, and he made friends. He hadn't written to any of his old friends back in America in months. What was the point? Berlin was their home now. Father was married to someone from the city, and they had more here than they ever had in America. *Am I ever going back? Will I ever see my old friends and neighbors again?*

It was best to put them out of his mind and focus on the present. He was proud of Father for bringing them here and for what he was building. Maureen still complained that he wasn't around enough, but she would do the same if he was home all day. Michael enjoyed the fact that he didn't have to answer to her anymore. Lisa was gentle with her discipline. She seemed to know not to overstep the mark, and besides, her mother took up almost all of her time. With Father at the factory so much, and everyone else occupied, he had more freedom than he ever had in Newark. Using that freedom was fun.

Michael finished his homework in double-quick time. His new teacher didn't assign as much as they had in America. She encouraged the kids to get outside and play once they got home, and he intended to do just that. Maureen was in the dining room, doing her own work, and the other two kids were playing on the floor. The new nanny was with Hannah. Lisa was out with his father, making arrangements for the funeral.

It was still light out and not as cold as it had been. The doorbell sounded, and Michael ran to get it. Dieter and Kristof were standing there. Dieter lived next door. He was smaller than Michael, with a round face and red cheeks. Kristof lived just up the road. He was the biggest kid they knew and was shaving already. No one was going to mess with them when he was around.

"You coming out?" Kristof asked.

"Give me a minute," Michael replied and went back inside the house. "I'm going out with my friends," he shouted.

"Be back in time for dinner," Maureen responded.

Michael grabbed his jacket and made for the door. The boys turned and ran with him as he slammed it behind him.

It wasn't far to the local park, and several other kids were waiting for them there. They decided to play cops and robbers but with a twist. Michael, as usual, was cast in the role of Eliot Ness, the incorruptible cop with a cohort of untouchables. The rest of the kids played bootleggers under the control of Al Capone. Dieter liked to play the famous gangster and used a few English phrases like, "Let 'em have it, boys," to spice things up. It was a change from cowboys and Indians.

Michael led his band to where the bootleggers had stashed the hooch, an opening among the trees where cutoff stumps doubled for barrels. The bootleggers scattered, and it was up to the cops to track each of them down. It was Michael's job alone to go after Capone, the big fish.

"Come get me, copper," Dieter called out in English as Michael took chase. The smaller boy was fast, and Michael had to sprint through the trees after him. The other kids receded into the background as Dieter ran on. Michael wasn't about to give up.

"You'll never escape," he called out in English. "There's no getting away from the long arm of the law." He got most of the phrases from books.

Dieter burst through the tree line and out into a field beyond. A group of ten boys, around their age and younger, was marching in step. They were dressed in brown shirts with dark ties and shorts. Each had an emblem on their armbands—the same one he saw at the Nazi rally in the Tiergarten—the swastika.

Dieter didn't seem to notice them and was looking back to taunt Michael as he ran into the middle of the group, knocking one boy off his feet. The others immediately surrounded him.

"What do you think you're doing?" one of the boys asked and pushed Dieter.

"I'm sorry, it was an accident. We were chasing—"

"You'll have an accident yourself," the boy he knocked over said as he squared up to him.

Michael was panting as he came to the group. His first instinct was to go back for Kristof and the others, but how could he leave his friend?

"Ok, let him go," Michael said. "We were just playing."

The boy Dieter knocked over turned to Michael with fire in his eyes. "Stay out of this unless you want some of this too," he said, shaking his fist.

Dieter went to say something, but the boy shoved him in the face. Michael's friend fell back, and the boy in the brown uniform jumped on top of him, punching him in the arms as Dieter tried to shield his face. Michael rushed in to pull the boy off his friend, but the others surrounded him. One of them punched him in the face and he fell back onto the grass, his head spinning. Dieter was screaming now, and another boy kicked Michael in the chest. He tried to get up, but was pushed back down.

He had taken beatings before—every boy had—but there was something different about this. It felt dangerous. He tried to call out for the others, but knew they were too far away. He wanted his father—anyone. The boys in the brown uniforms were jeering him, cheering on their friend as he punched Dieter. Michael yelled to stop, but was met with a kick in the chest with a black boot. He doubled in pain, holding his ribs.

"All right, that's quite enough," a voice called out. "Get off him."

Michael looked up in a daze. An older boy, perhaps eighteen or so, was walking toward them. He didn't seem in a huge hurry. The kids crowded around Michael parted, and he was able to get up. The older boy pulled Dieter's attacker off him.

"That'll do. Enough of that."

The older boy had bright blue eyes and chestnut brown hair. He reached down to help Dieter up, who was nursing a bloody nose. The leader of the boys turned to them.

"There is a time for fighting, but we must reserve it for our true enemies—not for some petty scuffle in the park. Come here," he said to Michael and Dieter. His voice commanded authority.

"What are your names?" he asked. They told him. Neither complained about what had just happened, and he seemed to respect that. "I saw some of the incident. You didn't chicken out. Particularly you," he said to Michael. "If you want to join our group and become part of the revolution that's happening in our country, you come see me. My name's Ulrich. We'll find a place for you."

The two boys looked at each other. Ulrich motioned for them to leave, and they ran back through the woods toward the safety of their friends.

9

Monday, February 27

The same pressure Seamus felt when he left his children back in '30 seemed to be building to a crescendo once more. It was with him in everything he did. There was nothing he could do about most of it, of course. Ingrid's death and Lisa's subsequent emotional turmoil wasn't anything he could affect in any meaningful way, but that didn't stop him from feeling guilty. He could do little more than offer comfort to his new wife, and that was all she expected, but it didn't seem enough.

He fantasized daily about a miraculous return to the normality they'd only known for a fraction of their time together. He fantasized about earning Maureen's forgiveness and being whole as a family once again. Michael came back from the park with bruises the day before. What happened there? He said it was roughhousing gone wrong, and didn't seem to care that no one believed him. There hadn't been time to go over it with him, as he had to deal with Ingrid's funeral arrangements with Lisa. His new wife needed him and the children were in bed by the time she settled down. He came into work early this morning for a meeting. The chance to speak to Michael again never arose.

Seamus was in his office going over some paperwork. The factory wasn't doing as well as he pretended. Only he, Helga, and Bernheim knew the truth. If things didn't improve soon, they'd have to start laying off workers. A knock on the door interrupted his thoughts, and he invited the person in without looking up.

Andrei Salnikov, the Russian foreman of the metal polishing section, walked in smoking a cigarette. "Can we talk?" he said in heavily accented German.

"Of course," Seamus responded.

Salnikov sat down in the chair on the other side of the desk. Seamus put down the papers he was reading.

"I need some time off," the Russian said. He took his cap off and placed it on the desk.

"Fill out the usual paperwork," Seamus answered. *Why is he coming directly to me for this?*

"It's more than that. I need an advance on my wages."

Seamus sat forward. "What's going on?"

"My daughter, Maria. She's sick. I didn't want to bother you about it. She can hardly get out of bed."

"I'm so sorry. Have you been to a doctor?"

"We went to all kinds when we first found out, but they were too expensive, or didn't give us any hope. We finally found one who's researching a new treatment. He says he might be able to help her. We're desperate."

"I can imagine. Who is this doctor?"

"Dr. Walz—have you heard of him? He has a clinic in Reuterkiez. Ottmar Laufenberg from metal polishing recommended him. He charges a fraction of what other doctors do, and even treats the homeless and the poorest of the poor for free."

"What's wrong with Maria?"

"The doctor says it's in her brain. Blood flow or something. He's not sure yet."

"Your poor daughter. I'll do whatever I can to help."

"She's had a hard life. She was born slow—not like her sister. Baby Anastasia's sharp as a tack. Maria is different."

"When is your appointment with Dr. Walz?"

"Tomorrow morning. She'll need to stay overnight too."

"Why didn't you come to me sooner?"

"It came up at the last minute. We could have waited a few months but—"

"I understand."

"I'll need the day off tomorrow. My wife will need to go with her."

"So, you'd have to stay home to look after the baby?"

"Yes."

"There's no one else?"

"Not that can come tomorrow. That doctor's seeing her at nine in the morning...if I can get the money together."

"How much do you need?"

"A week in advance, to pay for the doctor."

"I'll have to get Helga to sign off on it."

"Is there any way around that? It's delicate with her. Let's say she doesn't approve of my political affiliations. It's a hard time to be a member of the Communist Party, even a junior one."

Seamus thought for a few seconds. Helga would try to use this as an excuse to drive him and the other Communists out.

"Give me until the end of the day," he said. "You need tomorrow off?"

"Yes. I'm so sorry."

"Come see me before you leave. We'll sort something out."

Salnikov stood up and shook Seamus's hand. "I know your uncle would be proud of you," he said. "Thank you." He walked out without another word. Seamus watched from his window as the Russian made his way back to the factory floor.

Seamus went to the door and made his way down to Bernheim's office. The factory manager was eating lunch at his desk.

"Gert, I need a favor."

"What is it?" He put down the newspaper he was reading.

Seamus changed his mind as soon as he saw his manager's face. *I can cover it,* he said to himself. *Helga will veto it and pressure me to fire him if she finds out.*

"Actually, it's nothing. I can get it done."

"My favorite kind of favor," Bernheim said.

Seamus thanked him and left, passing Helga on the walkway. She smiled and said hello. He returned the sentiment before descending to the factory floor.

Salnikov pulled back the protective mask he was wearing as Seamus tapped him on the shoulder. The two men stepped away from the other workers to talk.

"I'll get you the money tonight. I'll try to come to your house. If I can't get away, I'll have it for you here tomorrow morning first thing."

"Thank you, Herr Ritter."

"No problem. Write down your address for me."

The Russian took the pen and piece of paper Seamus gave and scribbled down directions.

Seamus waited until after dinner to go. Lisa was in their room, lying on the bed.

"Are you sure you don't mind me going out?"

"No. We have to get on with our lives. I just hope that doctor can help Salnikov's daughter. I'm going to bed as soon as Hannah falls asleep. You don't need to hurry home."

His new wife was pale and drawn, cold to the touch. He

kissed her where she laid on the bed. "Get some sleep. I'll be back later."

She raised a hand to him and he left.

Hannah was on the living room floor with Conor and Fiona, playing with a train set Uncle Helmut had brought them just before he died. Maureen and Michael were listening to the radio—live jazz gyrated through the air. The children kissed and hugged him goodbye before he put on his coat and walked out to the car.

The cash was in a brown paper bag in the trunk. It was most of what he could take out of the business for himself that month. He was thankful he didn't have to pay the mortgage on their enormous house, or that Christmas wasn't coming up. They would have to go without some luxuries for the next few weeks, but what other choice did he have?

The car started and he pulled out of the driveway. The traffic was light at this time, but he hardly noticed it. He drove northeast across the city to a neighborhood he didn't know in Kollwitzkiez. A sour smell of trash hung in the air as he got out of the car. He checked the address on the outside of the apartment block against the piece of paper Salnikov gave him. This was it.

The car door closed with a bang, attracting the attention of two boys, about Fiona's age, who were playing with a mangy old dog on the side of the road. He went to the trunk and took the brown paper bag of money he'd drawn from his personal bank account in his hand.

"Nice car," one of the boys said. He had a long scar down the side of his dirty face. His friend smiled beside him; the dog forgotten.

Seamus wasn't sure what to say in reply. "Thanks."

"Be a shame if something was to happen to it," the same boy said.

"Can you help me with that?" Seamus reached into his

pocket for a few pfennigs and tossed them to the boy. "I'll only be a few minutes."

"We'll keep an eye on it for you," the other boy said. "And we'll set Marco on anyone who tries to mess with it."

The dog didn't seem capable of troubling a rogue hamster, but Seamus nodded at the boys nonetheless and carried on inside.

No one passed him on the flight of stairs. One door had a swastika on it, daubed in black paint. He kept on until he reached Salnikov's apartment. Seamus knocked and knew he had the right place when heard the sound of Russian being spoken inside. Andrei Salnikov opened the door.

"Herr Ritter, thank you so much for coming," he said with a smile and gestured for Seamus to come in.

Seamus handed the envelope to him. "Three hundred Reichsmarks," he said. "Just give it straight back to me when you can. No need to tell anyone else."

"Thank you. I wouldn't have asked, but it was all last minute."

"Not a problem," Seamus said and put his hand on the Russian's shoulder.

The apartment was neat, the furnishings colorless and simple. The stark contrast to the house his uncle left his family wasn't lost on him. Two rocking chairs sat in front of a fire. Salnikov's wife stood up with a young baby in her arms. She was pale and thin, with blond hair and skin like marble. The baby was about a year old.

"Herr Ritter. It's so good of you to come," the woman said. "I'm Nikita, and this is little Anastasia."

Seamus held out a hand to Salnikov's wife and then took one of the baby's tiny fingers. She smiled a little and they all laughed.

"She's pleased to meet you too," Nikita said. "Will you take a seat?" She gestured toward the rocking chair beside hers.

"I'd like to meet Maria," he said.

"Of course," Andrei said. "Come with me. Fix Herr Ritter a drink while we're gone. Will you have a glass of vodka?"

"Just one."

Salnikov led him through the kitchen and down a narrow hallway. The bedroom door was open. "I think she's still awake," Salnikov said. He pushed into the bedroom and called the little girl's name. She stirred and sat up, her mess of blond hair falling about her shoulders.

"Can you say hello to the nice man who's going to help you get better?"

Seamus got down on his haunches and smiled at her. "Hello, little girl. I hope you're feeling better."

Maria didn't answer, just stared past him.

"It was good to meet you," he said and stood up. "We should let her sleep. She has a big day ahead of her tomorrow."

Salnikov nodded and tucked his daughter back in. The two men returned to the fireplace, where Nikita had poured each of them a stiff glass of vodka. They toasted Maria's health, Andrei pulled up another chair, and they sat down together.

"I'm so sorry to spring this on you at the last minute," Nikita said. "We only heard about this opportunity on Friday. The doctor had an opening in his schedule."

"I'm glad to help. Andrei mentioned a new treatment he was going to employ. Do you know anything about it?"

"Not a lot other than the doctor is a brilliant man—a pioneer. He told us he believes he can cure Maria's illness, and even her mental condition." Nikita rocked the baby a few times.

"Have you seen his results?"

"He's hugely respected. He has awards all over his office," Salnikov said.

"What's Maria been diagnosed with?"

"He thinks she has a tumor in her brain, but we'll find out more when she goes in. The amount of money he charges is nothing when you consider the care Maria's going to get. The man is a saint," Nikita said.

"Well, here's to him and Maria's treatment. With any luck, she'll be back to full health soon."

Seamus stayed with them another hour before making his way back to the car. He hoped their faith in this doctor was well placed.

The two kids and their dog were sitting by the car as he came out. He tossed them a couple more coins, ignoring their voices in his ear. The car started and he drove toward home, thinking about Lisa.

The sound of sirens cut through the air like a ghost wailing in the night. An irregular glow against the dark sky grabbed his attention as he drove over the Kronprinz Bridge. *Something isn't right.* He pulled over to the side. An icy wind hit him as he walked to the edge of the bridge. The Reichstag building was glowing in the distance. He ran back to the car and continued down to Platz der Republik.

The glow against the night sky grew more acute as he neared the parliament building by the river. He blinked to make sure his eyes weren't deceiving him—the Reichstag was consumed by flames. Fire engines stood in front of the burning façade as he parked the car. Morbid curiosity dragged him out of the car to join the crowd of onlookers. Firefighters were rolling out hoses, and police held the masses back from the blaze. Flames seemed to flicker everywhere behind myriad glass windows of the massive parliament building. A firefighter smashed a window with his axe, showering broken glass on the concrete. The crowd, 100 strong, was muttering about Hitler and the Communists.

"The Reds did this," a brown-shirted Stormtrooper called out. Several people cheered in response.

"Why would the Communists do this?" Seamus asked out loud.

A man in a flat cap with a bushy mustache turned to him. "They're animals, trying to tear this country apart at the seams. I just hope Hitler and the Nazis have the stomach to stand up to them."

Seamus turned back to watch the burning building without responding. Somehow, he thought that they'd respond with gusto to tonight's events.

The glass dome that crowned the colossal building was glowing, illuminated from the inside as if someone had flicked on some massive light bulb below it. More fire engines pulled up, some directed to the sides. It seemed the entire Reichstag was on fire.

Questions bounced through his mind. How could the fire spread so quickly and evenly throughout the structure? This wasn't an accident. Something accidental would have been easier to contain. What would the Communists gain from setting the parliament building alight? Didn't they know what this would mean for them?

A loud crack interrupted his thoughts as one of the glass panes in the dome shattered in the heat. Another one popped seconds later.

The police cordoned off the onlookers as the horrific spectacle continued. Seamus stood transfixed for a few minutes before the crowd parted.

It wasn't more than a few minutes before several Stormtroopers formed a path for an enraged fat man to barrel through. Seamus recognized him as Hermann Göring, recently appointed Reich Minister and Commissar for the Prussian Interior. He marched toward the burning structure, shouting instructions at the orderlies who accompanied him. What were they doing here, and how did they know to come so quickly? Several people gave the Hitler salute as Göring passed. He took a second to turn around and return it before he and his men disappeared around the side of the building. The place the

Nazis abhorred so much was aflame. Another pane on the dome cracked and fell through. Several Stormtroopers in the throng of people watching cheered its demise.

Seamus stood and watched with the growing crowd as the firefighters struggled, and ultimately failed, to bring the flames under control. The massive building was gutted.

It felt like something had changed.

10

Tuesday, February 28

Andrei Salnikov was dreaming about a lake in the summertime when a thundering sound jarred him from sleep. Nikita, his wife of five years, jutted upright beside him and jumped out of bed. The hammering on the door came again. A truck pulling up on the street outside sent tendrils of fear down his spine. Andrei turned the bedside light on. The clock on the wall said it was past three in the morning.

His wife turned to him. A single tear broke down her cheek as the hammering on the front door build to a crescendo. The sound of breaking timbers flooded up the stairs, and Nikita grabbed the screaming baby in her arms. Andrei leaped out of bed, taking a few seconds to throw on a pair of pants as the jackboots came up the stairs. His wife screamed, and he ran to Maria's room. He got as far as the doorway before he was met with a fist to the jaw. He fell back onto the wooden floor. Blinded by pain, he tried to raise himself up, but was kicked in the chest and stomach.

"Nikita," he said as another boot connected with his arm. The men were in Stormtrooper uniform. He tried to say something, but was kicked again. His only thoughts were of his wife and daughters. Nikita screamed as one of the Stormtroopers dragged her out of Maria's room, carrying Anastasia in her arms.

"Commie cow," the man said and threw her down on the ground. She managed to fall in such a way that her baby girl didn't hit the floor.

"She's just a baby. What is this about?" Andrei asked.

A middle-aged man in Stormtrooper uniform with a twirling mustache stepped forward. "It's about protecting our country from the like of Communist scum like you."

He produced a sack, such as you might get from the greengrocer for an order of potatoes, and threw it over Andrei's head. Everything went black. The SA men raised him up by the arms and dragged him down the stairs.

"Nikita," he screamed as the men took him.

"Andrei," she shouted in reply, and it gave him some comfort. He was in the cold night air for a few seconds before they threw him in the back of a waiting car.

"Don't move, or I'll bash your skull in," said a gruff voice.

Andrei nodded, trying to disguise his terror as bravado, or something else noble or brave. The civil war between the Nazis and the Communists had raged on the streets for months, manifesting itself in brawls, and even dead bodies. Apparently, it was coming to a head. Even though he was never involved in any violence and had only attended rallies and meetings to promote the system he believed in, they had come for him. It seemed like he was to be on the losing side.

He sat there for ten minutes or more, wondering when they were going to drive him away, and begging whatever God who might have been listening for them to leave his wife and child out of this. He heard the sound of another man being bundled in beside him and then another.

"Igor, is that you?" he asked when the Brownshirts seemed gone. Igor Kamenev was his neighbor from Moscow.

"Yes," he said in Russian. "What triggered this?"

"I don't know," Andrei replied.

The other men stayed silent. A few seconds later, he heard the sound of the door closing.

"You'll keep quiet back there if you know what's good for you," came a voice from the driver's seat, and the car moved off.

It was hard to know for how long they drove. Keeping track of time sitting in silence in the dark was impossible. The blood from his head wounds was sticking to the fabric of the sack by the time they arrived at wherever they were. They might have driven five miles, or twenty-five.

Igor and the other man were dragged out of the car before he felt arms on him again. A voice cursed him as they pulled him along, and he felt the thud of a truncheon against his chest. The pain was such that he screamed like a little girl. Laughter ensued. He was carried down a flight of concrete stairs and thrown onto a hard floor.

"On your knees."

He did as he was told. The sack was ripped off his head, and he found himself staring into a 40-watt bulb.

Two Stormtroopers sat behind a desk. Andrei squinted to make them out, but wasn't able to. "Name?" one of them demanded.

"Andrei Salnikov. Where is my wife?"

"Put him with the others," the SA man said.

Two SA men dragged him to his feet and brought him down a hallway adjacent to the room he was brought into. Sewage pipes and electrical wiring lined the ceiling. About a dozen other men were already standing along the wall. Several were in tears. All had been beaten. Andrei knew he'd be lucky to get out of this place alive.

"No talking. Not a word or it'll be your last," the SA said and walked off.

Another Stormtrooper brought Igor along a minute later and threw him down. He repeated the same sentiment as the last man and left.

Andrei waited until he was sure the Stormtroopers were out of earshot before whispering to his friend. "Where are we?"

"No idea, but this is something to do with a fire in the Reichstag."

"A fire in the Reichstag?"

"Yes. They're blaming it on us and every other unfortunate with a Red tint in the city."

A Stormtrooper marched over with a clipboard and called out a name. A man limped up, and was promptly grabbed by his beard and dragged back toward the room where the SA men were sitting behind the desk. The sound of the man being beaten soon followed. Andrei knew his turn wouldn't be long coming.

Seamus was behind his desk, going over numbers for upcoming orders. The newspapers were dominated by the fire he saw with his own eyes the night before. The Nazis were blaming the Communists, and the rumor was they were about to make an announcement about limiting the powers of the government. So much had happened and it was still only ten thirty in the morning.

Problems of his own drew his attention back to the numbers on the page. He put the ledger down and picked up his bank book. The more than 4,000 Reichsmarks in his account was enough to sustain his family for months. Where was the money going to come from to pay the workers? The answer was in the ledger.

Thorsten Klink was the head of a chain of grocery stores that ordered a massive shipment of pots and pans. The first payment was due. Seamus picked up the telephone on his desk and asked to operator to patch him through to Klink's personal line.

"Hello? This is Seamus Ritter from Ritter Metalworks."

"Hello," came the cold reply.

Seamus had never met Klink in person, but his uncle dealt with him for many years. Like most of their accounts, it was one his uncle cultivated years before. He knew enough about the man on the other end of the line not to bother with small talk.

"I'm calling about the monies we're due—"

"I'm not sure about that at all," Klink interrupted. "I'm very disturbed by the situation in Berlin."

"The government is getting things under control. I can assure you it won't affect our schedule."

"And I hear you're employing all manner of Kosis and Jews in your factory."

The words took him aback, and he had to take a deep breath before he could proceed. He knew *Kosi* was the slang word for a Communist.

"My employees are not your concern, Herr Klink. Haven't we always provided you with the best service, and products to match?"

"I'm not sure I can do business with a company run for the benefit of traitors to the Reich. I'll send on the check, but cancel the rest of the order. I'll be buying German from now on. I advise you to take a good look at your staff and clean out the bad apples. Until then, I'll wish you good day, sir."

The line went dead.

Seamus stood up from the desk, drenched in panic and anger. Was this Helga's doing? No—why would she undermine her own business? He ran to the door and down to Bernheim's office. The office manager was reading over some reports when he came in.

"Do you know anyone in Klink's company you could talk to?"

"Yes. Why?"

"I just spoke to Thorsten Klink. He says he doesn't want to do business with a company full of Reds and Jews anymore."

"Do you think this has something to do with the Reichstag last night?"

"That's what I intend to find out. Call your man."

"I haven't spoken to him in a while," he said as he reached into a drawer for an address book. His demeanor didn't change, even with the news. He was still calm. That was part of what made him excel at his job.

He picked up the phone. It took a few seconds to connect the call.

"Karsten? It's Gert Bernheim."

The small talk they made for thirty seconds was a necessary agony.

"I wanted to ask, is Klink annoyed with us? Ritter just spoke to him and he said he wasn't going to do business with us anymore on account that the factory was full of Kosis and Jews."

Bernheim listened for a minute before thanking the man on the other end and hanging up.

"What is it?" Seamus asked.

"Klink's prejudices are a factor, but not the deciding one. Apparently, Milch Industries is offering them the same produce at less than cost price."

"They're undercutting us at a loss?"

"It seems Herr Milch is the one behind this revelation."

"The line about the Jews and the Kosis is just an excuse."

"It might be, or it might be part of the reason. Either way, Helga's going to use this to her advantage."

"Why does he want this place so much?"

"There's a bonanza coming: rearmament."

"They can't do that. It's against the terms of the Treaty of Versailles."

"You think Hitler cares about that?"

"Thanks, Gert."

Seamus got up and jogged back to his office. His body was stiff with rage as he picked up the phone again. He reached into his desk drawer for the card Milch gave him at the dinner and called out the number to the operator.

"What are you doing, Milch?" he asked when the old man picked up.

"Trying to prosper in tumultuous times, like everyone else."

"By undercutting me? You're willing to take a loss to drive me out of business?"

"I can live with a few bad months, or even a few years. Can you?"

"You won't get away with this," he replied, although he had no idea why he wouldn't.

"I'll call you again soon with a revised offer to buy the factory. It won't be as generous, but you might be happier to consider it."

Seamus hung up.

Martina Sammer appeared at the door.

"Come in," he said.

"Sorry to interrupt, Herr Ritter, but Andrei Salnikov's wife is here to see you."

The Russian hadn't shown up for work this morning for the first time in years.

"Show her in immediately," Seamus said.

"Thank you so much for seeing me, Herr Ritter," Salnikov's wife said.

Seamus showed her to a seat in front of the desk.

Salnikov's wife wore a plain gray dress with a hat to match. Anastasia was in her arms. She tried to smile as he shook her hand, but it came out more of an expression of pain.

"Shouldn't you be at the doctor's office with Maria? Is that where Andrei is?"

Her face turned red and she started crying. She brought her hands up to her face to hide the tears. "I don't know where else to go. Andrei always said you look out for the workers. I don't know what to do."

"Where is Andrei? What's this about?"

"They took him."

"Who?"

"The SA. They came in the middle of the night and dragged him out of our house. They bundled him and a few of our neighbors into a car and drove them away. I have no idea where he is, or even if he's alive...or dead."

"Why would they come for him?"

"I don't know. We're from Russia."

"Is Andrei a member of the Communist Party?" She hesitated a few seconds. "You can trust me, Nikita."

"Yes, he is, but we're not involved in any violence. We just want a quiet life."

"What about the other men? Your neighbors?"

"They're members of the Party too. None of their families have any idea where they were taken. No one knows anything. We called the police, but they're not helping—they're obsessed with rounding up Communists too. They say we're to blame for what happened at the Reichstag last night. I can't look myself; I have to get back to the clinic. The doctor said I could have an hour, but he needs me back there. I had no choice. He said if I missed the appointment today, it would be months before he could see her. I didn't have anyone else to go to, so I came here."

Seamus's promise to his uncle was front and center in his

mind. This was the price he had to pay for the big house and the factory. Helmut's last wish was that these workers that he thought of as family be looked after.

"Let me make some calls. I know some people who might be able to help us. If the police aren't going to help you, it's likely no one will. Do you have a telephone?"

"We'll be staying in a hotel tonight. Here's the number and of the doctor's office too." She pushed a business card across the table. Her makeup was running down her face. "I won't keep you any longer."

"Leave this with me. I'll call you later whether I find him or not."

"Thank you," she said and left, hushing the baby as she went.

Seamus waited until she left to pick up the telephone. The operator put him through and Clayton answered in seconds.

"I was just about to call you," he said. "Did you hear what the Nazis said on the radio? They're blaming everything on the Communists. They're issuing an emergency decree, suspending the power of the Reichstag in the interests of public safety. The city's going crazy."

"I need to see you."

"I'll be at my desk for the next hour."

"I'll be there in fifteen minutes."

Seamus hung up the phone and jogged to the door. Several workers stopped him on his way down the stairs to ask what was going on. Without the time to go into it in any detail, he replied that he didn't know and carried on into the parking lot. He got into his car and drove to Clayton's office.

Linda Thomas of the *Chicago Daily News* was standing talking to Clayton as Seamus burst in.

"Never a dull moment in this city," Linda said as she shook Seamus's hand.

"I was at the Reichstag last night."

"Not with a bunch of firelighters and some matches, I hope," Clayton said.

"No, but I saw it."

"Did you hear they dredged up a suspect?" Linda asked.

"No. Who?"

"Some Dutch comrade, but I'm surprised he's not Danish, because something is rotten in the state of Denmark here," Clayton said.

"What do you mean?"

"None of it makes sense," Linda said. "If the Communists really wanted to go for the Nazis, why not hit them where it hurts? Burn down the Reich Chancellery, or one of the SA bases all over the city. Two weeks ago, Göring said all enemies of the state should be gunned down, and now they do this? Now they give them every excuse they'd ever need to hunt each one of them down like dogs? It doesn't make sense. They're Communists, not idiots. And why choose some lowly Dutchman to carry it out, and how could he have burned it all down alone?"

"That's what I thought last night," Seamus said.

"And the election's on Sunday. How's this going to play out?" Linda asked.

"I think the question one has to ask oneself is, who stands to gain from this?" Clayton asked.

"The Nazis themselves," Seamus said.

"They issued an emergency decree this morning, suspending personal freedoms, freedom of expression, and assembly. And, of course, freedom of the press," Clayton said.

"Such is how democracy dies," Linda said.

"One of my men got grabbed and bundled up in the back of a car last night."

"Was he a Red?" Linda asked.

"A Russian. Any idea where they might have taken him?"

"Word is hundreds were picked up in the early hours.

They're being held in basements and warehouses all over the city," she said.

"How can I find him?"

"Go to the local police station," Linda said. "Ask for this man." She picked up a piece of paper and scribbled down a name. "If he won't tell you, I suggest going to the SA. They're the ones holding them. What's his name?"

Seamus told her and watched her write it down. "I'll see what I can find out. I'll let the man you're going to see know."

"Andrei's wife came to me this morning. They're good people."

"My advice is to bring some cash," Clayton said. "No one's going to tell them to release him—there's no one left. You're going to have to bargain for your friend."

Seamus nodded and the phone rang. Clayton excused himself as he went to answer it. His face drained white as he held the receiver to his ear. He thanked the person on the other end of the line and hung up. His voice was weak. "They took Hans Litten last night."

"The SA? He wasn't a Communist," Linda said.

"No—just someone who stood up to Hitler. This wasn't political. It was personal," Clayton said.

"I've got to make some calls," Linda said and rushed off. Clayton had to go too. His hand was cold as he shook Seamus's hand.

"Good luck finding your man," he said. "But be careful. Think of that family of yours."

"Thanks," Seamus said and left. He thought back to the conversations he'd had with Hans Litten and how the lawyer had refused to leave Germany. Courage like his was a rare thing. Perhaps taking him in was a warning, and the SA would release him soon. They'd find out he had nothing to do with the fire, and Hitler would forget his vendetta and move on. The thought of this might have comforted him if he believed it.

It took ten minutes to make his way across the city to the address of the police station on Mohrenstrasse Linda had given him. He heard the pandemonium 100 yards away. Several suspects were dragged up to the door, calling out in Polish or Russian or some language he didn't understand. Seamus inched inside, waiting until the last man was booked and hauled back into the station before approaching the desk. A young, irritated-looking officer was sitting behind a pane of glass.

"What?"

"I'm looking for Heinz Anker."

"And you are?"

"Seamus Ritter. I believe Linda—"

But the man was out of his seat, peering back into the station behind him already. He disappeared for a few seconds before he came back and told Seamus to sit on a bench that ran along the wall.

A middle-aged man with a thick black mustache and thinning hair came through the station door a few minutes later. He motioned to Seamus to follow him out onto the street. Anker stopped a few yards down the road and had already lit a cigarette when Seamus reached him.

"Linda called me—told me about your man. Salnikov?"

"Yes. His wife came to me this morning in a desperate state."

"Her and half of the Red side of this city. It's Christmas for the Nazis—if your idea of a holiday is hauling people out of bed at three in the morning and beating them to a pulp."

"Sounds like them. Any idea where Salnikov is?"

"I heard they took him here." Anker took a piece of paper out of his pocket and slipped it into Seamus's hand. "It's not a lot more than a basement underneath an old office building. God knows what the neighbors upstairs must be thinking."

"Can you help me get him out of there?"

The detective shook his head and took a drag on the cigarette. "Not a chance. With the emergency decree they passed, my hands are tied. It's all legal. The Nazis are smart enough to make sure everything they do is aboveboard. They learned their lesson back in '23, I suppose."

"Any suggestions?"

"On getting your friend back? You have money? If he's not a big fish—"

"He's not."

"Well, then, once they figure that out, they should release him, but heaven only knows what kind of state he'll be in by then. The Stormtroopers have been waiting for this moment for a long time." Anker threw down his cigarette. "Good luck with your friend."

Seamus thanked him, and the policeman was gone.

He walked back to the car, trying to process what he knew he had to do. The faces of his family, of Bruno, of Ernst Milch lying in a pool of blood, invaded his consciousness like a plague. He started the car. He ignored the idea of going to pick up Nikita and her daughter. The SA didn't seem to feel compassion or remorse. They would laugh at the Communist's wife and daughter and make them even less likely to release him.

No, he had to go alone: an upstanding citizen, a loyal German. He'd have to cover his accent. He had a new piece of paper with an address written on it, and he looked at it as he sat in the car, trying to summon the courage to face the insanity of the SA fully unleashed. He started the car and drove north.

It took almost half an hour to drive to the address in Prenzlauer Berg. He had to stop to ask for directions twice, his voice shaking like a leaf as he spoke each time. *How am I going to face down an officer in the SA?*

He pulled the piece of paper out of his pocket, looking for the address of the building the cop gave him, hoping somehow it was a mistake and he'd have to go home and hope that

Salnikov made it out himself. But it wasn't. He found the address and saw the SA men standing guard outside the entrance to the basement. Finding a parking space was easy.

He took a minute to compose himself, to reach inside for the courage to do this. The car door shut behind him with a *bang* as he strode to the Brownshirts standing on the street.

"Hello, gentlemen," he said in his most Teutonic accent.

One looked him up and down with a level of disgust usually reserved for something you'd dig out of your ear, but the other, younger man, was friendlier.

"What can I do for you?" He was blond, tall, well-built. The other man was plump and in his early forties.

"I have to speak to the officer in charge. I believe you're holding one of my men." Seamus pointed down toward the basement and reached into his pocket for a business card with his other hand. He handed the card to the younger Stormtrooper.

"I need my man back. He's the foreman in my factory. The whole operation's going to come crashing down without him. I have no idea why you men took him in the first place, anyway. He's a nobody—no threat to the revolution. You're wasting valuable time with him."

The younger man looked at the business card before handing it to his colleague. The older man smirked. "Get out of here," he said. "We've got a job to do—"

"And so do I. So do the hundreds of loyal Germans working there waiting for this man. He's the vital cog in the machine. Why do you think I'm here bothering you? I know you haven't got time for the likes of me, not while you're trying to hunt down the Red scum that carried out the attack on the heart of our government last night. I was at the Reichstag. I saw what they did, and if I wasn't serving the Fatherland in other ways, I'd be right here beside you. But you have the wrong person."

The younger Stormtrooper looked at his colleague, who

was shaking his head. "What's your man's name?" the younger SA trooper asked.

"Here it is," he said and handed over a piece of paper with Salnikov's name on it. "All I ask is that you check and let me inside to speak to one of your superiors. I know they'll see sense. My business might not survive without this man."

"Keep walking," the fat SA man growled.

"Stay here," the younger man said. "I'll have a word with Sturmhauptführer Lessing. Wait here." The SA soldier turned and jogged down the steps into the basement. Seamus stepped away, wary of spending one second longer with the other Stormtrooper than he had to.

Seamus walked to the other side of the road and lit up a cigarette. It was finished by the time the younger SA man came back with another man with him.

"Sturmhauptführer Lessing?" he asked, holding out a hand to greet the SA officer.

"Yes. Why am I standing here with you?" Lessing was several inches smaller than Seamus, but with a harsh voice that commanded respect in seconds.

"Did your man explain the situation?"

"Why should I release a dangerous suspect to you, or anyone else? For all we know, this man could have been involved in the plot to burn down the Reichstag last night."

"He was in bed with his wife at the time. I'm a loyal German—"

"You don't sound German," Lessing said.

"I spent some time in America until I realized I had to come home to help the Fatherland prosper once more. I'm a business owner—an employer. My entire operation has come to a halt because of this one worker."

"The man you seek is still under questioning. If we find he's not an enemy of the people, he'll be released. Not before then. Good day, sir."

Lessing turned around and walked back down the stairs. Before Seamus had a chance to speak again, the door slammed behind him.

"Time to leave," the portly SA man said. "If you know what's good for you."

Seamus thought about arguing, but knew it was no use. He had one card left to play. The vise around him tightened further and a thousand thoughts pelted his mind like hailstones. But the conclusion was the same from every scenario he imagined: He couldn't let Salnikov die in some hole. The SA might beat him to death trying to extract some kind of confession or implicate another poor soul.

No, he's my man. One of Helmut's men. And I'm going to get him out of there.

Some things were fleeting, but he'd sworn to himself the promises he made never would be again.

He got into his car and drove to the bank, where he withdrew 1,500 Reichsmarks. They still had plenty of money, and he'd figure out how to save the business from Otto Milch. They'd make it through. Perhaps Andrei wouldn't without this.

His heart broke for the hundreds of others taken, for Hans Litten, but he couldn't save them all. Linda and Clayton would get their lawyer friend back. Seamus was sure he'd be having a drink with him the next Saturday night, listening to the story of how he was snatched from his bed in the middle of the night.

Seamus pulled up right outside the basement this time. The same two SA men stood on guard.

"You again?" the fat man asked.

His blond colleague was once again friendlier. "You're back," he said with a tiny smile.

"I need to see Sturmhauptführer Lessing."

"We've done this already," the older Stormtrooper barked.

"Something came up. I'm not leaving until I see him."

They argued back and forth for several minutes before the

younger man relented. Lessing emerged, angrier than before, about ten minutes later.

"This had better be good, otherwise you'll be down with the Bolsheviks," he snarled.

"Sturmhauptführer, may I speak with you alone, please?"

The SA officer seemed to sense an opportunity and followed Seamus around the corner. "I need my man back—today. Now," Seamus said. He reached into his jacket for the envelope he'd stuffed most of the money he had left in the world into. "I was hoping we might come to an arrangement."

The SA officer's eyes lit up at the sight of the envelope. He poked a finger inside to expose the banknotes. "I think we can accommodate your request. After all, the wheels of commerce must keep turning."

Seamus thought to say something back and play this man's game, but the level of disgust he felt didn't permit him to do so.

"How do I know you won't come for him again?"

"His name will be stricken from the list. So, as long as he keeps his nose clean, our business with him will be concluded."

Without another word, the Sturmhauptführer turned on his heels and strode back toward the basement. "Wait here," he said to Seamus as they reached the other men.

Twenty minutes passed before the door opened once more and two Stormtroopers appeared, their arms over Salnikov's shoulders to prop him up. His face was a bloody mess and so swollen that Seamus wouldn't have recognized him. The SA men helped him up the stairs as Seamus opened the car door. The Russian was barely conscious. It was hard to tell if he registered what was happening. The Stormtroopers laid him down on the back seat of the car, and Seamus drove away.

He called her at the doctor's office from the telephone in the waiting area of the hospital. A nurse answered on the second ring and ran to get her.

"I have him," Seamus said.

It took her several seconds to recover herself enough to speak, and when she did, it was through tears. "Thank you so much. Oh, thank you."

"We're at the Charité Hospital. The doctors are with him now. The SA beat him up pretty badly, but he's going to be ok."

Twenty minutes later, she arrived at the hospital and threw her arms around Seamus's shoulders, sobbing on his neck.

"How is Maria?" he asked when she regained herself.

"I haven't seen her since early afternoon, but the doctor is confident. He said she should be coming home later this week, hopefully cured."

"That's wonderful," he said.

He left her in the hospital. It was time to get home to his own wife and family.

11

Wednesday, March 1

Seamus spent the morning scrambling to shore up the accounts Milch hadn't stolen yet. Clients who dealt with his uncle for years weren't returning his calls. He and Bernheim sat together, wary of telling Helga, but they both knew it was only a matter of time before she found out. They were halfway through the list of calls they needed to make when she burst into his office.

"I told you this was going to happen."

"Take a seat, Helga."

She did as Seamus asked. "What are you doing?"

"Trying to convince our customers not to leave us in the lurch when we need them most," Bernheim said.

"And trying to hide how desperate we are," Seamus added.

"And this is all because of your insistence that this place be a haven for traitors to the Reich—people who would subvert every belief we have."

"People like Jews, Helga?" Bernheim asked.

"I didn't mention you."

"But what about Leonard Greenberg, Judith Starobin, Robert Greenfield? I could go on."

"The new government isn't friendly to their interests. I'm not saying we should throw them out on the street."

"What are you saying, then?" the factory manager asked.

Seamus had never seen him lose his cool before. "Ok, this isn't getting us anywhere. We need to band together."

"Or sell. Why don't we give Milch what he wants?" Helga asked.

"Because he'd get rid of our entire workforce," Seamus said.

"And Seamus wouldn't get a pfennig," Bernheim said.

"We could come to an arrangement. I would make sure Seamus was compensated."

"That wasn't what your father wanted. He put strict guidelines in his will to prevent the sale of the factory." Seamus held up the list of clients. "This is what's important now. We need to retain the business we have. Will you help us?"

Helga took the list in her hand. "Yes." She picked up the phone and called the first name on the sheet of paper. Two minutes later, she hung up.

"They're staying with us." She put a check on the piece of paper.

They pored over the accounts for another hour after the final phone call. The factory was in trouble. Milch had poached almost half of their accounts. The Cologne account was their last hope. If they lost it, they'd have no choice but to lay off much of the staff, or even close. Bernheim insisted on making that call himself. Seamus and Helga watched him until he hung up the phone.

"He didn't say if Milch was in contact with them, but I think they're going to stay with us."

Seamus breathed a sigh of relief and slumped back in his chair.

Near the end of the workday, Seamus was resting on the

railing outside his office, looking out over the factory floor. Salnikov waved up to him. His daughter was still in the clinic. The mysterious procedure to cure her brain tumor and even her mental condition was well underway.

He went back into his office. Martina Sammer, the secretary he, Helga, and Bernheim shared, knocked on his door.

"Herr Ritter?"

"What is it, Martina?"

"There's a gentleman here to see you. He says it's important. I looked at the schedule, but it doesn't say you have any meetings."

"What's his name?"

"He didn't give one. He just said you knew him and would want to see him."

"I thought this day couldn't get any stranger. It seems I was wrong. Send him up."

"I'll let him know." The young secretary turned to walk back down the stairs to the factory floor. Seamus reached for the coffee mug on the table in front of him. The contents were cold, and he put it back down. He reached for a packet of cigarettes as the knock on the door came again. It was Martina. Seamus couldn't make out the man standing behind her.

"The gentleman is here to see you, Herr Ritter."

"Send him in."

A man in a worn gray suit stepped past the secretary, who took the opportunity to take her leave. The man strode to his desk, but didn't offer a handshake. The side of his face was covered with an ugly scar. He wore a patch over one eye, and his arm was gone. Realization hit him like a bucket of ice-cold water. It was the man from the basement, from the steps outside the Kaiserhof Hotel.

"Recognize me?" the man asked in a gravelly voice.

"Who are you? What are you doing here?"

"You can call me Bruno, and I'm here to get what I deserve."

Bruno took a seat. Seamus was on his feet, though he didn't remember standing up. "Take the weight off. We need to talk."

The suit he wore was in stark contrast to the rest of his appearance. He smelled of whiskey, and his fingernails were long and chipped and black with dirt. The condition of his jagged and broken teeth matched his stringy and uneven hair. His one visible eye was streaked with red blood vessels.

"Why are you in my office?"

"You know why I'm here."

"I can assure you—"

"Don't waste my time. Let me tell you a little bedtime story." He flashed a warped smile before continuing. "One night, I was in the basement of an apartment block on Würzburger Strasse. I was minding my own business, settling down in a warm, dry place to spend the night when who did I see coming down the stairs? You and your little girlfriend carrying a rolled-up carpet, stained red on the underside. What were you doing carrying a rolled-up carpet down the stairs in the middle of the night? Seems like a strange time to rearrange the furniture."

"I have no idea what you're talking about."

Saying those words came as a reflex—he knew they were pointless. This would be about damage limitation. The structure of their entire lives was about to come crashing down around them.

"Don't interrupt when I'm telling the story. Anyway, you paid me off with a few Reichsmarks and sent me on my way. The whole night didn't mean whole lot to me, if I'm honest. When you've been living on the street as many years as I have, you start to feel detached from society. It's almost like nothing going on around you affects you. Your only concern is where you're going to stay the night, or where the next meal or bottle is coming from. I ignored what I saw for months—I don't keep up with the news or current affairs. But the time came when I saw a story in an old paper about a rich man's son going missing the night I saw you and your girl. It seemed like too much of a coincidence, so I went back to the basement to jog my memory. It all came flooding back. I've been searching for you for quite a while, Seamus Ritter. And here we are. What's to be done?"

"I have no idea what you're talking about."

Bruno laughed. "How about one of those cigarettes for a start?" He motioned to the pack on the desk. Seamus passed one to him and lit it with a match. The homeless man took a long drag and sat back on the chair.

"You found me at the dinner the other night. What took you so long to come here?"

"I had to find you. But these are details. Who cares about details? What matters now is you and your girl staying off the executioner's block. It'd be a shame for her to have her pretty little head chopped off, wouldn't it?"

"Get out of my office."

"What are you going to do? Call the police? Go ahead."

Seamus stayed seated. He wanted to jump out of his chair and pummel this man.

"We need to focus on the bigger picture here."

It wasn't hard to see how much he was enjoying this.

"Perhaps you think what happened that night wasn't murder. Maybe you'd call it justice. Would Otto Milch see it that way? Would Ernst Milch's wife and children see it that way, or his mother?"

Bruno paused before an ugly smile spread across his face. "You didn't kill him, did you?" Seamus stayed silent. "This wasn't a plan. She killed him and you helped her cover it up. The things we do for love, eh? I must admit, she's quite the dish. I mean, you wouldn't risk your life for just any woman, now, would you?"

Bruno finished the cigarette and stubbed it out. "You got

anything to drink around here? I think it's only fitting that we have a glass in our hands as we negotiate."

It was quitting time on the factory floor, and the workers were packing up to go home. Helga came to the door to say goodbye, but seeing he had company, waved through the glass instead. Seamus waved back before reaching into the bottom desk drawer for a bottle of Scotch. He took glasses from another drawer and pushed one across to the homeless man.

"Who's going to believe you? The word of a homeless man against a respected member of society like me? Give up this charade."

"You would have thrown me out long ago if you really believed that, but in answer to your question—the police...and Otto Milch. I'm guessing that once the investigation begins with my eyewitness account to back it up, you'll end up feeling the sharp end of the executioner's axe."

Bruno stood up. "Perhaps you're right, and I should go to see Herr Milch. Maybe he'll be more interested in what I have to say."

Seamus filled his glass and pushed it across the desk. "Sit down."

Bruno took his seat once more, savoring the fine whiskey. "We both know what I saw, and what my testimony could do to you and your little girlfriend."

"What do you want?"

"The reward money."

"Five thousand Reichsmarks?"

"I don't care who it comes from. Whether from Herr Milch or you makes no difference to me. That money buys what I saw that night. And once I have it, the information goes no further."

"I don't have that kind of money."

Bruno took a generous sip of the Scotch. "I think you do. This is your business, isn't it? You were at that dinner the other night with the richest men in Germany—Otto Milch included."

"I've only been at the helm a few months. I share the profits with my cousin..."

"Seems like you've got it hard, all right. Don't play that card with me. Why don't you step with me for a day? I'll show you a side of life you couldn't imagine."

Seamus took a sip of whiskey, trying to dismiss thoughts of Lisa being caught, or of his children being orphaned. The irony was that he'd seen poverty, but he'd never make this man believe that. To him, he was just another fat cat, and this was the chance of a lifetime.

"You want 5,000 Reichsmarks?"

"I didn't set the price, but it seems fair."

"You're going to have to give me some time."

"You have one week. I'll come back here in seven days. If you don't have the money, I'll go to Milch, or the police, or both."

The homeless man stood up and downed the rest of his whiskey. He slammed down the empty glass. He made for the door, parting with, "One week."

Seamus couldn't move. He felt like he was drowning.

"Think, goddammit, think," he said out loud. "There has to be some way out of this." *Why don't you call the police?* He didn't have that much money. Not nearly. After bailing out Salnikov, he had two or three thousand left at most. He had been cast in the role of a rich industrialist, with everything but the bank account to match. He was due a large chunk of money in the next few weeks when the Cologne contract came through—if it came through. Helmut had forged alliances with the city council there, and Ritter Industries was due a check for goods to be delivered to them in three or four weeks. The cash would be more than enough to cover the cost of keeping this Bruno quiet and keeping Ritter Industries in business, but he couldn't wait that long.

This was a short-term issue that would work itself out. No need to bother anyone else with it.

Is there any way Bernheim can appropriate the money for me through the accounts, as I did for Salnikov earlier today? This was a far greater sum, and how could he ask him to do something so blatantly illegal? The money for Salnikov could have been sneaked through and replaced easily enough. Five thousand Reichsmarks would leave a hole in the accounts at that time, bigger than the Brooklyn Bridge. Helga would find out and sue him, and that would be the end. He doubted the money was there in the first place, anyway. It didn't seem possible. He could extend the line of credit the business had with the bank, but Helga would have to sign off on it, and Bernheim would find out the next day. Another dead end.

A thought came to him and he jogged out of his office and down the stairs. He was in his car in two minutes, and home in ten. The house was quiet. He walked up the stairs to where he knew his wife would be. She turned to him with tired eyes. Hannah was on her lap, reading a book.

"Why are you home?" Lisa asked.

"I forgot something important," he replied. "How are you?"

Lisa shook her head. "Do you mind taking Hannah for a few minutes?"

"I can't stay long."

"Just a few minutes. The nanny left for the day. I have to call the undertaker."

Seamus opened his arms and the little girl ran to him. He took her out to the backyard, where they kicked through leaves for a few minutes before returning to the foyer. Lisa hung up the phone.

"Thank you," she said. "The funeral will be on Friday."

"I'll let the staff at work know. I just need to get something before I leave," Seamus said.

"Ok," Lisa replied.

He held her in his arms for a moment before she told him to get going. He ran up the stairs and went to the bedroom and pushed back the painting of the royal palace on the wall to reveal the safe underneath. The combination was the day Helga was born. He almost hoped he wasn't able to open the safe, and was disappointed when he could. It opened with an audible *clunk* and Seamus reached for the necklace inside. He hadn't opened the safe since Helmut died, and no one else knew about the necklace. Helmut never told Helga, who would have received it on her wedding if that day ever came to pass. Not even Lisa knew it existed.

At first, he wanted to keep it as a surprise, and then forgot about it himself. The necklace was worth more than the entire house, but Helmut made him promise to pass it onto Maureen on her wedding day and fulfill his mother's last dying wish. This one piece of jewelry could solve the problem with Bruno. He was sure it was worth far more than 5,000 Reichsmarks—more like double or triple that.

It was hard to believe it had come to this. Helmut's words about passing the necklace on to Maureen at her wedding rang in his ears as he lifted the heavy diamond necklace. He stuffed it into his pocket, not wanting to behold its beauty. He shut the safe and replaced the painting.

"What are you doing?" came a tiny voice behind him. Hannah was standing at the door.

"Nothing, my darling." He scooped her up in his arms and brought her back downstairs to Lisa.

"Who were you talking to?" his wife asked.

"No one, just myself."

"Don't lose your mind on me. We can't afford that right now," she said with a forced smile.

"I'll do my best." He kissed her on the lips.

Seamus got in his car and went straight to the bank, in a daze as he drove. The weight of what he had to take on was crushing him. He longed to tell Lisa, to share the burden of paying off Bruno and pawning his uncle's necklace. It would feel so good to talk to her, but keeping this secret was his way of shielding her from it, and leaving her to concentrate on the greater pain of losing her mother. He remembered back to when he lost Marie. If he had to deal with the likes of this Bruno person and Otto Milch then, he would have lost his mind. His duty to protect the woman he loved came before his own feelings. It was up to him to bear the brunt of this—Lisa could never know.

His hands were sweating as he reached the teller. "How much do I have in my account?"

The teller, a woman around his age with thick glasses and streaks of gray through her slicked-back hair, pointed to this bank book. "It's written in there."

"I just thought—"

She reached across and took the little blue book out of his hand. "You have 3,012 Reichsmarks in your account."

It was everything he had in the world, and all the family would have to live on for the next few weeks.

"I'd like to withdraw 3,000, please."

"Will you be closing your account with us?" the teller asked.

"No."

The lady behind the counter disappeared a few moments before returning with a wad of cash in her hand. She counted it out in front of him, put it in an envelope, and placed it in his hand. He thanked her under his breath, put the envelope in his jacket pocket and went back to his car.

He lit a cigarette, banging on the steering wheel of the stationary car. Thoughts of how else he could get the remaining 2,000 ran through his mind. *Is there any other alternative to pawning the necklace? No way am I asking any of my friends for the money.* It was hard to think of anyone who'd have that kind of cash lying around, apart from Helga, and he wasn't going to crawl to her. He dreaded to think how she'd leverage a debt to her. All confidence she ever had in him would be destroyed, if she even gave him the money. What would he tell her it was for? He'd have to lie again. Heaven only knew where that web of lies would lead him. No, going to Helga wasn't an option, so it seemed he had only one chance left.

The thought of what he was about to do was like a dagger in the chest. He remembered the look on Helmut's face when he showed him the necklace, when Seamus gave him his word.

But what other choice do I have? Perhaps this isn't the betrayal I'm making it out to be. I can pawn the necklace, get the money for it, and come up with the cash to pay it back later. But where am I going to get the money to pay it off? I'll have to worry about that when the time comes.

He drove to Wedding, the area he stayed in as a child, figuring to find a pawn shop there. He couldn't find any at first and had to ask a policeman for directions. He pulled up on Kameruner Strasse, made sure the envelope of money, as well as the necklace, were in his pockets, and pushed the door open to the pawnshop.

All manner of furniture, musical instruments, tools, and bicycles were on display. The man at the back counter, who was small, balding, and in his fifties, looked up. "Can I help you, sir?"

"I have an item here." Seamus reached into his pocket.

"To pawn or sell?"

"To pawn."

"Interest rate is 20 percent per month."

That beats the 20 percent per week I'd pay to a loan shark.

"I need 2,000 for this," Seamus said and placed the necklace on the table.

The pawnshop manager looked at him, and then the antique jewelry again. "Give me a moment," he said and took the necklace into the back of the store.

He emerged five minutes later. "It's real. I'll give you the 2,000 with sixty days to pay the pawn back."

"You drive a hard bargain," Seamus said.

"You understand what this means? I'm effectively giving you a loan that uses the necklace as collateral. Once the sixty days is up, I'm free to sell the necklace as I please."

"I understand. I'll be back."

The pawnbroker gave him a look that said he'd heard it all before, but kept his mouth shut. Helmut's necklace was on the counter, and Seamus stared at it one last time before the pawnbroker swept it into an envelope. He reached down to a safe deposit box and counted 2,000 Reichsmarks. Seconds later, Seamus had another envelope to deposit in his pocket.

"Don't lose this," the pawnshop manager said and handed him a ticket. "The first interest payment is due one month from today."

"I'll see you then."

Seamus felt empty, drained, but he had the 5,000 Reichsmarks. He went home and put it in the empty safe where the necklace had been.

12

Friday, March 3

T he weather was suitably cold, the sky colorless for the morning of Ingrid's funeral. Ingrid's warning about Lisa's father bobbed up and down in Maureen's mind like corks in water. Lisa sat at the end of the pew, her head on her new husband's shoulder for much of the ceremony. *How can I tell Lisa? How can I destroy her mother's memory on the day of her funeral?*

The church service ended and Seamus helped carry out the ornate casket he bought for his mother-in-law. Maureen didn't recognize any of the other pall bearers. Lisa assured her they were cousins, but she didn't seem to know them well, or hardly even at all. The small crowd followed the casket out of the church and watched as it was loaded into the hearse to be taken for burial. Maureen stood with her siblings. Their father came to check up on them.

"How are you?" he asked for the third time that morning.

"Fine," Maureen said.

"I'm ok," Michael added. The other two nodded in agreement.

Perhaps seeing their mother die had hardened them to this, or maybe it was just that they never really knew Ingrid. Either way, Maureen was proud of how her siblings handled the day. Lisa walked out last, holding Hannah. They were both crying as everyone lined up to receive the handful of mourners.

A small woman with glasses was first. She embraced Lisa, who introduced her to the rest of the family.

"This is my mother's cousin, Liesl."

Maureen shook the woman's hand. *What do you know about what Ingrid said?*

"Can we talk?" Lisa asked Liesl as she was about to walk away.

"Perhaps later," she replied and faded into the crowd.

Maureen wondered again about what Ingrid told her. Should her words die with her? Was she even serious about what she said? Lisa had warned them about the drugs she was on at the end of her life. Perhaps she made the whole thing up on the spot. Should she risk telling Lisa about something that might have been an elaborate hallucination? Lisa's father was long dead. Why would Ingrid warn her against trying to find him? It wouldn't be right to bother her with it, particularly at this time.

A woman appeared through the crowd and went to Maureen's father. She was thin with blond hair, her skin streaked with tears. Maureen was standing next to her father.

"Nikita," he said. "Why are you here? How is Andrei?"

"Still in hospital," she said. "I had to come and pay my respects after everything you did for our family."

"How is Maria?"

"She died last night," Nikita said. "The doctor said she took a turn for the worse and never woke up this morning."

"Oh, no. I'm so sorry."

"Thank you for what you did for us." She turned away and wandered back toward the street.

"Who was she?" Maureen asked.

"One of my employees' wives. Her little girl was sick for a while." ˒

"What did you do for them?"

"Not enough."

Lisa returned to her husband's side and the conversation ended.

They walked to the car that was to take them to the cemetery when Maureen spotted a face in the crowd.

"Thomas?" she asked.

Her new friend from school was standing alone, looking so handsome in his suit. The feelings he prompted in her didn't seem fitting here.

"I just wanted to pay my respects."

"But you should be in school."

"My parents let me take the day off."

She held her hand out to him. It felt warm in his. "I need to go," she said.

"Until Monday," he replied.

She got into the car with her family and they drove away.

Wednesday, March 8

Bruno was giddy as he got off the tram. A week had passed, and it was time to pick up the money from the American. He felt little guilt and had slept more soundly these last seven nights than for many years. The American could afford it.

He should be grateful. They wouldn't be in this mess if she hadn't killed him, or they hadn't killed him, or whatever had happened.

Either way, that wasn't his concern. All he cared about was

taking advantage. What would 5,000 Reichsmarks mean to a man like Seamus Ritter, anyway? One less pair of diamond earrings for his murdering girlfriend? He doubted a man of his means would even miss it, but it would mean everything to him. It was his ticket to a new life—a way to get over the past and to put the horror of the war behind him. It was like he was being born this very day, and that nothing that had gone previous to this day would ever matter again. It was a good deal. All parties were getting a new life from it.

He met the same secretary as he had the previous week at the door to the factory, but this time she let him in without question. She led him up the stairs to the level where Ritter's office sat overlooking the factory. The floor was empty, the machines off. It was difficult waiting around all day, but he had ceded that small favor to the man who was about to give him 5,000 Reichsmarks. It was hard to keep the smile off his face as he walked into the office. Ritter was considerably less jovial and looked at him with daggers in his eyes. Bruno sat down at the desk opposite him. The secretary said goodbye, but neither man looked up.

"You have the money?"

"I do." Bruno edged forward, but Ritter held his finger in the air. "Do I have your word of honor that you will never breathe a word of this to the police, or Milch or anyone else?"

"As a loyal German. This is what getting away with murder costs. You could spend it on fancy lawyers and still face the axman, or give it to me. This is the smart choice."

"I never want to see you again," the American said.

"You won't." Bruno turned and walked out of the office.

It was dark as he stepped out onto the street outside the factory. Willi, waiting for him, could hardly contain himself.

"Did you get it?" the newsie asked.

"I got it."

Willi punched the air in triumph and let out a whoop under his breath.

"Control yourself. Someone could be watching."

The boy seemed to understand. "I'll take my share and be on my way."

They found a deserted alley. Bruno counted out 500 Reichsmarks and handed it to him.

"Thanks, Bruno. Am I ever glad I ran into you! You come see me again if you ever need anything, all right?"

He stood and watched as Willi got on his bike and left. Bruno felt like he was losing something.

He walked a few minutes before the paranoia gripping him became too much and he flagged down the first taxi he saw. The car took him to a fancy hotel. The man working at reception eyed him like something he just found on the underside of his shoe.

"I'd like a room. Sorry about the smell—I was in an accident and I'm in need of a bath. I'll take the finest suite you have." The man looked as if he was about to call the police until Bruno produced a wad of banknotes. "Is there a problem?"

"No," the clerk said. "Everything is in order. How many nights will you be staying?"

"Let's try five to begin. We'll see from there."

The man checked him in and gave him the key. The fact that he was wearing a respectable suit seemed to matter little. People still stared at his scars and his missing eye and arm on the way to the elevator, and a couple waiting there refused to share it with him. That was nothing a bath couldn't sort out. Bruno tipped the elevator operator for keeping his mouth shut. The room was like nothing he'd ever experienced before. During the war, in the early days, when they were pushing into France, one of his friends told him they'd be in the Palace at Versailles soon. This was what he imagined that palace to be. Chandeliers and thick carpeting. Paintings adorning the walls, and even a grand piano in the corner by the balcony. Bruno picked up the telephone by the bed. It took him a few seconds to work out how to use it, and then he ordered three bottles of the finest Scotch they had. It arrived as he was getting into the bath.

He raised a glass in the air. "To Ernst Milch. I'm sure you got what you deserved, but thanks to you, so did I."

Friday, March 24

Thomas was waiting for Maureen as she walked in. He stood up, a handsome smile on his face as she zigzagged through tables. Once again, he had asked to meet at the Romanisches Café on Kurfürstendamm. Thomas was attracted to the site on account of its reputation as a place where artists met. It was as if by being there, he could inhale some inspiration.

He greeted her with a kiss on the cheek just as a fleeting thought of Leo flared inside her. She hoped he wasn't still waiting for her—their time together was over. Her life was here, in this beautiful, maddening, exciting, insane city. It was time to move on. Thomas reached across and took her hand as she sat down opposite him. He wore a smart gray suit with a matching tie. It had taken her an hour and a lot of input from Lisa to choose her outfit. In the end, she went for a blue floral dress with a beret. She took the hat off as she sat, resting it on the table beside her. She was fifteen minutes late—by design—and Thomas was halfway through the beer on the table. He attracted the waiter's attention, and Maureen ordered a beer too. *Why not, when everyone else is?*

The café was packed. Dozens of tables sat in the ample space, and they had to lean across to hear each other above the loud chatter in the room.

"I didn't see you in school today," he began.

"We don't have class together on Fridays, remember?"

"Doesn't mean I didn't want to see you."

His blue eyes sparkled and a devilish grin came over his face. The waiter returned, and Maureen leaned back to give him space to place the drink down. She thanked him and took a sip, wondering if he realized they were both seventeen. No one seemed to care here.

Thomas had a folded newspaper beside his beer. He saw her eyes on it and held it up. "You read about this?"

The headline read NATIONAL SOCIALISTS PASS ENABLING ACT.

She nodded, feeling empty.

"They're calling it a law to remedy the distress of the people of the Reich."

"I read that."

"You know what this is, don't you? It's the death of the Republic." He smacked the newspaper with the back of his other hand. "Hitler and his cronies have used the crisis to steal the power they could never win at the ballot box. Even with incumbency and everything else at their disposal, more Germans voted for other parties in the March 5 election than the Nazis, but none of that matters now. Are you worried?"

"I grew up in a democracy. This is alien to me."

"So did I," Thomas replied. "The rights of free speech and free assembly are gone. Same with freedom of the press and due process of law. I can't believe it's come to this but we're at the mercy of these people now. I just hope the German people know what they've been signed up for."

He took a sip of his beer and drew a pack of cigarettes out of his pocket. He lit one before continuing. "Hitler will be making up the laws himself now. No one can stop him."

"He's doing exactly what he said he'd do."

"What's that?"

"To sweep all the other political parties out of Germany. The Nazis are the only ones left standing."

He took a drag on his cigarette. "I'd hate to think you and your family are thinking of leaving Germany because of this. We've only just started to get to know each other."

"We've had the conversation in the house, but the truth is, we've nothing to go back to. We were poor in America, and we have a big house in Berlin. My father is doing well in his job here, but had nothing at home. We can't leave. We're as stuck here as anyone else."

"Hoping that the National Socialist Party does a good job for Germany?"

"Like everyone else. My father lost a friend to the arrests after the fire—Hans Litten."

"I think I read about him. He was the lawyer who cross-examined Hitler?"

"They took him the night the Reichstag burned down. He's been in protective custody ever since. That's what the SA call it, at least. My father knows a lot of journalists, and they've been lobbying for his release, but the Nazis aren't budging. He's stuck in Spandau Prison."

They finished their beers and ordered another round. Maureen wondered for a few seconds how her father would react if she came home drunk, but dismissed the thought. She'd been old enough to look after her siblings at fourteen, so wasn't she old enough to enjoy a few beers at seventeen?

The conversation moved away from politics to their peers and what was going on in school. It felt good to be young and to make him laugh. He was so handsome when he laughed. She managed to forget about her family for a while, but the knowledge lurking below the surface emerged after she drank her second beer. Before she knew it, the words in her mind were on her lips.

"Lisa's mother told me something before she died."

Thomas put down his beer. "What?"

"She was on morphine, and I suppose she thought I was Lisa..."

"She couldn't tell?"

"I heard some things—private things."

"I don't want to pry, but you wouldn't have started this conversation if you didn't want to tell me."

Maureen took another gulp of beer, wondering if she did want to keep on with what she started. Once this genie was out of the bottle, there would be no putting it back. Telling Lisa what she heard would change both their lives.

"I thought Ingrid would be the one to tell her before she died."

"Oh, come on. You have to tell me now. You can't do this to me."

"I've been carrying this around like a millstone around my neck."

"Would sharing it with me make you feel better? I won't tell a soul." She turned away. "Come, now. I'm hardly about to march down to your house, knock on the door, and spill the beans to your stepmother, am I?"

Maureen had only known Thomas a few weeks. She finished her beer without another word.

"I can't help you if you don't let me in." He reached across the table, his hands warm on hers.

The act of sharing what she knew would be cathartic in itself. She told him what Ingrid said in the most detail she could. Thomas didn't interrupt as she spoke, but his face betrayed his shock.

"Where is her father?"

"He died nine years ago."

"What did she mean by it's too dangerous, then? It doesn't make any sense."

"That was one of the reasons I didn't tell Lisa. I had no idea what Ingrid was on about. I thought it'd be better to let her tell her daughter herself."

"They're Jews? You didn't know that?"

"I don't think Lisa does either."

"Are you going to tell her?"

"I decided to wait until after the funeral. Lisa was so upset. I didn't want to sully her mother's name."

"Alive or dead, her mother won't be the same in Lisa's eyes once she hears what she kept from her. It all depends who your loyalty is to—Lisa or Ingrid?"

"Lisa, of course."

"Telling her isn't the easiest thing, but it's probably the right thing."

Maureen didn't answer, just gazed out at the crowd. "I wonder if Remarque or Billy Wilder is here today?"

"I heard Billy Wilder is off to Hollywood, and the Nazis are no fans of Erich Remarque's novels either. *All Quiet on the Western Front* doesn't tally with their vision of German patriotism and the glory of war. Anyway, don't change the subject."

"I love Lisa. Her mother's death devastated her, but knowing her mother lied to her all these years could destroy her."

"Were any of her family at the funeral?"

"A few distant relatives. Her cousin Liesl was the only one she stayed in touch with, but she barely said a word. We exchanged hellos, but not much more, and she left without saying goodbye. As far as I know, she drove straight home after the service without talking to anyone. I thought she might know something, but she didn't say a word."

"It's up to you."

"Don't remind me."

"You want my advice?"

"That depends on what it might be," Lisa said, remaining taciturn.

"You might be surprised at what she already knows or suspects. Perhaps you telling her will be the last piece of the puzzle. Perhaps it won't, but that knowledge burning inside that pretty head of yours doesn't belong to you. It's Lisa's."

"What about her mother?"

"It's not an easy time to be Jewish in Germany, but Lisa needs to be given the opportunity to find out who she is for herself. But then, you knew all this already, didn't you?"

"Yes."

"When are you going to tell her?"

"Tonight. How did you know I'd already made up my mind to talk to her?"

"I know you."

"We've only been friends a few weeks."

"I know enough."

They sat in the café another thirty minutes or so, but Maureen's mind was elsewhere. Thomas walked out with her, holding her coat and then the door. A cold wind scythed through them as they stood facing one another on Kurfürsten-damm. She raised her scarf up over her neck to ward off the cold, making sure to leave her lips free.

"Good luck with Lisa. Let me know how it goes, and if you need anything—"

She rose up on tiptoes and kissed him on the lips before he had a chance to finish. A smile burst across his face.

"I was wondering when you were going to do that, so I had to take the lead," Maureen said. "A girl can't wait around forever."

Thomas shook his head, still smiling. "I'm glad you did."

Her tram pulled up, and he bent down to kiss her again. It was slower, more satisfying. *Perfect.* The bell rang on the tram and she jumped on. Thomas held up a hand, and she took a seat at the back as he receded into the distance.

The children were playing in the living room as she got

home. Conor was running a toy train up and down the rug. Michael had set up toy soldiers and was preparing an ambush among the pillows strewn on the floor. Fiona was practicing her dance moves. Hannah was tucked up in bed.

"How's your new boyfriend?" Fiona asked. The boys laughed.

"He's very well, thank you."

Maureen hung up her coat and went into the kitchen. Her father was sitting at the table, holding Lisa's hand as she drank a glass of wine. They looked years older. They both tried to smile, but the pain only showed through more.

"We kept you some dinner," her father said.

Lisa took a plate of food out of the oven. "How was your evening?" she asked.

"We had a lovely time."

"I'm so glad you're making friends," Lisa said.

Her father stayed quiet. The beer glass on the table in front of him was empty. Maureen sat down with them, expecting them to leave, but they didn't. Maureen couldn't tell her like this—not in front of her father.

She spoke about her date with Thomas. It felt safe to call it as much. Her father bristled as she spoke, but didn't verbalize what she knew he was thinking.

"He's a lovely young man," Lisa said. "We'll have to invite his parents for dinner soon."

Maureen finished her food and took the plate to the sink to clean it off. She turned to the table once she finished. "Lisa, can we talk?"

"Of course," Lisa said.

"Why don't you two ladies go for a stroll around the block, and I'll prepare the kids for bed?"

"Thanks," Maureen replied. She stood still as her father came to her. He hugged her, and she reached her arms around to reciprocate. It felt good. He left without another word as Maureen and Lisa went to get their coats.

The full cloak of darkness had fallen, and the ladies walked in silence under a cloudless sky. Maureen's hands were sweaty and shaking so much, she had to keep them rammed into her pockets.

Lisa was the first one to speak. "I'm so grateful to you all. Thank you for taking Hannah and me in as part of your family. It hasn't been an easy time."

"We're lucky to have you."

"You've had so much thrust upon you. New city. New friends, new school. My mother's death." Lisa reached out to curl her arm inside Maureen's and they walked together. "I'm so sorry."

"You have nothing to apologize for."

"I do. I'm sorry we made you lie to the police for us. I never told you how grateful I am for what you did. I never thanked you."

"You don't have to."

"I do. Thank you for saving our family."

Maureen thought to ask why she had to lie for them, but knew better.

"I can't believe you had the presence of mind to say what you needed to. You amaze me every day."

Lisa brought her hand up to the swirl of Maureen's hair before bringing it back down to link arms again. The streetlights illuminated the street, and a man out walking his dog tipped his hat to them as he passed. They didn't speak for a few seconds. Maureen knew the time was now.

"There's been something weighing on my mind, something I heard your mother say before she died."

The moment felt surreal. She envisioned saying these words to Lisa so many times, it was hard to believe it was happening. They kept walking.

"You told me she said she lied to me about my father to protect me."

"That wasn't all she said."

"What?" Lisa asked.

The words caught in her throat as if they were shards of broken glass. "It's hard to say exactly—she was on those heavy painkillers at the time."

"What else did she say?"

"She said, 'Don't try to find him. It's too dangerous.'"

"What? Don't try to find my father?"

"I know. It's so ridiculous—he's been dead for nine years."

"Was there something else? Why would it be dangerous?"

"She said he didn't marry her because you're Jews."

"We're Jews? What? We're not Jews. We were never church-going types, but we're Lutheran, not Jewish. Did she explain any more?"

"No, she passed out. That was all she said."

Lisa let out a moan, and a tear broke down her face. "I heard her and Liesl talking about something when we visited Rostock a few weeks ago. Liesl referred to something I couldn't quite hear, but my mother said the past should be left in the past. Liesl told her that everyone deserved to know who—" She stopped, as if afraid to go on.

"Who what?"

"Who their real father is." Lisa stopped. She took her arm from Maureen's and used her hand to wipe her wet face.

"What else did she say?" Maureen asked.

"That she didn't want her good name tarnished by a mistake she made thirty years ago." Lisa found a bench at the edge of a darkened park and flopped down. "Liesl didn't seem to know many details."

Maureen sat beside her.

"I asked my mother about it afterward. She admitted that

the man who raised me wasn't my real father, and man who was died years ago."

"That doesn't tally with what she said to me, but maybe that was just the morphine. She probably didn't know what she was saying."

"Maybe, or maybe it was a deathbed confession and she was trying to clear her conscience."

"I'm sorry I didn't tell you sooner. I wanted to give her the opportunity—"

"No, it's not your fault. I'm sorry you've been carrying the weight of this around for the last few weeks. I can't imagine how difficult it must have been for you."

She put her hand on Maureen's. "Liesl knows something. She never said a word at the funeral and ran off before I got the chance to ask her any questions." Lisa's voice was weak as she spoke, as if all the energy drained out of her.

"I suppose she was trying to respect your mother's last wishes."

They sat there a few more minutes as Maureen went over every last detail she remembered. Lisa was calmer when she finished.

"I think my mother wanted to tell me at the end, but she wasn't able to get the words out. Why did she wait so long?" she asked, as if to herself.

A few minutes passed before the bite of the night air became too much to bear.

"Let's go home," Lisa said.

The two women trudged back toward the house. "I didn't think I'd be going back to Rostock so soon," Lisa said.

"I'll come too—if you'll have me."

"Of course," Lisa said and put an arm around the younger woman's shoulder. They walked in silence until they came to the house. The children were in bed.

"Is everything all right?" Maureen's father asked.

Maureen left them to talk and traipsed up the stairs. She barely had the energy to change for bed and was asleep seconds after her head hit the pillow.

Lisa waited until the children were settled to tell Seamus. He sat in the living room with a bemused look on his face as Lisa spoke.

"She told Maureen? That sounds like your father is still alive."

"I know. Why else would she warn me off looking for him? What harm would there be in looking for a gravestone?"

"You want to find him, don't you?"

"Wouldn't you?"

"Yes. What about your mother's warning?"

"I don't know. I've been wracking my brain to figure that out. Maybe he's a criminal, or in jail? I have no idea."

"What about this assertion that you're Jews? Where did that come from?"

"I have no idea. We're Lutheran. My family was never religious, but they never mentioned anything about being Jewish."

"You think your grandparents were Jews? Maybe your mother converted?"

"I don't know, but it's not a good time to be a Jew in Germany."

"But you're not a Jew, so you don't have to worry. The Nazis' twisted obsession with them has nothing to do with you. How can you be Jewish if you never even knew you were? And even if your grandparents were, your mother must have converted when she was a child."

"Maybe she was born a Jew. Doesn't that make me ethnically Jewish?"

"Does it matter?"

"To the Nazis? It might. They've already banned Jews from working in the civil service. What's next?"

"Even if your mother was born Jewish—and we don't know that—you didn't know about this your whole life. How would they find out?"

"I don't know."

He put his hands on her cheeks. "You don't have to worry, my sweet."

"I'm sure you're right. Our National Socialist friends will be gone soon enough, anyway, I'm sure. Hindenburg's got to come to his senses sooner or later."

"Exactly."

"You do know I'm going to try and find my father, though, don't you?"

"I wouldn't expect anything less from you."

13

Saturday, March 25

L isa woke before dawn, finding it hard to say how many hours she slept. Perhaps two or three. She and Seamus stayed up talking long into the night until he passed out after one o'clock. The same thoughts and questions bounced around her mind unanswered. She tried to picture her father and why Volker Geisinger, the man who raised her and gave her his name, never spoke up. A thousand questions and no answers. The dull sun of early spring was limping over the horizon, doing little more than brightening the gray clouds covering it.

The plush rug was soft beneath her feet as she got out of bed. She was packed and ready to leave in minutes, but Seamus was still asleep. It was hard to know what was affecting him so much these last few weeks. Her mother's death and the new job would have been enough to send anyone over the edge, but her intuition pointed toward something else. What was troubling him that he hadn't told her about? Now wasn't the time to ask Seamus what his troubles were, but a dagger of guilt pierced her heart as she turned to watch him sleep. She hadn't been present for him—her mother's death blinded her to everything else. She would make it up to him later.

She went to the kitchen and prepared breakfast for the family before going to Maureen's room when she couldn't stand to wait for her to wake any longer. The young girl greeted her with a tired smile and went to the bathroom to ready herself for the day. Hannah was more difficult to rouse, and she felt terrible doing it but fought through the guilt. The little girl clung to her like a barnacle. Lisa had to pry her off her body to bring her to the bathroom and get her dressed.

Thirty minutes later, and just as the rest of the house woke up, they walked out to the car.

"How are you feeling?" Maureen asked from the passenger seat.

"Determined," Lisa replied and started the car.

Hannah sat in the back, reading books and playing with dolls as the other women spoke in the front. They talked about the same thing over and over. With little else to say, the conversation faded until all they heard was the sound of the tires on the road.

They were an hour from Rostock when Lisa broke the silence. "I wish I knew my mother's reasoning for keeping it from me all these years."

"Loyalty to Volker, perhaps. He raised you as his own."

"Almost, yes. I used to think the gap between me and my brothers was because of my gender, but I know better now. He and my mother never seemed happy. I suppose that's what happens when you settle for the safe option."

"You think she wanted to be with your real father?"

"That's one of the many things I intend to find out."

"What if Liesl's not home?"

"She'll be there. One of the few things she told me at the funeral was that it had been more than fifteen years since she was in Berlin, and more than ten since she left Rostock. She'll be there all right."

A gentle rain began as they pulled in front of Liesl's house, the North Sea greenish-gray for miles behind them. Lisa bounded out of the car and went to get her daughter.

"You were such a good girl on the way up here," she said as she reached in for her.

Controlling herself was going to be a challenge. She took a few deep breaths to slow down her racing heart. Maureen went to the front door, waiting for Lisa to catch up. Before she had the chance, Liesl appeared.

"Lisa, and little Hannah! What are you doing here?"

The lines Lisa rehearsed in the car on the way up dissipated like smoke in the breeze. "Can we come in?" she asked. "This is my stepdaughter, Maureen. You met her at the funeral."

"Pleased to see you again, young lady," she said and took the girl's hand. "Of course. You came all this way. Was it to see me?"

"We need to talk," Lisa said. She kept Hannah in her arms as she entered the tidy little house. The fire was already started. A half-drunk cup of tea was sitting on the table in front of the couch, and the book Liesl was apparently reading was turned upside down on a cushion.

"Please, take a seat," Liesl said. "What brings you all the way up here from Berlin?" Lisa put her daughter down and took a seat with Maureen in the armchair perpendicular to them.

"Some things my mother said before she died, and a conversation I heard when we visited before."

The color drained from Liesl's face. "Can I get you something? I was drinking tea."

"I'd rather talk," Lisa said. "Please join us." She patted the couch beside her and sat back. Hannah spilled onto the floor and made her way to the window, where she watched the rain running down the glass.

Liesl took a seat in silence.

"My mother was in great pain before she died."

"The poor dear. It breaks my heart," Liesl said.

"The doctor prescribed morphine, but warned me about the side effects. She was in a drug-induced haze for the rest of her time with us. Every trace of her personality disappeared, and we never spoke again. But she did call out. Just words at first, but after a while, she began to speak in coherent sentences. She told me she loved me over and over, but then something changed. Some kind of guilt came over her. One night she woke while Maureen was there. My mother thought she was me and warned her off looking for my father. She said she lied to protect me."

Liesl took a sip of her tea and put the cup back on the saucer. She brought a handkerchief to dab her eyes.

"I got up to get a glass of water the night we stayed here," Lisa said. "I heard you two talking about my father, and how Ingrid never told me the truth."

"You must have been mistaken. And your mother was delirious. Heaven only knows what she was talking about in that state."

"I heard the conversation you and she had that night about my real father, and she admitted it to me the next day. You said then I deserved to know. Don't you think I still deserve that much?"

"I don't know what you're talking about." Liesl started to get out of the seat. Lisa put an arm on her shoulder and, using a firm but gentle touch, eased her back down. "I'm going to find him, with or without you. Don't make this harder. Do me that favor."

Liesl put her face in her hands. "I swore I'd never say a word."

"The person you swore to is dead. She wanted me to know the truth."

"Ingrid was so secretive about it. There's so much she didn't tell me."

"Who was my father? Do you know his name?"

Liesl shook her head. "She never told me, but she did say he was a doctor. Your mother was working as a part-time nurse before you were born. It was something she always wanted to do, and Volker didn't care. They weren't getting along well. He was brash and rude—at least, that's what she told me."

"Where did she meet this doctor?"

"After they moved to Berlin. They were married ten years or so and the boys were old enough to go to school alone. Volker got a job in a hotel there, working at the front desk. They needed the money. Ingrid also found work."

"Did you ever meet him?"

"Oh, no. Ingrid never would have allowed that. I was still here in Rostock. All I knew was through her letters."

"Do you still have any of them?"

Liesl finished her tea and put the cup back down. "I'd have to look in the attic."

"We drove from Berlin."

The older woman got up without another word and left her guests alone. Lisa brought Hannah out to the back garden. It was enclosed, and the rain had stopped, so she slipped a pair of galoshes on her and left her to play in the puddles. Ten minutes passed before Liesl returned with an old box.

Her mother's cousin sat down once more and put the box of letters on the table. "Let me see," she said as she went through it. "Here's one." She found three more and placed them on the table. "This is the first, written just after she began working in the hospital." She handed it to Lisa. It was short, not more than eight lines, just as her letters always were. It was dated January 2, 1902. She read it out loud.

Dear Liesl,

I've taken a job at the Charité Hospital as a nurse. It's

PART TIME AND I'LL STILL BE ABLE TO LOOK AFTER THE BOYS WHEN THEY'RE NOT IN SCHOOL. ANYTHING TO GET AWAY FROM THAT BUFFOON, VOLKER...

Lisa held up the letter. "Most of the rest of it is about my brothers." She put it down and picked up the next, dated March 6, 1902.

DEAR LIESL,

I'M SORRY I HAVEN'T WRITTEN IN SO LONG. I CHERISH YOUR LETTERS, AND OFTEN FEEL YOU'RE THE ONLY PERSON I CAN TRUST. VOLKER AND I HARDLY TALK THESE DAYS. HE SPENDS MOST OF HIS TIME AT WORK, AT THE BAR, OR PERHAPS WITH A FANCY WOMAN. HE'S RARELY HOME, AND I HONESTLY DON'T CARE.

HIS INADEQUACIES AS A HUSBAND ARE ALL THE MORE APPARENT WHEN I COMPARE HIM TO J, THE YOUNG DOCTOR I'VE BEFRIENDED. HE'S EVERYTHING VOLKER ISN'T—HANDSOME, FUNNY, INTELLECTUALLY BRILLIANT, KIND, AND GIVING. I FIND MYSELF THINKING ABOUT HIM ALMOST ALL THE TIME WE'RE NOT TOGETHER. WE EAT DINNER ALONE TOGETHER SEVERAL TIMES A WEEK. IT'S A STRANGE FEELING TO KNOW WHAT YOU'RE DOING IS WRONG, YET NOT CARE ONE JOT.

SOMETIMES HAPPINESS ISN'T A STRAIGHTFORWARD MATTER. SOMETIMES WE HAVE TO CONSTRUCT IT FOR OURSELVES. I'M SURE ALL THIS WILL BLOW OVER SOON, AND I'LL BE BACK WITH VOLKER. IN THE MEANTIME, I KNOW YOU'LL KEEP MY SECRET.

LOVE,

INGRID

Lisa was finding it hard to breathe. It was difficult to match the woman she knew with the person who wrote this. Her mother seemed alive within those words. It was as if she could see her as a young woman, trying to justify her passion. "What did you respond?"

"Just to be careful, and to make sure of every step she took. She seemed happy."

"Did you ask her who the doctor was?"

"Yes, but she refused to tell me. I stopped asking after a while. I thought it would all blow over, like she wrote, and it did, but after I thought it would."

Lisa picked up the following letter.

JUNE 26, 1902

DEAR LIESL,

I HAVEN'T WRITTEN IN SO LONG. I HOPE YOU DON'T THINK ANY THE LESS OF ME. MY LIFE HAS SPIRALED TO PLACES I NEVER DREAMED OF, AND THE SITUATION I FIND MYSELF IN NOW IS UNTENABLE.

I DON'T LOVE VOLKER. I DON'T THINK I EVER DID. I LOVE THE DOCTOR. I'VE NEVER KNOWN A MAN LIKE HIM. HE IS SINGLE, FROM A GOOD FAMILY, AND IS VERY MUCH LOOKING FORWARD TO THE REST OF OUR LIVES TOGETHER. I KNOW YOU'RE DYING TO KNOW HIS NAME AND I'LL TELL YOU SOON, ONCE ALL THE DETAILS OF OUR GETTING TOGETHER ARE IRONED OUT. HE ASKED ME THAT I NOT REVEAL HIM TO ANYONE JUST YET.

VOLKER DOESN'T KNOW ABOUT US, BUT SOON WILL, AS I'M WITH CHILD. HE WILL KNOW IT CAN'T BE HIS. OUR BABY IS COMING NEXT FEBRUARY. MY LIFE IS ABOUT TO BE TURNED UPSIDE DOWN, BUT I'M HAPPY. HAPPIER THAN I'VE EVER BEEN. SURELY THERE CAN BE NO BETTER WAY TO BRING A CHILD INTO THIS WORLD? I'M IN LOVE, AND THINGS WILL WORK OUT.

LOVE,

INGRID

Lisa fought back the tears as she reached for the final letter. The tragedy of her mother's affair was unfolding in front of her all these years later.

AUGUST 5, 1902

DEAREST LIESL,

I REALIZE NOW HOW STUPID I'VE BEEN THESE LAST FEW MONTHS. YOU WERE RIGHT. VOLKER HAS AGREED TO TAKE ME BACK. THE BOYS NEED A MOTHER, AND HE NEEDS A WIFE. MY INFI-

DELITY WILL REMAIN A SECRET AS THE SHAME WOULD BE TOO MUCH TO BEAR FOR OUR FAMILY.

I'VE LEFT MY JOB AT THE HOSPITAL. THE DOCTOR IS GONE—HE TRANSFERRED HIMSELF TO LEIPZIG—BUT THE LESS SAID ABOUT THAT, THE BETTER. I AM JUST THANKFUL THAT VOLKER HAS AGREED TO STAND BY ME. I SOMETIMES DOUBT WHETHER HE WOULD HAVE IF IT WEREN'T FOR THE BOYS, BUT HE HAS, AND THAT'S ALL THAT MATTERS. I FEEL LIKE SUCH A FOOL.

LOVE,

INGRID

"Is that all?" Lisa asked. Liesl took a few more seconds to recheck the box before nodding.

"I'll go check on Hannah," Maureen said and got out of her chair.

Lisa was in a daze. Her body felt as if it weighed 1,000 tons, and she let her torso fall back on the couch. It was impossible. She reread the letters for any clues to who her father might be. *Should I be referring to him like that? As my father?*

"Did she ever speak about the doctor again?"

"Not much. I asked her, of course, but she wanted to leave the past behind."

"And when I was born?"

"She moved on. She and Volker were determined that the boys never find out, and knew you would be the easiest one of all to keep it from. They got on with their lives, and in time, she forgot about the doctor. You were her daughter. That was all that mattered."

"But she didn't forget about it. Why else did she bring it up with you? Was it something you discussed often?"

"I don't think we spoke of it in twenty-five years."

"Who brought it up when she visited?"

"It was she who broached the topic. It was weighing on her mind."

"Was she looking for advice?"

"Do any of us ever really seek out advice, or are we looking for affirmation? Gazing into the abyss causes us all to examine the choices we've made in life, and whether we could have done anything differently. I think she wanted to calm her mind."

"Mother was fifty-nine. He's probably around the same age. I know he's alive."

"You don't know that, or anything else."

"My mother said something else. She said the doctor didn't marry her because she was Jewish."

"She never told you, then," Liesl said.

"Not until the end."

"Your grandparents were both Jews. We all converted back in the 1880s. The stigma was too much to live with. I never knew that the doctor found out and refused to marry your mother because of it. I suppose it's possible. Your mother wanted to leave that part of her life behind, so much so that she never even told you about it. I'd advise you to do the same. I certainly won't be publicizing it now the Nazis are in power."

Lisa stood up and went to the window, watching Maureen chasing Hannah around the yard. "You think it'll come back to hurt us?"

"Not if the Nazis never find out."

"My mother said it was too dangerous to look for my father."

"She must have meant that the secret of her past—that she was a Jew—might come out. I think you should take her advice. Let the past be past."

"He's alive. I know he is. I can't just ignore that fact. I'm not Jewish myself, so what do I have to worry about?"

"The mother passes on Judaism."

Lisa strode back to her mother's cousin. "She converted, and besides, being Jewish is nothing to be ashamed of."

"I know that, but do the Nazis? They've already started

cracking down on Jewish civil servants and college students, and they've curtailed the number of Jews in the medical and legal professions. What's next? You can't risk this. Your mother was right—it's too dangerous."

"I'll make up my own mind."

"I don't know anything else. I wish I could help you more."

"If you wanted to help so much, why didn't you tell me this before?"

"I was in a difficult position. I had to balance my loyalty to your mother with what I thought was the right thing to do."

Lisa took the letters and put them in her bag. "Well, you've no need to worry anymore. The secret's out." She stood up and called Maureen and Hannah.

"You're not staying?" Liesl asked.

"Too much to do. I have to get to the Charité Hospital."

"He transferred to Leipzig years ago."

"Yes, but they'll have records. It's a start."

Liesl stood up from her seat. "This is a bad idea. He rejected your mother, he will reject you. And it's far more dangerous now to be found out as Jewish."

Lisa put her hands on Liesl's shoulder. "Not if I don't tell anyone. This is about me and my life. You'll come down and see us in the city sometime?" She embraced her mother's cousin, knowing it would likely be for the last time.

"Travel doesn't agree with me much these days, but you never know."

Maureen came in carrying Hannah, who had mud splattered all over the hem of her dress.

"I'm sorry you overheard us, and that I didn't have the courage to tell you myself," Liesl said to Lisa.

"I understand," Lisa said.

Liesl embraced the two younger girls and stood at the door as they got into the car. Lisa started the engine and sped down the dirt track toward the highway, never taking the time to look back.

As they arrived in Berlin, Lisa told her, "I need to go to the hospital."

"On a Saturday?"

"Someone there can answer my questions."

"You can leave Hannah and me off at the house. I'll watch her."

"Thank you."

The others weren't home as Lisa dropped Maureen and Hannah off. She'd have to wait to tell her husband the story, and would go to the hospital alone. It was fitting. This was her life and hers to find out who her father was. She planned a dozen different ways to try to sit down with the personnel manager at Charité, but in the end, settled for the truth and the hope that human charity would prevail.

Lisa parked on Luisenstrasse. The old gray visage of the hospital dominated the street as it had for over 100 years, stretching almost the entire block. The only new additions were the Nazi flags fluttering in the wind.

She pushed through a massive black door and into the bustling lobby. Nurses passed, steering patients in wheelchairs, and a young man in an SA uniform sat with a stained handkerchief over his bloody nose. The woman behind the front desk raised an eyebrow when Lisa asked to see someone with access to personnel records. Lisa didn't accept her snub and the woman soon realized she wasn't going to get rid of her. She told Lisa to sit down while she went to call someone.

Ten minutes passed before a small man with fluffy gray hair and thick glasses emerged from behind a white door.

"I am Herr Hoffer. Can I help you, fräulein?"

The man looked old enough to have worked there before she was born. A flame of hope flickered inside her. "I'm looking for someone who used to work here in 1902. Do you have records going back that far?"

"Why do you need this person?"

"He's my father."

Herr Hoffer looked at her for a few seconds before motioning for her to follow him. He led her up a staircase to a small office and bade her sit down at the desk opposite him. A door to the right said HOSPITAL RECORDS on it.

"I've been here twenty years, but the records go back further than that. What can you tell me about this man you're looking for?"

"Not a lot. He was a doctor here in 1902, but transferred to Leipzig soon after. His first name might start with J, but I'm not sure."

"Not a lot to go on."

"He was young, probably in his early thirties."

"Leave this to me. It's going to take some time to access the records from 1902."

"Would it be faster if I helped? I can lift boxes and go through the records. Please? I've been waiting all my life for this."

The old man took off his glasses. Lisa realized that she'd have to use what she had at her disposal—what she always fell back on in moments like this.

"I just don't know what I'll do if I can't find him. I'm so sorry to put you in this position. I know you have a job to do."

It was a challenge to look both pretty and upset simultaneously, but she thought she pulled it off.

"Just a few minutes," Herr Hoffer said. "If we're caught in the records room—"

"How often do other people go in there?"

"Almost never."

"I'd be forever grateful. You're the best chance I have to find my father. I need help."

The older man stood up and shuffled to the door without another word. He turned and motioned for her to follow as he inserted a key from his pocket into the door. He flicked on a light, illuminating the ample space. Three rows of shelves, each full of boxes, stretched from one end of the room to the other. Each stack of shelves had three layers. It was hard to even guess how many boxes were on the shelves. A hundred on each?

"Now, the boxes from the early part of the century are over on the other side."

She followed him along the first shelving unit and around the corner. The thought that she was alone in this enclosed space with a complete stranger appeared in her mind. Hoffer seemed trustworthy and was old enough to be her father himself, so she persevered. She wondered if any man would ever need to have these same thoughts in the same situation.

Hoffer came to an unmarked section and a row of boxes that looked like all the others.

"These boxes contain the records from the early years of the century." He reached in and plucked out the first piece of paper that came to hand. "Ah, yes, an employment record from 1901 for a Horst Meier. He was a janitor in the psychiatric ward."

"Are they organized by year, or by profession?"

"Some might be by year, but finding a random doctor among the hundreds who worked here would be difficult, even if we knew his name."

Lisa felt the walls of the musty old records room close in on her a little. "We can try, can't we?"

"For a while," Hoffer said. "You search these three boxes here, and I'll look through the others." She took the boxes on the bottom shelf and another to sit on.

It took an hour to go through the employment records in the first box. None of the names fit. The few doctors she found were too old, or weren't transferred. She and Hoffer spoke little as they worked.

Another hour passed before the old man spoke. "My shift is ending in half an hour, and my wife is expecting me home."

"Just a few more minutes."

Hoffer nodded and kept on reading. Fifteen minutes later, he stood up. "This might be something." The excitement in his voice was contagious. "A list of new doctors from 1901, some of whom were eligible for transfer."

He held up the piece of paper, and Lisa had to stop herself from grabbing it out of his hand. "What are the names? Any beginning with J?"

"Three. Johann Gutz, Josef Walz, and Jonas Littbarski."

"Do you know any of them?"

"I do. Dr. Littbarski is a surgeon in the pediatric ward."

"Does it say if he was transferred?"

"No record of that, but he likely knew the other men. I'd speak to him, if I were you." He handed Lisa the piece of paper. "You can keep this."

"How can I get an appointment with this man? Can you help me?"

Hoffer nodded. "I'll make a call as soon as we get out of here, and then I'm going home for my dinner, all right?"

"Of course," Lisa said. "Thank you so much."

He led her out of the records room and left her clutching the piece of paper in the lobby. He emerged fifteen minutes later with his coat and hat on and an umbrella tucked under his arm.

"Dr. Littbarski will see you on Monday morning at ten. We have some mutual friends, so he fit you in as a favor."

"Thank you, Herr Hoffer. How can I ever repay you?"

He put a hand on her shoulder. "Find your father. I had one son—I lost him in Flanders in 1916. Nothing is so precious as time. Don't waste any more."

He smiled and she threw her arms around him, hugging

him in the lobby. He tipped his hat as she let him go and strolled out into the evening air.

Seamus was waiting in the living room, listening to the radio, when she got home. Hannah was playing on the floor in front of him. Lisa picked up her daughter and planted a kiss on her husband's lips.

"Maureen told me what happened in Rostock." He switched the radio off and returned to his seat.

"I think we found him. I went to the hospital, and I have a list of three men from that time who were transferred."

She handed him the piece of paper.

"Dr. Josef Walz? I've heard of this man. Several of the families in the factory have seen him in the past. He was the one treating Salnikov's daughter."

"The one who died?"

"Yes. He returned the fees they gave him, and paid for the funeral himself. He works with the unfortunates in society all the time. They say he's a good man."

Lisa took the piece of paper back from her husband and put Hannah back on the floor.

"What about you? Are you all right?" she asked. "You seem stressed."

"Work is difficult. We're struggling to make ends meet, but we'll make it through. I should know more next week."

"Next week should reveal a lot in that case."

"Indeed," Seamus said.

Monday, March 27

Lisa was tired as she bade the nanny and her daughter goodbye that Monday morning. Sleep had not come easily the night before. Her mother's words echoed through her mind over and over. The house was soon quiet. Coffee was all she could manage, as her stomach was a tight, knotty mess. *This was what Mother wanted—at the end, anyway.* She didn't know whether to feel angry or happy or sad. The list of doctors Herr Hoffer gave her was on the table in front of her. She knew every wrinkle on the page, every blotted letter. What if he had his own family and denied his past with Ingrid? Would she ever know the truth?

She went upstairs and readied herself to leave. It seemed fitting to wear her best dress on the day she met her father.

She drove through the city in a daze and pulled up outside the hospital in almost the same spot she parked in two days before. It was only nine thirty, but she couldn't stay away any longer. A gentle drizzle licked the skin on her face as she strode toward the foyer of the pediatric wing of the Charité. A child with a bandage obscuring one half of his face bounded past her up the stairs. His mother called out after him, but he kept on and ran through the doors. He was waiting as Lisa came through. She returned his smile and went to the young nurse behind the desk.

Twenty minutes crawled by before the nurse summoned her to Dr. Littbarski's office. She waited outside in the hall another twenty before the heavy wooden door creaked open. A small man with a thin gray beard and a visible hunch in his back greeted her with a stern countenance. She knew instantly he wasn't her father. He invited her into the office, and she took a seat opposite him.

"What can I do for you?"

"I'm looking for someone who used to work here back in 1902."

"And why are you coming to me?"

She pushed the personnel record across the desk to him. "This was in the records office downstairs. Were you ever transferred to Leipzig?"

"No, but I know these men."

"Still?"

"Well, Dr. Gutz is dead, five years or more, but Dr. Walz? Yes, I know him. He was transferred out of the hospital after we served our residencies here together back in '02. I don't remember why. We kept in touch."

Lisa tried to disguise the fact that her heart was aflame in her chest. She could tell by the look on Dr. Littbarski's face that she wasn't achieving her goal.

"I believe he's still here in Berlin."

"I'm not surprised you've heard of him—he's been lauded many times for his work with the poorer people in our city. He runs a clinic over on Hobrechtstrasse in Reuterkiez, for ten years or more. Why are you looking for Dr. Walz?"

"My mother knew him when they were young. She's ill now, and wants to see him before she dies." It seemed easier to lie. The good doctor might not be so cooperative if he knew she was his friend's long-lost daughter.

Littbarski smiled. "I can call him for you and make an appointment."

"Please."

He picked up the phone on his desk. "Hello? This is Dr. Littbarski over at Charité. Can I speak to the doctor?" He waited a minute or so before he began speaking again. "Josef? I have a young lady here to see you. Are you free this morning? Can you fit her in? Thanks. I'll speak to you soon." He hung up the phone. "He'll see you at 11:45."

"How can I ever thank you?"

"Just tell Josef I said hello, and let your mother know her old friend is a good person. His clinic gives free health care to veterans and the homeless. He's a brilliant man. Here's the address." He handed her the piece of paper.

"I can't tell you how grateful I am."

Lisa shook the doctor's hand and left his office. It was hard to believe this was real. She was sure Dr. Walz was her father, and she would meet him in a little over an hour. Breaking the news would be a delicate matter. She'd have to explain piece by piece. No sense in overwhelming him—she couldn't risk chasing him away after all these years. How much did he know? Did he know Ingrid had her, or realize she was even pregnant?

The rain had begun in earnest, and she had to run to the car to escape it. She checked her makeup in the mirror—it was still good. She started the engine and drove across town, her fingers tingling on the wheel.

The rain stopped as she pulled up on Hobrechtstrasse. *Should I have brought Hannah along? Would Dr. Walz recognize her as his granddaughter?* Her hands were shaking as she locked the car door. It was only 11:05, and the thought occurred to her to sit in the café on the corner while she waited, but she couldn't be anywhere else. It took her two minutes to walk to the health clinic, and she shoved the door open as if she were late for her appointment.

Lisa took off her hat as she approached the counter. The middle-aged nurse looked up at her and directed her to take a seat in the waiting area. Lisa sat beside a man in his sixties, and another wearing a tattered old coat and torn shoes sat across from them. A young mother with three children emerged from the back room. The man in the ragged coat was called back.

The walls were covered in pictures of the doctor meeting important people—the mayor, Vice-Chancellor Papen, President Hindenburg, and a fat man in a Nazi uniform she recognized as Hermann Göring. Lisa got up to stare at each one. Dr. Walz was a tall, clean-shaven, handsome man with short gray hair and a bright smile. He wore the same expression in each photo whether meeting liberal, conservative, or even Nazi dignitaries. Several awards for service to the city's homeless and poor populations hung beside the photographs, including the one he received from President Hindenburg.

It was all too much and she stepped out onto the street to get some air. What if she never saw him? This was her last chance to heed her mother's warning. It only took a few seconds to make up her mind. She wasn't going to run away from her past.

She strode back to the doctor's office. The man in the tattered coat was gone, replaced by a young mother with a baby in her arms. The little boy provided some distraction, and Lisa spent the last few minutes talking to his mother.

The nurse called her name. The vise inside her chest constricted until her heart felt like it would explode. Lisa took a seat, trying to regulate her breathing, wondering what she would say to this man. Was this a moment she'd never forget? Would her entire life change on meeting the doctor?

The door opened and he walked in. He was as tall as Seamus. His sallow complexion was lined around his brown eyes—eyes just like her own. His wedding ring finger was bare, but an indentation was still visible.

"You were sent over by my old friend Dr. Littbarski at Charité?"

It took her a second to clear her dry throat. "Yes. He was very kind."

"He didn't mention what the problem was."

"I saw your awards on the walls outside."

"Yes, for my work with the poor and homeless. I've always made time for those less fortunate in society. I suppose you could say it was my calling."

"I was in the records room at the Charité on Saturday."

"Sounds ominous," the doctor said and took a seat on a stool opposite her.

"Something my mother said led me to search for someone

she once knew a long time ago. I found a list of names at the hospital that mentioned you."

A confused, suspicious look crossed the doctor's face. "I'm not sure what we're discussing here. Do you want me to examine you?"

"I just want to talk."

"I'm a busy man, miss..." He looked at the chart. "Mrs. Ritter. I have other patients to see, so unless you have a medical issue, I'll wish you good day." He stood up.

"My mother's name was Ingrid Geisinger. I think you knew her once."

Dr. Walz's face dropped, and he sat down again. "That's a name I haven't heard for thirty years."

"She was a nurse in Charité with you, wasn't she?"

"Yes." He nodded. "A long time ago. How is she?" His voice was gentle now.

"She died a month ago. Cancer."

"I'm sorry."

"She mentioned something to me on her deathbed, something additional to a conversation I overheard her talking about with a confidant. What was your relationship with her?"

"Your mother was married when we met," he said, huffing and puffing.

"That's not what I asked."

Dr. Walz took Lisa's papers and threw them down on a table before walking to the window. He stared out as he spoke. Silence fell like a curtain. She gave him the time he needed to compose himself.

"I was young, just out of medical school. I was born in Breslau, so I didn't know anyone in the big city. Your mother was a good nurse, a better friend...someone who was there for me when I needed them. I knew her for a time. We became close, but I was transferred to Leipzig a few months later. I made a life for myself in my new home and moved on. You're her daughter?"

"Born in February 1903."

The doctor turned to her. "When?"

"February 23, 1903." Lisa inhaled and pressed on. "My mother was in a state of heavy sedation at the end of her life. The physician told me her personality would disappear under the weight of the morphine he prescribed, and he was right. But she did say some things."

The color was gone from the doctor's face. He sat down opposite her once again. "She mentioned my name?"

"No. I had to go to her cousin's house to see the letters she wrote in 1902 telling her about the young doctor she met and fell in love with."

"I never knew," he said.

"You never knew what?"

"That she was pregnant. I transferred in August, just a few months after we met. She never said a word. Never even wrote."

It was difficult to talk now, but she found the strength to get the words out. "She told me she referred to my father as J. Nothing else, just that one initial. So I looked for young doctors whose names started with J who worked in Charité before I was born. That's how I found you."

Dr. Walz's eyes were dewy, and he was struggling to look at her now. "I married in Leipzig. Angela died in '21, the year before I moved back to the city to set up this place. We never had children of our own."

"Mother never told you she was pregnant?"

He shook his head. "She never told me about you."

She didn't want to cry in front of him. Not the first time they met. What would he think of her? A tear broke down her face. She caught it before it got to the bottom of her cheek.

"I have a daughter," she said and reached into her wallet.

The faded photo of Hannah was over a year old. "She's older now. This was when she was two."

"She's beautiful—just like her mother." He handed back the photograph.

"I have four stepchildren too, with my new husband."

"I'm so very happy for you, Lisa."

"Maybe...you could come over and see them sometime." The tears were uncontrollable, and she stopped trying to hold them back.

"I'd like that," Dr. Walz said. "I think I'd like to do that as soon as you allow me."

14

Tuesday, April 18

T he table was set, and the smell of roast beef wafted from the kitchen. Lisa went to the mirror in the dining room to check her makeup. She, Seamus, and all the children were in their Sunday best for her father's first visit to the house. She'd met him several times briefly, but he was always too busy to come over until tonight. It was a fine spring evening, and the kids amused themselves in the backyard. Michael and Conor were playing soccer with Maureen, while Fiona and Hannah wandered around looking for fairies. Seamus was in the kitchen, a beer in his hand.

"Has that money come through from Cologne?" she asked.

He shook his head in response. "It's going to be another lean month."

"And I thought I was marrying a rich industrialist." She kissed him on the lips. She turned away and opened the oven to check the beef, prodding it with a fork. It was almost done, and the potatoes were nearly boiled. She stood back and faced him.

"We'll be ok," she said and took him by the lapels. "Money's overrated anyway."

"I just didn't think we'd be back in this position. I thought the days of struggling were in the rearview mirror."

"You'll turn things around for us." She kissed him again, and then once more. "Is there anything else you need to tell me? Is it just money?"

"The political situation isn't much of a comfort either, but it's mainly my own bottom line I'm worried about right now."

"You and everyone else. That's why those fat cats gave so much to the Nazis—they're trying to cash in on the new regime."

"I'm not supporting that bigoted rabble."

"Nor would I want you to," she said and kissed him.

Seamus finished his beer and put his glass down on the sideboard. He lit up a cigarette and stared out the window at the children in the backyard.

The doorbell sounded, and Lisa ran to get it. Dr. Walz stood with a smile on his face and a bouquet of carnations in his hand. Lisa took the flowers and hugged him with her other arm.

"Hello, Father."

"Good evening," he said. "Thank you so much for having me over for dinner."

"It's our pleasure. The children are excited to meet you."

"Where are they?"

"Playing in the backyard."

They strolled down the hallway to where Seamus was waiting. Lisa's father greeted him with a firm handshake.

"Josef. Good to see you again."

"And you. Shall we go out and see the children?"

Seamus led him out the back door as Lisa checked on dinner once more. Ten minutes later, she called them all in to sit at the dinner table.

Hannah and Conor were last to enter the dining room, holding hands.

"Hello there," Dr. Walz said to the little girl. She hid behind her stepbrother. "You don't have to speak to me if you're shy. As long as someone will sit beside me."

Conor took the bait and sat in the spare seat. Hannah took her place beside her mother opposite.

Lisa stayed silent for much of the meal, watching the man across the table interact with her husband and children.

Dinner ended, and the children ran out to the backyard once more. Seamus moved around the table, collecting the plates.

"Let me help you with that," her father said and began the job of clearing the remnants of dinner off into the kitchen. Lisa walked in to join them, sitting at the kitchen table as the two men did the dishes.

"Why did you start the clinic?" Seamus asked as Josef handed him a clean plate to dry.

"I worked as a surgeon at the front during the war. It was horrific."

"I can only imagine," Lisa said as she took a sip of wine.

"One thing that struck me, however, was that every man who came in for treatment, whether he was a general or a cadet, received the same level of care. That wasn't true after I came home. Too many people in our society were falling through the cracks. I moved back to Berlin in '22 to start my own practice. I was shocked by the number of homeless on the streets, many of whom served the Kaiser during the war, only to be discarded after. I wanted to do something for them. Everyone is welcome in my clinic, and those who can't afford the best care still receive it."

"How many homeless people do you see?" Seamus asked.

"As many as I can. Our patients are too poor to go anywhere else. I wish I could see more. I raise money from the rich to help cover the costs of their treatment and my research."

The men finished the dishes in minutes, and Lisa, her father, and her husband went out to take their seats in the backyard to watch the children. The daylight was fading to a different hue. The evening air looked gritty and thick, almost like one could reach out and feel it.

Seamus went inside to get brandy, emerging a few seconds later with two glasses. Lisa was happy to stick with wine.

"Have you told Hannah about me yet?" Josef asked.

"I'm working up to it. I thought I'd get used to the idea first."

"I never dreamed of this—that I had a daughter and a grandchild. The last few weeks have been a revelation."

"In more ways than one," Lisa said.

"It's a shame I never met Hannah's biological father."

"Seamus is fifty times the man he ever was," Lisa said and put her hand in her husband's lap.

"Still, the study of genetics fascinates me. I'd have liked to have met him just for that. Have you heard of the new science of eugenics?"

"No," Lisa said. Seamus shook his head.

"It's a system to make the human race better—to eliminate the mistakes of the past."

"What do you mean?" Seamus asked.

"Certain genetic mistakes are passed along from one generation to the next, leading to blindness, or disease, or idiotic traits. Eugenics is the study of ridding society of these miscreant faults."

"How?" Lisa asked.

"By isolating those traits and making sure they aren't passed on from one generation to the next. The idea originated in your country, Seamus. The Rockefeller Institute is the major benefactor for the Kaiser Wilhelm Institute for Anthropology I helped found." He took a sip of his brandy. "It's a science in its infancy, but any way to improve humans as a species fascinates me. Imagine a world without feeble-minded people. How can they be expected to lead productive lives? They're to be pitied."

"Who makes that decision? Who decides whose life is productive, or worthy?" Seamus asked.

"I think you'd agree our society would be improved without sexual degenerates, criminals, and those who suffer from debilitating disease?"

"Wouldn't that be playing God?" Seamus asked.

Dr. Walz laughed. "Isn't that what I do every time I treat a patient who would otherwise die? If we left God to his own devices, the science of medicine wouldn't exist. I can assure you, the study of eugenics is a benevolent movement. It won't harm a single person. It's a way to make us better, more productive, happier human beings for the short time we have to spend on this Earth. I understand your feelings. All new sciences make people nervous."

"I read the Nazis are planning to invest in doctors willing to study the betterment of society as they see it," Lisa said. "What are your thoughts on their policies?"

"Yes, our new overlords, eh? They've certainly left their mark on the city already. Sometimes I ask myself who's making all these flags, and how do I invest in them?"

Lisa laughed, took a sip of wine, and repeated the question.

"Regarding their views on eugenics? They're quite forward-looking in some regards. Hitler's always been interested in the idea of a purer society."

"At the expense of whom?" Seamus asked.

"No one, I hope."

Lisa changed the subject, ready now to talk about the issues plaguing her mind.

"It's strange to think of my mother as a young woman embarking on a passionate love affair."

"She was a bright, strong, beautiful woman. Just like you,"

the doctor said. "Yes, you remind me of your mother in many ways. She was sharp as a tack, in both senses of the word. It's amazing to see her in you."

"Did you want to marry my mother?" Lisa asked.

"It was a difficult situation. My parents never would have approved. They were old-fashioned Prussian nobility—bigoted and unaccepting."

"Because Ingrid was poor?" Seamus asked.

"Yes, but more because she was born a Jew."

"How did they find out?" Lisa asked.

"They had a police detective friend of theirs look into her background when I told them about her." Her father put down his drink.

"She never told us she was Jewish. I only found out after she died. It's scary. I never thought the Nazi rants about the Jews would apply to me, or Hannah. I can't believe she was that ashamed of her heritage that she never told me."

"There's been a lot of unreasonable hatred toward the Jews for a long time now. Ingrid obviously wanted to protect you from it," the doctor said.

Seamus took her hand. "The Nazi hatred toward the Jewish population won't apply to you. You're not a Jew. How can you be Jewish if you never even knew you were?"

"He's right," her father said. "The government won't bother with the likes of you and Hannah, and even if they were to, how would they find out?"

"The same way your parents did—by looking into birth records." She got out of the seat. The men were still talking, but she wasn't listening now. Hannah was hiding alone in a bush and held a finger to her mouth. Conor and Fiona were calling her name, pretending to not see her, and she thought it was hilarious. She waved to her mother, and Lisa huddled in beside her, planting a warm kiss on her smooth cheek before she walked back to where the men were sitting. The question on her lips came out before she reached them.

"Do you believe Jews are genetically inferior?" Lisa asked.

Dr. Walz put down his glass, watching all the kids playing soccer now. Maureen lifted Hannah up to kick the ball past Michael, who flailed as he pretended to be unable to save it.

"Can I have a cigarette?" he asked. Seamus reached for his pack and gave him one. The doctor lit it with a match and stared out at the children again.

"I don't agree with the Nazis' statements on the Jews. I know dozens of brilliant Jewish doctors—men working for the betterment of society every day."

"Einstein renounced his German citizenship a few weeks ago because of the Nazis," Seamus said.

"He's not the type of Jewish doctor I was referring to, but I understand the point. Perhaps the great man was a little too taken with the bright lights of New York, and the funds available for his studies there."

"Or perhaps it was because of the new laws forbidding Jews from teaching and researching in universities, or even being civil servants," Lisa said.

"Such a waste. So many brilliant minds set adrift," her father said. "The new government is far from perfect, but I'd ask you give the National Socialists some time. Hitler's been chancellor less than three months. I've spoken to several representing his government, and believe me, I had my reservations at first. But I was surprised by their intelligence, and passion, to get Germany back on the right track. I think you might be pleasantly surprised in time. I hope to be."

"What about their crackdown on the Communists?" Seamus asked. "One of my workers was snatched out of bed when the Reichstag burned just because he voted for the Communists. Another friend who antagonized Hitler hasn't been seen since."

"Have you been saving up these questions?" her father asked. He finished the cigarette and stubbed it out. "It seems the Communists were trying to launch an insurrection. The Nazis did what they deemed they had to do to counter the threat to the legally appointed government. I'm sure mistakes were made, and I hope your friend gets out soon. The Nazis are a passionate bunch, and their obsession with bettering Germany can border on the fanatical at times. I think they have the best interests of the Fatherland at heart."

"I just hope Hitler's obsessive hatred of the Jews doesn't come back to bite us," Lisa said.

"I'm sure it won't, but in the meantime, we keep your mother's heritage to ourselves. We mention this to no one. Agreed?" her father asked.

"Yes," Lisa said.

"That seems prudent in this climate," Seamus added.

Maureen broke away from the game and came running over. She pulled up a chair and sat down.

"You have quite the left foot," Seamus said.

"Thanks. I thought it was just for standing on before today, but turns out I was wrong."

"We enjoyed the game," Dr. Walz said. "It's such a treat for me to find I have a family. I can't tell you how much."

"Ask him," Lisa said.

"I've always wanted to become a doctor," Maureen said.

"Have you now?" Lisa's father asked.

"Ever since she was a little girl."

"More and more women are training as doctors these days," Dr. Walz said. "I'd be delighted to help you in any way I can. How about you come in and shadow me for a day when you're not in school? I'm in the clinic all afternoon on Saturdays."

"That would be incredible," she said. "What do you think, Father?"

"Is it appropriate to have her in your office? What about the homeless men coming in?"

"Rest assured they want the same things you and I do—to be cared for. They don't start trouble. I think it would be an invaluable opportunity for the young lady."

"Come on, Father," Maureen said.

"All right. Saturday, it is."

His words brought a bright smile to his daughter's face. "Thank you," she said.

They sat watching the kids play until night descended, and Lisa's father made his excuses and got up to leave. He promised he'd be back to visit in a few days and left the last word for Maureen. "I'll see you on Saturday."

Lisa walked him to the door.

"Thank you so much for having me over," the doctor said. "I hope I didn't scare you off with all the talk of eugenics and purity. You know I don't mean you."

"No, of course not." She leaned in to hug him for the first time. She felt his arms around her and leaned her head against his shoulder. It was hard to break away. He was smiling as he drew back.

"Good night," he said.

She watched him walk to his car, holding her hand up to wave as he drove away.

Wednesday, April 19

Bruno woke up alone, his eyelids stuck together. The pain hit him in seconds, and he raised his hand to his throbbing head. The curtains were half open, and the bright light of morning gushed inside. His throat felt like he'd ingested a handful of sand, and he reached to get water from the nightstand beside his bed, finding only a drained bottle of whiskey with cigarette butts floating at the bottom. He was still in his clothes from the night before and had his shoes on also. They were scuffed and in need of cleaning.

Every part of his body ached. Thirst forced him off the bed and to shuffle through the mess of clothes and trash. He found a jug of water on the table by the window and let the liquid slide down his throat. He wiped his mouth and grunted, realizing he was still drunk from last night. *Where am I? Who was I out with?*

Memories of a bar and some other homeless men he knew flashed through his mind, but not as anything solid. Feeling something in the pocket of his pants, he fished out a casino chip for one Reichsmark. The essence of being in the casino, of playing roulette, appeared and disappeared in his consciousness. He didn't chase the memories. He knew he lost.

Sitting down, he took off his shoes and massaged his feet. The blisters had faded, but the calluses from almost fifteen years on the street remained. The thought to see how much he lost the night before emerged from the mire of his mind. He searched the room for cigarettes first and found an unopened pack underneath a two-week-old newspaper. He lit a cigarette, taking a few seconds to inhale the smoke before he went to the chest of drawers against the wall. He opened the sock drawer and reached inside. It took him a few seconds to count the money he pulled out. A flash of panic hit him, and he counted it again. *How can I only have 1,000 Reichsmarks left? What did I spend all that money on? In a month?* It didn't seem possible.

A fit of rage came across him like a dark cloak, and he threw the money at the wall. He collapsed onto his haunches, his hands over his face. A dozen or more empty whiskey bottles littered the hotel room. The maids hadn't been in for days. The clothes and magazines he bought were strewn all over the floor.

At this rate, he'd be back on the street in a week or two. He needed more money, and knew where to get it.

The mirror painted a sorry picture, and he ran himself a bath. Once he was clean, he had a shave. Feeling almost human again, opened the closet. The one new suit he hadn't worn yet hung beside his old army overcoat.

"Cowards," he said, referring to the November criminals—the politicians who surrendered to the Allies in 1918, the Nazis mentioned so often in their speeches. "Traitors."

Five minutes later, he was dressed in the new suit and looked like a different man. Inside, he was the same.

The lobby of the hotel was busy. Several men in suits stood at the front desk, arguing in French. It was funny to hear that frog language here in Berlin. Times had changed since the war.

He reached the bottom of the stairs and was stepping toward the front door when he heard the voice of the hotel manager, Herr Koeberlin, calling from behind. Bruno swiveled around to see the manager standing in front of him. He was a large man in his mid-fifties, with a massive bushy mustache.

"Herr Kurth, may I have a word?"

He had no choice but to stand and listen. "Yes."

"This is a respectable establishment, and we pride ourselves on certain standards. Given that our guests are different types of people, from all manner of backgrounds, we are flexible in the behaviors that we will tolerate, but you, sir, have stretched our patience to breaking point."

"I paid in advance."

"This isn't about money. This is about the standards we expect of our guests, and of the image we wish to portray as an organization. The night porter saw you vomiting in the lobby last night after four in the morning. The evening before, we almost had to call the police when you got into a fight with one of our other guests in the hotel bar."

Bruno didn't remember getting back last night, but the guy

in the hotel bar had it coming. "I'm a guest here like anyone else. I've paid my money—"

"Only until the end of this week," Koeberlin said. "After that time, you'll be asked to check out of your room and not return."

"I understand," Bruno said.

"Good day, sir," the manager said. He turned and walked away.

He wanted to say something clever or memorable, but the chance was gone. His hungover brain was mush, anyway. The thought to go after him crossed his mind, to remind him that he and other brave men had fought for this country. He had seen and done things that men like that fat manager could never even imagine. Who were these people to criticize him? *They should be on their knees thanking me every day.* The manager was at the front desk. Bruno went to him.

"I never drank before I joined the army. Barely ever touched a drop, but when I got home, it was the only thing that dulled the nightmares."

Koeberlin took a second to answer. "This isn't about your service to the Reich, or the cause of your behavior. My concern is the image of our hotel you're portraying in front of the other guests."

"Your concern is covering your own hide, just like the November criminals who sold us out back in 1918." Bruno balled his fist but kept it by his side.

The manager didn't back down and stared back at him. "You have four more nights booked. Do you wish to take your leave right now, or will you calm down and see your time out?"

Bruno swallowed the words on the tip of his tongue and walked away.

The sun was high in the early afternoon sky. Hunger forced him to the café down the road. He wolfed down the sandwich they served him and was back on the street in less than ten minutes.

He walked for a while, denying to himself where he was going until he saw the newsstand in front of him. Willi looked up at Bruno with a smile. No one else greeted him like this.

"What are you doing back in the old neighborhood? I thought you'd be hobnobbing it with the rich and famous."

"You're still working here?"

"Gotta earn a living," the kid said.

"What did you do with the money?"

"Gave it to my parents. They paid off their debts, and we'll be eating good for months. They didn't ask where I got it— knew better. What about you?"

"I invested some. I've been looking into buying a farmhouse in Tauche, where I'm from." *If only that were true.* "But I decided to stay in the city."

"You looking for a job?"

"Why do you say that?"

"I just thought that might be your next move."

"Who's going to hire me?" Bruno asked with a laugh. "I've got one arm and a face to scare children."

"How about Ritter Metalworks? Go back there and demand a job. Say you'll blow the lid off everything if he doesn't hire you. Nothing like a steady wage." A customer came to the newsstand. "I gotta go. I'll see you around, Bruno."

"Ok, see you, kid," he said and drifted away.

He hailed a taxi and jumped in the back. The fat hotel manager's words stoked the anger within him, and his entire body was rigid as the cab pulled up outside Ritter Metalworks. He gave the taxi driver exact change and slammed the door behind him. The taxi driver said something, but Bruno wasn't listening and strode toward the factory.

A young secretary greeted him.

"I need to speak to Seamus Ritter," he said.

"Do you have an appointment?"

"Tell him Bruno Kurth is here to see him."

"Herr Ritter is a busy man. You can't just—"

"Tell him I'm here."

The young lady seemed to get the message and climbed the stairs up to Ritter's office. The clanking of the machines and the sparks flying in the dark corners of the factory floor made for an interesting sight as he waited.

The secretary appeared a minute later. "Herr Ritter will see you now, sir." Ritter was standing at the door to his office and extended a handshake. Bruno accepted it and followed him inside.

"I thought you said I'd never see you again," Ritter said as he closed the door. His voice was laced with invective.

"Situations change."

"You gave me your word."

"What's more important, my word or your freedom? Why don't we talk things over?"

Ritter walked back to his desk and Bruno took the seat facing him.

"Why are you here?"

"It's been a tumultuous time since last we met. So much has happened."

"I gave you 5,000 Reichsmarks. Have you blown it all already?"

"How is business? It seems like the factory is running like clockwork. The money must be tumbling in."

"For some. What is it that you want? I don't have any more money to give."

"Can I get a drink?"

"No. You gave me your word of honor. You told me I'd never have to see you again."

"I want a job."

"You want a job? Here?"

"Yes. Nowhere else's going to take me on with one arm and a face like this. I'm not asking for more money, just a second chance. But if you don't hire me, I might have to go to Milch and ask him for a job."

Ritter's face changed as Bruno mentioned Milch.

"Here's what we'll do," Ritter said. "You come here and work for me on a trial basis. We have need of an apprentice metal polisher."

"I'm not working for pfennigs—"

"You won't be. I'll arrange it so you receive the same wage as the man training you. It's the best I can do."

Bruno turned to peer down at the factory floor once more. What would it be to be part of something again? He was a valued member of a squad once. "Tell me more."

"You could be part of what we're building here, and be an important man again. Start over. Don't blow all your money on booze. Build a life."

Bruno pictured himself on the factory floor, earning a good wage. He'd never have a problem with the boss. What price self-respect?

"When do I start?" he asked.

"Monday morning at seven thirty. And no special treatment. I won't look at you any differently than any other worker here. No better, no worse."

Bruno walked back to the desk and sat down. "So, what do I sign?"

15

Saturday, April 22

Maureen tried to contain the churn of excitement and nerves inside as her father dropped her off at Dr. Walz's clinic. It was just before nine in the morning, and the first patients would be in soon.

"The longest journey begins with one small step."

She turned to him and nodded. "Let me go alone."

"Good—you don't need me. Go and take the first step."

She opened the door and got out. "Good luck," he said.

"Thanks."

He drove away, leaving her alone. The office wasn't open yet, and she had to knock on the door. A nurse in her late thirties with curly black hair answered it with a yawn.

"I'm Maureen Ritter."

"Oh, yes," the nurse said. "Come right in. Dr. Walz is expecting you."

The door to the back office was open. The doctor was going through some paperwork, but stood up as soon as he saw her.

"Maureen!" he said with an excited smile. "It's great to have you here. Are you ready for your first day?"

"I feel like I've been building to this for years. I'm ready."

"You won't need to do much, just observe. The doctor's life isn't an easy one, but the sense of gratification makes up for a lot. You need to be a certain type of person—focused on other people's welfare more than your own. It goes against many of our selfish human instincts."

"I think I'm that person."

"That's what we're here to find out."

The nurse introduced herself as Hilda and helped Maureen get ready. A few minutes later, the first patients started to drift in. She stood in the background as Dr. Walz welcomed a mother and her four-year-old son into the back office. The doctor introduced her as a medical student. The child's mother ceded her permission for Maureen to observe, and the doctor proceeded. It took him a matter of a minute to diagnose the young boy with whooping cough. He advised plenty of rest and fluids, and a trip to the country for some clean air. The mother shook her head at that. Neither she nor the boy had ever been out of the city.

Dr. Walz took Maureen aside after they left. "Even though the treatment here is often free, we're not able to help everyone. Living in squalor, or working in dirty, dusty conditions with air full of toxins, kills more people than all the diseases combined. I can only do so much."

"That must be frustrating."

"It's the world we live in. Perhaps medical science can improve it someday. I'm working toward that goal in my research."

"This next man, in his early forties, is one of the homeless I see. Like many of them, he's a veteran of the Great War. As you can imagine, they come with many ailments, some dating back to their time in trenches."

The man walked in wearing an army issue coat and torn pants. He was a mess. It was hard to believe he was only a few years older than her father. His skin was rough and worn, his eyes were bloodshot, and his breath reeked like the bottom of an empty whiskey bottle.

"How are you feeling today?" the doctor asked. "Are you ready for your medicine?"

The man nodded and took off his coat. Dr. Walz turned around and reached for a small bottle. Maureen couldn't make out the handwriting on the outside. He used it to fill a syringe. The homeless man rolled up his sleeve and the physician gave him the shot.

"I'm feeling better lately," the man said. "Calmer, but I've been having shooting pains in my chest."

"Let's try and figure out why." Dr. Walz took out a stethoscope to listen to the man's heart and lungs.

"Are you going to lay off drinking?"

The man didn't answer. Maureen felt uncomfortable looking at him.

"I don't have the money to pay you."

"No need," Dr. Walz said. "We're just happy to see you."

The branch was thick enough to take his weight, and Michael shimmied along it to peer down at his fellow scouts below. He was directly above Artur and Jacob's heads, and could hear them talking. Sports and outdoor activities had always come easily to him.

"Where is he?" Artur asked.

"You don't think I'd just go and find him if I knew?" Jacob replied.

The two boys shuffled on. It was difficult to resist the temptation of dropping something on their heads, but that would have given away his position. Being the American, the foreigner, was fun at first, and he enjoyed the talk of Babe Ruth and hot dogs, but it grew tiresome. It was time to earn their respect as a scout and show them he was more than just the cultural stereotype built up in their minds. He stayed still, barely breathing, as the boys passed. More came searching a few minutes later, with a similar level of success. He crawled back along the branch and rested against the thick trunk of the oak with a satisfied smile on his face. It was a long way down, but heights had never scared him, and climbing trees had always come easily. An hour passed. It wasn't until he heard Phillip, the scout leader, calling out that he knew it was time to come down and make himself seen.

He slid down the tree trunk, coming down on the forest floor with almost no noise. Artur and Jacob were twenty feet in front, making as much noise as two elephants trudging through the forest. He grabbed them from behind, shouting in their ears.

"What are you doing?" Artur asked.

Michael was red-faced, crying with laughter.

"You think that's funny? We've been searching for you for two hours," Jacob said.

"Looks like I won the game of hide and seek."

"Phillip wants us back at camp," Artur said. "He has an important announcement to make."

"That's why I came out of my hiding place. I could have stayed there until I was old and gray before you two found me."

"Where were you, anyway?"

Michael stood back and pointed up the tree. The two boys shook their heads and laughed before starting back toward the camp where they were to spend the night.

Phillip, the scout leader, a thin man in his late twenties, ran out to them as he saw them approaching. "Where were you?" he asked Michael.

"I thought the point was to hide somewhere you couldn't find me."

The scout leader took a second to study him before grabbing him by the shoulder. "Come on. We have some special guests."

Three men in brown uniforms with swastika armbands stood facing the thirty scouts. Michael recognized one of them —it was the Hitler Youth leader who pulled him out of the fight in the park a few weeks before. Michael and the other two boys took their places at the back. "What are the Nazis doing here?" Michael whispered. Neither of his two friends answered.

One of the men with the Nazi armbands cleared his throat and began to speak. "Good evening, young German patriots. I am Rottenführer Ulrich Prokop of the Hitler Youth. Earlier this month, upon the direction of our Führer, all youth organizations in the Fatherland were incorporated into the Hitler Youth umbrella. Raise your hand if you are fourteen or older."

About half the boys—Michael, Artur, and Jacob among them—raised their hands.

"You fine young men will be incorporated into the Hitler Youth. The others will train toward joining the older boys when your time comes." Ulrich motioned toward Phillip. "Rest assured, you'll still participate in the same fun outdoor activities, but from this point, we'll focus on learning about the history of our great nation and how we can prepare for the future. Make no mistake, the destiny of the Reich is in your hands. The Führer understands this better than anyone. Training you to become better citizens and servants of the Reich is his obsession. Your new uniforms will be ready in the next few weeks. As you can imagine, getting uniforms for millions of new recruits at once has been a difficult task."

Ulrich smiled at the two young men standing beside him, who nodded in agreement. "You will learn to march in step and sing songs recognizing Germany's greatness, all the while making friends and enjoying nature. Who is excited?"

Most of the boys cheered. Michael and his friends stayed silent. Phillip helped the three new leaders organize the boys into lines, and they were taught to march. It was fun. Some of the boys swung their arms as they went, goose-stepping like the soldiers they saw at the Nazi rallies in the city. Michael almost laughed, but knew this wasn't the time or place.

Ulrich brought the group to a dirt track that ringed the woods and had them march along. He called out the words of their first marching song, and they repeated them back as one. It didn't seem right not to join in. It all felt strange, but Michael wanted to be one of the group, not a pariah.

Raise the flag! The ranks tightly closed!
The SA marches with a calm, steady step.
Comrades shot by the Red Front and reactionaries
March in spirit within our ranks.
Clear the streets for the brown battalions,
Clear the streets for the Storm Troopers!
Millions are looking upon the swastika full of hope,
The day of freedom and of bread dawns!
For the last time, the call to arms is sounded!
For the fight, we all stand prepared!
Already Hitler's banners fly over all streets.
The time of bondage will last but a little while now!

It seemed a ridiculous song, and Michael couldn't understand all of the words, but he called out with the other boys, marching in step.

An hour of marching and more singing ended with lunchtime. The boys sat down and cooked sausages and beans over the campfires.

"What do you think our parents will make of all this?" Michael asked between bites. Artur and Jacob were sitting with him.

"Mine won't care—they love Hitler. I think my mother would rather be married to him than my father," Artur said.

The three boys laughed.

"I don't think my parents will be too happy, but what choice do we have?" Jacob said. "It's either stay with the group, or leave. I don't want to sit at home while all my friends are out here having all the fun."

"I don't either. My father's no fan of the Nazis, but what harm can all this do?" Michael asked.

"Exactly," Artur said before finishing the rest of his food.

"Lunchtime's over," Phillip said. "We have a special treat for this afternoon."

The boys lined up, some wiping the remnants of beans off their faces. Emil, one of the other new leaders, held up a bow and arrow. "Ever use one of these?"

A few boys raised their hands. Emil pointed to a tree ten paces away, drew back the string, and let the arrow fly. It struck the tree trunk with a harsh *thunk*. Bark broke off and fell to the ground. He spent the next few minutes going through techniques before setting up targets at the end of the campsite for the boys to have a go.

Michael was one of the last to try, but first to hit the target. The instructors clapped him on the back.

"Where are you from, kid?"

"Charlottenburg, sir," he said, trying to conceal his American accent. The question of his nationality would only muddy the waters with these people.

"Was that a fluke, rich boy?"

Michael drew back the bow and hit the target again. Phillip gave a proud, knowing look at the Hitler Youth leaders, who were chuckling to each other. The next boy stepped up and missed the mark. Michael sauntered back to where his friends were standing. Rainer Fay, who towered over the younger boys in the group and wore a heavy stubble on his face despite being only sixteen, glared at him.

"Lucky shot, Yank," Rainer said.

Michael did his best to ignore him, but when he glanced back ten seconds later, the older boy was still staring at him.

The remaining scouts took their turn with the bow and arrow. Three hit the target, but none repeated the feat as Michael had.

The Hitler Youth leaders gathered the boys. One of them had a large sack in his hand. Ulrich was the one to speak once more.

"We will practice with the bows and arrows until you learn to master them. We will be perfecting all manner of new skills, and playing new games to hone them. You will find yourselves growing stronger, more focused, and better able to serve the Fatherland, which has provided for you all your lives. In that vein, we will be playing war games this afternoon."

The leader beside him opened the sack. It was full of red and blue armbands. "Werner will be handing out different colors. If you receive a red one you are part of that team, same with the blue. Your job is to hunt down the members of the other team and rip off their brassards. The team with the last remaining armbands will be declared the winner."

Werner walked the lines of boys, handing each a brassard. Michael was assigned to the red team, while Artur and Jacob were both on the blue team. They stood up to divide into two separate squads. Rainer shifted his sleeve up his thick bicep, standing almost a head taller than most of the boys. His group moved away. The leaders stood back, observing.

"We have to organize ourselves," Michael said. Walter Brandt, who had just turned fourteen but looked at least two years younger, stood beside him. Michael put his hand on the smaller boy's shoulder. "You stick with me."

"Thanks," Walter said.

The twenty boys of the blue team had already disappeared into the woods.

"Here's what we'll do," Michael said. His group seemed to consist of the younger, punier boys. Winning with this lot was going to be a challenge. "We'll split up." Several of the boys groaned. "No, hear me out. We take them in a pincer movement. I read about it in one of my war comics a few weeks ago. If we take them from both sides, they won't be able to escape."

"They're bigger than us," Walter said.

"But we're smarter."

They stood in a circle going over the plan for another few minutes. Michael and Walter volunteered to venture into the woods to locate the blue team. Walter was small but quick and quiet through the undergrowth. They soon found the main force of the blue team in an opening in the forest. They seemed to be waiting for the others to come at them. Michael guessed they were counting on their superior physical strength to pull them through. Artur and Jacob were milling around in the center. Rainer was laughing with a few of his friends.

The two scouts made their way back to where the other boys were waiting and split up. Each group took a wide berth to where the blue team was waiting. As ordered, each boy on Michael's team hid in silence to wait for the signal. Michael called out, and the red team burst out of the undergrowth, attacking in pairs. One boy held the blue team member while the other ripped off his armband. Michael and Walter ran for Jacob, who laughed as the smallest member of the group ripped off his armband.

Michael's tactics worked well for the first few seconds, but the blue team's greater size and strength soon overtook them, and most of the red squad fled back through the woods. About eight blue team members chased the ten or eleven remaining red team members. Michael got separated from Walter and noticed him running from Rainer. The two boys disappeared through the undergrowth. Michael pushed Jacob off.

"Got you already," he said before rushing after Walter.

Rainer leaped onto the younger boy's back like a lion bringing down an antelope. Walter fell, and Rainer jumped on top of him, unleashing a storm of punches. Twenty paces back, Michael screamed. The bigger boy turned just as Michael jumped on him. Walter lay on the forest floor, his face beaten and bloody.

"What are you doing?" Michael shouted, but Rainer didn't answer, just threw another fist at him. It caught Michael in the chin, knocking him to the forest floor. Rainer tried to hit him again, but Michael jumped to his feet and caught the bigger boy with a left hook to the side of his head. Then he charged at him, unleashing several hard hits to his stomach. Rainer caught him with an uppercut before he hit back with a right hook.

Michael's face felt like it was on fire. Rainer's nose was bloody and his lip had burst open. Walter was still on the ground, crying. Rainer grabbed Michael, twisting him around so he had him in a headlock. Michael felt the breath leave his body. He elbowed the bigger boy, but the grip tightened.

"All right, that's enough," came a voice from behind them. "Let him go." Ulrich was standing there with his arms folded. "I think we've seen enough for today."

Rainer let go, and Michael's lungs filled with air once more. He went to Walter and picked him up off the floor. The little boy cried in his arms.

"What did you do?" Michael screamed. "He's half your size!"

"Let's get back to camp," Ulrich said. "We'll talk this over later." He put his hand on Rainer's shoulder and led him away.

Michael and Walter followed them back a few minutes later.

It took Walter an hour to stop crying after Phillip patched

him up with some bandages. Michael, Artur, and Jacob sat with him for dinner, though the little boy barely said a word.

Night fell, and Ulrich called Michael and Rainer aside. The light of a massive bonfire danced in the Hitler Youth leader's eyes as he spoke.

"I want you two boys to clear the air."

"With him?" Michael asked. "Did you see what this thug did to Walter?"

"He's weak. If he's not able to stand up for himself, he shouldn't be out here," Rainer said.

"Listen. All these boys, all of us here, are one community, bound by our nationality and our blood."

"The Yank's not even German," Rainer said.

"He's got German blood running through his veins, don't you?"

"Yes, I do!" Michael nodded.

"Our Führer Adolf Hitler wants to change the world, but he needs our help. Our faith in him is our strength. If we stand behind him and his ideals as one, we can defeat anyone. We're not here to chase each other around the woods. We're here to better ourselves. We're here for unity—for community and strength. You understand that, don't you?"

The two boys nodded.

"I'm not saying we never have to fight. Sometimes we do, and blood will flow. But together and against the enemy, not each other. Then we can achieve anything. Don't fool yourselves. Our enemies are lurking out there, plotting to derail the new Germany our dear Führer is working so hard to build. Our enemies are everywhere. In our towns, in our schools, and even in our own families. The only way we can fight them is to stick together. Do you understand that?"

"Yes, Rottenführer, sir," Rainer said.

"What about Walter?" Michael asked. "Is he going to stop picking on him?"

"I was only trying to toughen him up."

"Not against each other, remember? Save your energies for the fight that's coming, because, believe me, boys, it's closer than you think," Rottenführer Prokop said.

Monday, April 24

Dr. Walz nodded at the doorman and proceeded up the steps to the Kaiser's Club on Schadowstrasse. Streetlights illuminated the outside of the building, which was unchanged in more than 150 years. The legend was that no woman had set foot in here in more than 100 years, and the last one that tried was promptly shown the door.

"Dr. Walz," the doorman said.

"Hello, Völler," Walz replied as he continued through the thick wooden door. Pictures of kings hung on the walls—Wilhelm I, Friedrich III, and, of course, Wilhelm II, who was forced to abdicate after the mess of the Great War. A photo of Wilhelm II inside the club a few years before, sat beside an ornate mirror on the wall. He took a second to look at it before continuing on.

Walz strolled past the billiard room and up the stairs. Being here was a distraction, but a necessary one. He intended to keep his time in the club as short as possible, as he had pressing work back at the clinic. The death of the young Russian girl a few weeks before was unfortunate, but perhaps it was just the dose he gave her. Her death might lead to a better life for millions, which was a worthy demise for a feeble-minded young girl with little future ahead of her. The parents would never understand, of course, but that was to be expected. Paying for the child's funeral expenses was the least he could do. In his work, mistakes were bound to happen. Changing the world wasn't easy. The Nazis knew that, and so did the men in this building.

Walz pushed through the carved wooden doors into the smoking room, where ten or so men sat in leather armchairs smoking cigars and drinking brandy or schnapps. Dr. Walz nodded greetings to a few men before spotting a raised hand beckoning him. Two men dressed in tuxedos stood from their armchairs to greet him, drinks in hand and cigars hanging from their mouths. Walz knew one of them, but the other was a stranger.

"Dr. Josef Walz," Otto Milch said with a smile on his face. "I'd like to introduce you to Gustav Krupp."

The doctor recognized Krupp as soon as Milch introduced him. The man was in the papers often enough that most would have.

"It's a pleasure, sir," Dr. Walz said. He shook both men's hands and sat down. A waiter arrived within a few seconds. The doctor ordered a whiskey, Milch ordered another brandy.

"My friend, Otto, told me about some of the valuable work you're doing," Krupp said.

"Yes. I'm fascinated by the idea of preventing disease before it has the chance to gestate within the body and corrupt the cells around it."

"And how do you go about doing this?"

"It's a complex science we're only just beginning to gain an understanding of, but much of it is to do with breeding and the eradication of unworthy traits being passed down to the next generation."

"Seems like common sense to me." Krupp puffed on his cigar. "That's what separates the upper classes from the homeless that plague our streets, and the criminals who'd shoot us for the contents of our wallets."

"I'm working toward the betterment of our society."

The waiter came back with the drinks and placed them on

the table. *These conversations with rich men are always so awkward. It's humiliating to have to sell myself at this stage in my career.*

He longed for the day when the government would formally recognize his work and he'd no longer have to come to this place, cup in hand. He sat with the two rich old men for another hour discussing the chances of eradicating not just disease, but crime and malevolence in society through controlling the gene pool. The clock on the wall struck ten and Krupp rose from his seat.

"It's time I got home. It was good to meet you, Doctor," he said. "Be sure to give me a call if you need anything in your quest to better the human race."

Dr. Walz stood up and shook the man's hand again. There would be no check for his research tonight, but he was confident that next time they met, the industrialist would reach into his deep pockets.

"You have some more time to talk?" Milch asked as Walz sat back down.

"Of course."

"Gustav is a valuable contact to have—just the kind of man who can bring research like yours to the attentions of the highest echelons of society. Perhaps even Herr Hitler himself."

"I'd imagine so."

"Was there another reason you asked to meet me tonight, other than to tug on the purse strings once more?" Milch asked with a wry grin.

Taken aback by the old industrialist's comments, the doctor finished his drink and put the glass back on the table before speaking.

"I have some information you might be interested in."

"Do you? That would make for a pleasant change. I'm as much for the betterment of society as the next man, but we businessmen are a selfish breed at heart—always wondering what's in it for us."

"I have a new intern in my office."

"So?"

Walz knew he had to be prudent in how he presented this. The matter of his paternity was private. If the upper echelons of society Krupp referred to knew he had a half-breed Jewish daughter and granddaughter, his funding could be in jeopardy.

"Her father is the American you mentioned in passing last time we met—Seamus Ritter."

"Is that right?" Milch asked.

"Yes, and I've gotten to know the family."

"How?"

"I saw some of his factory workers and met him from there. The young girl is interested in becoming a doctor."

"A female doctor? She should be at home learning how to cook." He picked up his cigar from the ashtray and lit it again. Clouds of pungent brown smoke filled the air between them. "But this could be useful. Do you think you could get into the factory? See how things run in there?"

"For what purpose?"

"I'm trying to buy the man out. I want to give him a fair price. Some inside information might help me, and then I'd likely be even more generous with your funding next time."

The doctor didn't respond. This was such a coarse business, and he didn't like the idea of interfering in Seamus's business, but looking around a little? What harm could it do?

"I'll arrange a visit to the factory," Dr. Walz said.

"Excellent," Milch said. "I'll have my people deliver a check to the clinic later this week."

16

Tuesday, April 25

T he ashtray was full, and Seamus tipped it out into the trash can before stubbing his cigarette out. The man in Cologne wasn't returning his calls, and Seamus picked up the phone again. The operator seemed insulted by his tone and he had to apologize before she put him through. The phone rang a few times before a voice came on the other end.

"This is Amon Goldberg,"

"Herr Goldberg," Seamus said. "I've been trying to get a hold of you for a week."

"Yes. I do apologize."

"I'm following up on the order you placed with us last year. It's due for payment. When can I expect the check?"

"I meant to speak to you about that. Unfortunately, we're going to have to defer payment for a while."

"What?" Seamus had to stop himself from shouting. "For how long?"

"It could be six months."

He almost dropped the receiver. The money he was depending on wasn't coming for six months.

"This is most irregular, Herr Goldberg—"

"I must apologize. We're dealing with a severe shortfall in funds this quarter. Your uncle was always understanding of such circumstances in the past."

Seamus remembered his uncle telling him of the same circumstances back in '30. A dark veil seemed to fall across Seamus's vision. They spoke another few minutes until he realized it was no use. The bonus he was counting on wasn't coming until the end of the summer. He was going to have to find another way to pay the pawn on the necklace. He hung up the phone and pushed it off his desk onto the floor.

He stood and went to the window. It took him a few seconds to pick Kurth out on the factory floor. The factory's newest employee was watching two other men work the sheet metal press. Seamus cursed him under his breath and returned to his desk. He picked up a folder and started leafing through pages of orders. *Where is the money going to come from?*

A knock roused him from his thoughts. Andrei Salnikov came in and closed the door behind him.

"Do you have a minute, boss?"

"Of course, Andrei. What's on your mind?"

Salnikov's face was healed now, but for the rest of his life, a scar above his right eye would remind him of the night the SA snatched him from his bed. The pain of losing his daughter would never heal.

"I wanted to talk to you about the new man, Bruno Kurth. Isn't he a little old to bring on as an apprentice?"

"He needs a second chance, Andrei. I think we can all empathize with that."

"Of course. But he came to work drunk this morning," Salnikov said in his Russian accent.

Seamus threw down the papers in his hand and cursed out

loud. How was he going to defend this man in front of the other workers, or Helga?

"I'll talk to him."

Salnikov's facial expression did little to disguise his displeasure, but his words were different. "Whatever you say, boss. I'll let him know you want to see him at the end of the day."

"No need. I'll find him myself."

Salnikov didn't move. "There's something else," he said. He took an envelope out of his pocket and placed it on the desk. "I'm sorry it took so long. This is the first payment. The money you gave me for Maria's treatment, and what you used to pay off the SA. It's 1,000 Reichsmarks. I'll get you the rest as soon as I can, but it might be a few months."

"Oh, no, Andrei. No need. Please keep it. You've been through enough, and the costs of the funeral for your daughter..."

"Doctor Walz returned me the cost of her treatment, and paid for the funeral himself. As I told you, he's a good man."

In another place and time, he still might have turned the money down, told the Russian to keep it and get his family out of Berlin. But that place and time wasn't here and now.

He reached across and took the envelope.

"I wanted to thank you again," Salnikov said. "I'm forever in your debt."

"I made a promise to my uncle before he died, and I intend to keep it."

"We all know you're a man of your word."

The Russian shook his hand before leaving.

Seamus waited until he was gone to inspect the contents of the envelope. It was all there—1,000 Reichsmarks. It wasn't his responsibility to figure out where Salnikov had come up with it in a month, as he knew what the man made. He went to the coat rack by the door and slipped the envelope into his jacket pocket. He took it on his arm as he made his way down the stairs.

Kurth was standing a few yards away. The other workers were expecting him to speak to him.

"Kurth," he called out.

Seamus motioned for him to come over. Kurth sauntered over with a ridiculous smile on his face.

"I heard you were drunk when you came into work this morning," Seamus said under his breath when he was sure no one else could hear. "How do you think that makes me look?"

"I was out celebrating last night."

"This is your second day on the job. I won't stand for this."

"I'm here to learn the trade. I won't do it again. Perish the thought of making you look bad."

"Don't make me come looking for you again."

Seamus walked away, not knowing how he could effectively threaten this man. The car his uncle left him was parked outside. Climbing in, he started the engine. Questioning himself had become a part of his daily life, and he did it again. Was what he was about to do the only way to keep his word to Uncle Helmut, the man who gave him all this? What was more important—his word to a dead man or the wrath of his wife and children?

He started the car and drove to Wedding. The brakes whined as he pulled up outside the pawn shop on Kameruner Strasse. This was a place he knew now. He was here last month to pay the interest on the pawn—400 Reichsmarks.

The shop was empty. The manager glanced up at him from behind the counter.

"You're early," he said. "The money for the pawn isn't due until next week."

"I want to pay off the loan."

The man looked disappointed as Seamus gave him the envelope.

"You're short. Almost 1,400 short."

"Come with me," Seamus said, leaving the money on the counter."

The pawn shop manager gave him a sideways look before apparently deciding he could trust him. Seamus led him to the sidewalk outside the shop.

"How much for the car? Fourteen hundred Reichsmarks?"

The pawn shop manager took a few minutes to inspect the American-built Ford his uncle had imported before agreeing.

The two men walked back into the store. Seamus handed over the keys and took the necklace in return. He said goodbye to the pawnshop manager, who knew the necklace was far more valuable than ten Ford Model A's.

Seamus didn't look at the car, just kept on until he came to the tram stop, where he found enough coins in his pocket for the fare. The surge of freedom he expected didn't come. It seemed like he swapped one cage for another.

It took over an hour to get back to the factory. Helga was at the door as he arrived.

"Where have you been? I wanted to see to you about the new man," she said.

"Can we talk later? It's been a tough day."

Seamus didn't wait for an answer and ran upstairs to the safety of his office. Sitting behind his desk, he reached into the bottom drawer for the bottle of whiskey he kept for business meetings.

"What on earth am I going to tell Lisa and Maureen?" he asked out loud as he poured a couple of fingers into a glass. The burn of harsh liquor felt good, and he settled back into his chair, staring out into space.

Helga came in later that afternoon to complain about Kurth. All her points were valid, and Seamus conceded every one of them. It was true—he didn't seem interested in the job, and he smelled of booze. He asked that she give him a couple of weeks to find his way. She agreed, with more than a little reluctance. His cousin stormed out of the room without saying goodbye.

Seamus stayed in the office until everyone else was gone. The sun was low in the spring sky as he emerged into the yard outside the factory. A pair of pliers served to break the lock on an old bike that had been chained to a pole outside since he first came here. He wiped down the saddle, oiled the chain, pumped up the tires, and cycled home.

Lisa and the kids were in the living room listening to the radio as he arrived. Conor ran to him, wrapping his arms around his body, and Seamus put his hands on his head. Lisa stood and kissed him on the lips. The others barely looked up from the magazines they were reading.

"Is Hannah in bed?"

"For over an hour," Lisa answered. "How was your day?"

"Exhausting," he said.

It was hard to know how to bring up the fact that the car was gone. Should he wait until someone noticed?

"I saved you some dinner," she said.

It was then he remembered that he hadn't eaten since breakfast. Lisa took him by the hand and brought him into the kitchen. The food was still warm in the oven, and she placed it down on the table.

"How are you today?" he asked.

"I'm taking life little by little. My father called at lunchtime. He wants to come over and see your office this week."

"Great," he said with all the enthusiasm he could muster. He forked a piece of chicken into his mouth and began to chew.

"What's wrong?" she asked, taking a seat opposite him.

It took him a few seconds to answer. "Something happened. I had to cover some short-term costs." He looked at his food as he spoke. "I had to use the balance in our personal account... and sell the car."

"You did what?" Lisa said.

"I had to sell the car."

Maureen came into the kitchen. "Father, where's the Ford?" she asked. "I wanted to take it out."

Seamus closed his eyes for a few seconds before repeating what he said to his wife. "I'm sorry. I'll make it up to you," he added.

"Does Helga know about this?" Lisa said.

"You'll wake Hannah," he said.

"I'd say that's about the least of our concerns right now," Lisa said.

"You did it again," Maureen said. Tears rolled down her face. "You haven't changed."

"I did what I had to do," he said.

"Oh, Seamus. Why didn't you tell me we were in trouble?"

"Your mother is barely in the ground. I didn't want to burden you any further."

"What are we going to live on? How are we going to eat, and pay the bills?" Maureen asked.

"We'll get through. We have money due in a few weeks. I thought I could cover it with the Cologne contract."

"You always have an excuse, don't you?" Maureen asked. "I thought you'd changed. I can't believe what an idiot I've been."

Lisa was crying now too. "I'm your wife. Let me decide what I can or can't handle."

Seamus shook his head and stood up. "I'm sorry. It won't happen again."

"What does Helga know about this? I spoke to her yesterday. She said things in the factory were difficult, but she never mentioned this."

"The Cologne contract didn't come through."

"So you had to sell the car?" Maureen asked. The other children appeared in the doorway behind her.

"I had no choice. I didn't plan any of this," he said. "Please don't tell Helga. She doesn't know about what happened."

"But she's your partner. You shouldn't have to bear the liability for the debts alone." Lisa said.

"That's the way it worked out. It's temporary. None of this is going to matter in a couple of months."

"That's what you say every time. I can't believe I trusted you!" Maureen stormed out.

"Are we going to lose the house?" Fiona asked.

"No, the house is perfectly fine," he said. "We'll get through this, just like we always do."

"Maureen..." Lisa hurried after her stepdaughter. Conor, Fiona, and Michael stood in silence, staring at him in shock.

"We'll buy a new car soon. I promise you."

"Ok, Father," Michael said.

Seamus excused himself and went upstairs to their bedroom. Lisa was next door with Maureen. He took the painting of the royal palace off the wall and opened the safe. The necklace was beautiful in the light. He slipped it back into the safe and closed it up.

17

Wednesday, April 26

Seamus rose from an empty bed. Lisa was with the children, getting them ready for school. He got dressed in his best suit and went downstairs. Conor was playing with Hannah in the living room as he passed through. The little boy ran to him and hugged his legs.

"Have a great day in school today, kid," Seamus said and patted him on the head.

Lisa glanced up at him with a tepid smile before returning to the dishes.

"You remember my father's coming in to see the factory today, don't you?"

"Yes."

"Good morning," Michael and Fiona said in almost perfect unison.

Maureen didn't look up from the magazine she was reading. Her breakfast was crumbs on her plate now. The coffee cup in front of her was empty.

"Good morning, Maureen, my love," he said.

She raised her eyes from the article she was reading. "Good morning. I have to get ready for school." She got up and left with the other children.

Seamus shook his head and went to his wife at the sink, wrapping his arms around her.

"My hands are wet," she said.

He nuzzled into her, inhaling the aroma of her hair. "Everything's going to be all right, isn't it?"

"Of course, it is. Where is this coming from?"

"When are you going to forgive me?"

She drew her hands out of the kitchen sink, dried them off, and turned around to face him. "When are you going to tell me the truth?" He remained silent. "I spoke to Helga last night. I didn't tell her about the car or our savings. She said you were a good manager, and that you were loyal to the workers—to a fault sometimes. What's going on?"

"You had so much to deal with when your mother was dying. I couldn't add to that."

"She's gone now. You need to tell me."

It was time. He couldn't hide from his wife forever. "The man from the basement on Würzburger Strasse found me," he said under his breath.

"What? The homeless man in the army jacket?"

"Yes."

Lisa's legs seemed to give way beneath her and she flopped into a kitchen chair. The sounds of the children getting ready for school bled through from the living room.

"Is he going to the police?"

"No. He tracked me down at the chamber of commerce dinner and then at the factory. He wanted the reward Milch was offering."

"Five thousand Reichsmarks?"

"That's where the money problems came from. I cashed out our savings and pawned a necklace Uncle Helmut left us. I paid him off and he gave me his word, but he came back again."

"For more money?"

"No, for a job in the factory. He wanted to get off the streets, and nowhere else would hire him."

"You didn't take him on, did you?"

"What other choice did I have?"

Lisa brought her hands up to her face. "I thought this nightmare was over."

"And that's why I didn't tell you."

"I can't believe you brought him in to work for you."

"I wanted to keep him under my control—not have him running around blabbing all over the city." He kneeled down beside her and put a hand on her shoulder, but received a swift rebuke as she shrugged him off.

"Things in the factory have been difficult. One of our competitors is undercutting us, trying to poach our client list so he can buy us out."

"But then we'll get nothing," Lisa said.

"And I'd be betraying my uncle's will."

"Are you going to lose the factory?"

"We're working on it every day. Even Helga is helping out."

"But she stands to gain everything if you sell now."

"She respects her father's wishes. She won't sell it out from under me."

"Are you sure about that?"

A tiny voice came from the doorway. "We're going to school now," Fiona said.

"Let's talk more about his later," Seamus said.

Lisa nodded and got off her chair. Seamus followed her out to the foyer, where all the kids had bags on their backs. Michael was already outside on his bike.

Seamus said goodbye to each of the children before putting an arm on Maureen's shoulder. "Can we talk for a moment?"

"I've got to get to school."

"I'll tell the teacher something came up if you're a few minutes late. I'll send a letter."

"Fine," she said.

Seamus picked up his briefcase and kissed Lisa on the mouth. She was numb, and it was like putting his lips on a statue.

Maureen waited for him while he got his bike. They ambled down the driveway to the road as the other kids disappeared into the distance.

It seemed impossible to begin.

"I want you to know how sorry I am, about everything— about leaving you with Maeve, and being a terrible father. I'm sorry I dragged you here,"

"I like the city," she said. "And we have a beautiful house."

"Thank you for saying that, but I know how angry you've been with me, and you were right to be. I can't defend what I've done other than to say everything I did was for the family."

"Selling the car? Leaving us broke when Helga said it wasn't necessary?"

"My cousin has no idea what's going on in our lives."

"Do you?"

They reached the end of the street and turned the corner onto another tree-lined street. People were emerging from the mansions on each side. Some were businessmen on the way to work, others children on their way to school.

"I never told Lisa what was going on either. I wanted to protect her, just like I wanted to protect you."

"Just like you did on the train from Hamburg, when the SA thugs attacked us."

"I'm so sorry I ever let that happen. I should have been there for you and the other children. I take full responsibility and ask for your forgiveness."

"I thought you'd changed, Father. I was starting to believe in you again...until you came home on that beaten up old bike and told us we were broke."

Seamus had no idea what to say or do. Once said, words could never be taken back, and Maureen was only seventeen. Could he trust her with everything? The temptation to tell her, to trust her with everything, was tearing him up inside. Would it finally fix their relationship and exonerate him in her eyes? Surely that would be worth anything? Yes, anything, but it would burden her with the weight of what he went through these last few months. She deserved to live her life free of the mess he'd fallen into. And no matter how good sharing the burden with his seventeen-year-old would have felt, he knew it was his to shoulder alone.

Seamus reached into his pocket for his pack of cigarettes before thinking better of it and putting them back.

"Someone told me once it's easier for a father to have children than for children to have a real father," he said.

"I'd say they were right."

"I want to be the father you deserve."

They stood aside to let several nuns in full regalia pass them. Seamus waited thirty seconds to begin again.

"Things have been difficult at work."

"Is that why you've been so stressed these last few weeks?"

"That, and Ingrid's death."

"It's been a hard time for all of us."

"I'm sorry for everything that's happened, sweetheart. I never meant to drag you into the mess we created. Seeing Ingrid die like that, and hearing what she said about Lisa's father, must have been difficult for you."

"It was, but I'm glad Lisa has her father now."

"You and I are the same in many ways."

"Don't tell anyone," she said after a few seconds.

"I'm proud of you."

He wanted her to say she understood what he was going

through in the factory, or even that she was proud of him too, but she didn't. They walked on.

"I'd better get to school. I might not be too late if I get going now."

"Ok," he said, his voice barely audible.

Maureen got on her bike. He stood and watched her, frozen in the moment. This was where he usually wished her a good day, but none of that seemed fitting.

His daughter went ahead a few paces before stopping. She turned to him. "Father?"

"Yes?"

"Good luck in work today."

Seamus nodded his head and his daughter pedaled away. Perhaps they would never make up the way he wanted, but it would be worth it to let her live the rich, free life she deserved. His own selfish feelings weren't important.

It took him a few minutes and a cigarette to compose himself enough to cycle to work. Once he was ready, he got on his bike and was there in twenty minutes.

Taking a handkerchief from his pocket, he wiped sweat off his brow. Georg Kaltenbrunner and Max Waldhausen greeted him as he locked his bike up along with dozens of others. The two men were outside having a smoke.

"What happened to the car, boss?" Max asked.

"I thought that with the weather getting a little better, I'd leave it at home. I could use the exercise too," Seamus said, patting his belly. It was a little after nine.

"How's the new man doing today?" Max and Georg, who were helping to train Kurth, looked at each other.

"He's not here," Georg said. "No sign of him."

Seamus tried to pass the news off as if it didn't worry him, and accepted it as he would any other conversation. "All right, then, get inside once break time's over and I'll see you men later." His two employees wished him a good day.

Andrei Salnikov came to him as he strode inside.

"I know, Andrei," Seamus said. "I heard he's not here again." Salnikov shrugged his shoulders.

Seamus knew what he had to do. Any other new employee would have been fired for less. *How will he react? I don't have any more money to give.*

Seamus went upstairs to talk to Bernheim, but found a note on his desk instead. He was out of the office for a few hours. He put the paper back and left.

Helga stood at the top of the stairs. A Nazi Party pin shone from her lapel.

"What's that?" Seamus asked. His words seemed to catch her off guard.

"I'm a member of the party. It's my right to display my loyalty."

"Not in here it isn't. I've told you before—this place should be apolitical."

"Everywhere and everything is political these days. We're in the midst of a revolution. You can get on board or resist, but let me assure you, the National Socialists are here to stay."

Seamus pushed past her, but she followed him into his office.

"Your man isn't here again today," she said. "If you don't dismiss him the next time he shows his sorry face in here, I will."

Seamus searched his mind for some kind of excuse, but couldn't find one.

"I understand your perspective."

"I hope you do. This factory seems to be going down the toilet. We'll be dead soon at this rate."

"We'll get through it."

"You'd better hope we do."

Helga left his office, and he slumped down in the seat behind his desk.

He sat back up and pored through the paperwork on his desk. *How much longer can the factory sustain itself? Three weeks? Four at the outside?* The prospect of laying off his uncle's workers sickened him. No one was hiring. They'd have nothing, and Otto Milch would get exactly what he wanted.

Seamus threw the papers down on the table before the sound of his door opening caused him to raise his head. Bernheim thundered through the door with an ill-disguised smile spreading across his face.

"What are you so happy about?" Seamus asked.

The manager walked to his desk. "This," he said and slapped a check down on top of the papers Seamus just threw.

He picked it up. "Forty thousand Reichsmarks?! Where—"

"I met up with Amon Goldberg this morning, of the Cologne City Council. He's soon to step down. The Nazis forced his hand with their new law preventing Jews from working in the civil service. He decided to give us a down payment on our delivery as his last act in office."

"They said they couldn't pay for six months, at least. How did you get this?"

"Amon Goldberg is a good man who appreciates what we're trying to build, and who our workforce is."

"Why didn't you tell me?"

"I didn't know. He called me yesterday to tell me he was in the city, but not why he wanted to meet."

"This is enough to pay our bills for months."

"Enough to see us through to winter, when the other monies will come in."

Seamus held the check in front of him. "This is life."

He stood up and embraced Bernheim. The two men couldn't help laughing as they drew back. Seamus ran to Helga's office with the check in his hand.

His cousin looked up from the papers on her desk.

"Excellent," she said with no emotion in her voice.

Seamus closed the door and went back to Bernheim to celebrate with a drink.

Three hours passed before a knock came. It was his secretary. "Dr. Walz is here to see you, Herr Ritter."

"Thank you, Martina. Show him right in."

Lisa's father entered, dressed in a smart gray suit. He offered a bone-crunching handshake before Seamus took his hat and hung it up for him.

"Thank you for letting me come in today. I've had a fascination with what goes on in factories like this since I was a child. It's a treat to be here. I often try to do interesting things like this on the days the clinic is closed."

"My pleasure, Dr. Walz."

"I think it's about time you started calling me Josef."

"All right, Josef. How about a seat and a drink?"

"Yes to both."

A minute later, they were sipping fine whiskey.

"It's good to get a chance to spend some time alone with you," Dr. Walz said. "The last few weeks have been a whirlwind, but I couldn't be happier. To have Lisa and Hannah, and all the rest of the family, has been the most wonderful thing I ever could have imagined."

"To Lisa and Hannah," Seamus said, offering his glass for a toast.

"And to Maureen, Michael, Fiona, Conor, and of course, your good self." Dr. Walz clinked his glass with Seamus's.

"We're a package deal," Seamus said and took a sip of his drink.

"If I'd known Lisa existed... We've wasted half a lifetime."

"Half is not the whole, and you have the rest of your life left. You've found each other. Nothing else matters."

"Yes. I like that."

Seamus took his father-in-law on a tour of the factory.

Several of the workers recognized him from his work with the underprivileged and shook his hand. Salnikov went to him.

"Again, I'm so sorry about your daughter," the doctor said.

"You did everything you could for her—I know that much."

"That I did."

Helga was on her best behavior, and the spat seemed to be over for now. The doctor's visit was a pleasant distraction. He seemed fascinated by the workings of the machines and remarked several times how much he was enjoying himself. A few men on the floor asked him about aches and pains, and one about an ugly ulcer below his armpit. Dr. Walz took each question with good grace, but advised that each person make an appointment to see him so he could examine them more thoroughly.

The two men climbed the stairs to Seamus's office once the tour was done. They lit up cigarettes and lounged at the desk. Talk of lunch would soon follow.

"What was Ingrid like as a young woman?" Seamus asked. "Do you see her in Lisa?"

Dr. Walz laughed and stubbed out his cigarette. "I see more of my mother in her, but Ingrid was beautiful, just like Lisa is today. She was stubborn and self-righteous."

"Sounds familiar."

"But she was intriguing—like no other woman I ever met. She had a sadness about her I found irresistible. I'm confident I would have asked her to be my wife had she not already been married."

"Was that why you chose to transfer to Leipzig?"

"It was complicated. We talked about her getting a divorce, but my parents didn't approve."

"Because she was married?"

"That and her...background. I think I could have persuaded them about the divorce, but they were so old fashioned. Bigoted, one might say."

A hammering sound on the door interrupted the doctor, and Helga stuck her head through.

"Seamus, the man we were talking about earlier has arrived."

It was almost two o'clock. Seamus got up from his seat. Kurth was on the factory floor, shouting and flailing his arms around—drunk.

"Helga, could you take our guest into your office for a few minutes? I'll deal with this."

"Dr. Walz, would you be so kind as to accompany me into my office?"

"Of course," he said.

Seamus ran to the door and down the stairs. Kurth was at his station with Salnikov.

"Bruno, follow me up to my office," Seamus said.

"Yes, sir, my American overlord." He gave the Hitler salute and clicked his heels together.

He was slurring his words, and the stench of stale liquor was almost overpowering. The new suit he was wearing was torn and ragged, and his expensive shoes were scuffed and muddy. Kurth followed him up the stairs to his office. The eyes of every man and woman in the factory were stuck to them like limpets.

"Sit down," Seamus said.

Kurth slumped in the seat with a ridiculous grin on his face. His eyes were bloodshot, almost entirely red.

"What can I do for you?" he asked and reached into his pocket for a crumpled pack of cigarettes.

Seamus reached across and swiped the cigarette out of his hand.

"You can start by getting the hell out of my office, and never darkening my doorstep again."

Bruno's eyes narrowed. "You can't fire me."

"Oh, you're wrong. I can, and I am firing you. Get out of here."

"Don't forget what I saw you and your wife doing. One word from me and her neck will be on the executioner's stump."

"No one will believe you. I offered you an opportunity to change your life and be part of something, but you threw it back in my face."

"You won't fire me. You don't have the guts."

Seamus stood up. "Our business is concluded. Get out of my office."

Kurth ran for the door and stood at the top of the stairs down to the factory floor. "Seamus Ritter is a murderer!"

Seamus grabbed the war veteran, but he slid from his grasp and stumbled down the steps to the factory floor. "Murderer! I saw him with my own eyes," he shouted.

Helga was on the landing outside her office, looking down. Dr. Walz was beside her.

Salnikov ran at Kurth, felling him with a right hook to the jaw, and the homeless man went down like a severed tree trunk. Seamus was beside him in seconds.

"Who is this man?" asked the doctor.

"I tried to give him a job, and he started spouting slanderous lies when I fired him," Seamus said.

"He's clearly delusional. Bring him to my car," Dr. Walz said. "I'll take him back to the clinic and give him the care he needs."

Bruno was semiconscious and muttered something about murder as the men carried him out of the factory to the doctor's car.

Seamus went with them and watched as they put him on the backseat.

"I'll deal with this," Dr. Walz said. He put a hand on Seamus's shoulder. "Don't worry about a thing. I'll take care of him."

"Thanks. I don't know what we would have done without you."

Dr. Walz got into his car and waved before driving away.

"I can't believe that just happened," Seamus said to Salnikov and the other men who were still standing with him.

"Let's get back to work," Salnikov said. "And don't worry, Herr Ritter. No one believes that idiot's lies. We all know what kind of man you are. Don't we?"

The four other men nodded and patted Seamus on the shoulder, then went back inside and got to work.

Helga was standing at the top of the stairs as Seamus ascended to his office. She gave him a long stare before disappearing into her own without a word.

The man in the back of his car came to. Walz looked at the him in the rearview mirror. Kurth was huffing and puffing, trying to right himself. It was apparent he was still intoxicated.

"Where are you taking me?"

"To the clinic," Dr. Walz answered. "Don't worry. I'm going to give you the care you need."

Kurth seemed to be in pain from where one of Seamus's men had punched him in the jaw.

"I'll get you some painkillers for that once we arrive."

"Take me back to the factory," he slurred. "I'm not finished with that murderer. He owes me."

"What does he owe you?"

"I kept my mouth shut. I could have gone to the police. Ritter and that wife of his would be in jail right now, or awaiting the executioner, if it weren't for me."

"Quiet down. We'll be at my surgery soon."

The man leaned forward. "You've got to believe me, Doctor. I saw them carrying a body down the stairs the night Ernst

Milch went missing. It took me months to clean up enough to realize it, but it's clear as day now."

"What on earth are you talking about?"

"I was in the basement looking for somewhere to sleep when they came down the stairs carrying a rug stained with blood. In the same building Milch went missing from."

The doctor remembered reading about the Milch case in the newspapers. The story was all the more interesting because of who the man's father was.

"I'm telling the truth. Take me to the police station, Dr. Walz. They wouldn't listen to me before, but they won't turn me away now. Not dressed like this and especially not with you by my side. That killer doesn't get to fire me. I'll have my revenge."

"I'd appreciate it if you kept your slanderous statements to a minimum."

"She killed him."

The way to deal with a man in a hysterical state was to ignore him, not give oxygen to the fire burning in him. Dr. Walz made sure his tone was calm and clear.

"Stop this. We'll talk more once we reach my office. I'll take you straight in for treatment."

The man ranted and raved all the way back. Dr. Walz did his best to block him out, but visions of what the man said he saw on that night in November haunted him. His hands grew tighter on the steering wheel with every word the man spewed, and he was gritting his teeth in anger as he pulled up outside the clinic.

"Get out," the doctor said as he held the car door open for Kurth.

"I need to go to the police."

"After your treatment, I promise. I'll take you myself."

The homeless man nodded in agreement and seemed to calm down.

The clinic was closed. Once a month, Dr. Walz gave the staff the day off in the middle of the week and didn't see patients. It gave him some time to be alone and to work on his research in peace.

He slipped the key into the door and led Kurth inside. "No need to wait today," he said and brought him back to the surgery.

Kurth sat down. "I'm feeling better now."

"Let me treat you, and I'll bring you to the police station to report this heinous crime. You mentioned the police wouldn't see you before?"

"When I was homeless and in rags. But I'm a different man now."

"Were you telling the truth about Herr Ritter in the factory? Don't lie to me—I'll know."

"Every word was truth. I was on Würzburger Strasse the night of November 15, the night Ernst Milch went missing. I was in the basement of his apartment building when I saw Ritter and his girlfriend come down the stairs in the middle of the night carrying a rolled-up rug with red stains on it. They were struggling with the weight."

"What happened then?"

"They paid me off and I left."

"Why didn't you go to the police at the time?"

"I put it out of my mind, since it was nothing to do with me. I saw the reward and used what I saw to get it. I'm a better man now."

"Are you? Tell me about your time in the war. Did you lose many friends?"

Kurth paused a moment before answering. Dr. Walz took the time to prepare a handkerchief he took from the cupboard.

"I lost the best men I ever knew. My brothers."

"Did you ever wonder why you were the one to survive?"

"Every day, Doctor. They were so much better than I am.

They all died. My best friend Charlie, and his brother Gereon, too. I think about them all the time."

"Keep them in your mind now. Take a deep breath. Close your eyes."

The man looked at him, and the doctor repeated himself. Kurth did as he was told.

"Picture your friends as the men they would be today. Do you see them?"

"Yes, I do."

"Picture yourself with them, and you're happy. It's a sunny day and you're by the lake together. Your families are there, your wives and children. The water is calm."

"It's beautiful," Bruno said.

The doctor held the chloroform-soaked handkerchief over the man's mouth.

"Now, breathe in," Dr. Walz said.

Kurth did as he was told, opening his eyes at the last millisecond as if he realized too late what was about to happen.

Dr. Walz laid his unconscious body down on the bench and started setting up the intravenous injection.

"This is a new technology," he said to Kurth, though he knew he couldn't hear. "It sends nutrition or medication to a patient's veins directly. It's useful for those who cannot, or will not—perhaps due to a deranged mental state, such as yours—take their medicine."

The doctor slipped a needle into a vein in Kurth's arm.

"In your case, however, it will be used to deliver a large dose of potassium chloride into your system. Enough to stop your heart."

Dr. Walz reached into the cabinet behind him for a bottle of the deadly compound and poured it into the container that fed the intravenous drip.

"You, sir, have proven yourself unworthy of life. My daughter? My only child—a murderer? Your best purpose is as a test subject so that others such as yourself, who are also unworthy of life, may take their leave of this existence. People like you are no more than a drain on public resources. And the act of slandering my daughter and her husband, in his place of work, no less? Count yourself lucky that I had the mercy to knock you out before I administered the potassium chloride."

The chemicals made their way down the drip and into Kurth's veins.

"This is the way of the future. Imagine a world without the likes of you. No more alcoholism or degeneracy of any kind."

Dr. Walz made the sign of the cross over Bruno's unconscious face and went to use the bathroom. When he came back, the man on the table was dead. Dr. Walz checked his pulse to make sure before going to the telephone at reception. His first call was to the police. His second was to the factory.

Seamus answered. "Josef. What happened with Kurth?"

Dr. Walz cleared his throat before continuing. "I'm afraid it didn't go well. I gave him some chloroform to let him sleep a while, but unfortunately, he suffered a heart attack. I've notified the police already."

"He's dead?"

"Yes, I'm sorry to say. He was a veteran of the Great War. Another of our brave soldiers has fallen."

Lisa's husband was silent on the other end of the line for a few seconds. "Did he say anything before he died?"

"Just more of the same slander he was spreading in the factory. But I wouldn't worry about that. Who's going to believe a man like that over a respectable business owner such as yourself? Today was a tragedy, but at least we won't hear those lies again. They died with him."

"I don't know what to say."

"This is part and parcel of my line of work. I'll deal with it from here. Get on with the rest of your day. Go home and look after my daughter and my grandchild, and I'll see you all in a few days."

"I will. Thank you, Dr. Walz," Seamus said.

The doctor hung up the phone before he hurried back to Kurth's body. He disconnected the intravenous drip and put away the sodium chloride. The coroner wouldn't ask any questions, and certainly wouldn't waste his time performing an autopsy. Walz reached into Bruno's pockets and pulled out a wad of banknotes.

"More than enough for a decent funeral," he said. "You surprise me."

Dr. Walz sat alone, wondering about the credence in what Bruno Kurth told him before he died. What reason did his daughter have to murder Ernst Milch? He dismissed the thought as soon as it entered his mind. Ernst was a blowhard and likely overstepped the mark with her, but it was as well never to know. His relationship with Otto Milch was too important.

There was no way he was going to jeopardize it by getting involved in a scenario where his own daughter had killed Milch's son. Who knew what an investigation might dredge up? His new National Socialist masters wouldn't appreciate Lisa's heritage, and his research was too valuable to risk.

Kurth was dead now. The matter was closed.

Friday, April 28

Lisa felt as if she'd been flushed into a giant whirlpool and spat out again. The one thing she still couldn't work out was why her mother urged her not to find her real father. Why was it too dangerous? She could only reason that she must have carried some bitterness from their breakup, or it was the morphine talking. Either way, her father was a kind, respected man.

The children were outside playing with the neighbors, and Maureen was in the city with her new boyfriend. Seamus came into the kitchen as she was clearing off the table. The remnants of the dinner she wasn't able to eat still sat on her plate.

"How are you?" Seamus asked.

Lisa checked to see if any of the children could hear them. They were all outside on the street. "Confused," she said.

"We'll get through the next few weeks. And the company's going to be fine."

"I'm not worried about money, and I'm glad the check came through. I just wish you came to me to share the burden."

"Your mother was dying."

"I know that, but we're married. We're meant to face our problems together. If we can't tell each other the truth, then what do we have?"

"I was trying to protect you."

"I'm your wife, not your daughter. We need to be united so we can protect them. If I can't trust what's going on under this roof, then I've no chance against the craziness of the world outside."

Seamus tossed the tablecloth in his hand onto the sideboard. "I'm sorry."

Lisa went to him and wrapped her arms around his waist. "I forgive you, you idiot."

He smiled, and she kissed him. "What's going on in the factory?" She let him go.

"Nothing. A few of the staff came to me to say they were glad Kurth was gone, and they didn't believe a word that came out of his mouth."

"What about your cousin?"

"Helga hasn't mentioned it."

"You think she suspects us?"

"I don't know, but even if she does, what can she do? All she heard was the ramblings of a disgruntled employee as he was being thrown out the door. She's not witness to any crime. She can't testify in court."

"She could tell Milch."

"You think she'd actively set out to destroy our family like that? You think that little of her?"

"No. She loves the children too much to do that."

"I'm sure Helga ignored what he said if she heard it at all. We've nothing to worry about from her. She's more concerned about my choice in employees."

Lisa went to the window. The sun was setting, casting down golden sabers of light. Michael was playing soccer with his friends, and Fiona and Hannah were hiding in the bush as Conor pretended to try to find them. Hannah giggled as he walked past calling her name.

Seamus came up from behind her and wrapped his arms around her chest.

"It seems like everything's ok right now, doesn't it?"

"Yes," she said.

"Bruno Kurth is dead, so he won't bother us anymore. We're going to get through this. The specter of Ernst Milch will disappear from our lives."

They were still looking out the window as a car pulled into the driveway. For a brief, terrifying second, Lisa thought it was the police. Then she saw her father in the driver's seat.

The children greeted him before he came to the front door, and Lisa went to get it. "I wasn't expecting you," she said.

"I was in the neighborhood and wanted to see how you were doing. It's been a stressful week."

"I think that's an understatement," Seamus said as he shook her father's hand.

They went inside and sat in the kitchen. Lisa made coffee.

"You want some Irish in that?" Seamus asked.

"Please," her father said.

Seamus plucked a bottle of whiskey from the top shelf of the cabinet and poured a little into each mug.

"What happened with Kurth?" Lisa asked.

"Heart attack brought on by stress. Years of abuse weakened his system. It's a miracle people like him live as long as they do."

"And he died right in front of you?" she asked.

"I've seen it many times. Goes with the job, unfortunately."

The doctor took a sip from his mug. "I presume your workers didn't believe any of that tripe he was screaming as they dragged him out."

"I don't think so. You never can tell, but nothing so far."

"Few things are as fragile as a man's reputation. Hard gained, easily lost. I've had slanderous statements thrown at me in the past, and even some libelous ones. You just have to ride it out. Grab on to the sail and wait until the storm diminishes."

Lisa was curious to know what libelous statements had been published about him in the past, but knew better than to ask.

"Herr Kurth, before he died, was in a paranoid, delusional state, ranting and raving about witnessing the two of you disposing of the body of Ernst Milch."

Lisa's blood ran to ice.

"I have no idea why he was saying that—" Seamus said.

"Why he said it isn't the important part. What's important is that the matter ends here. Is there anyone else who would echo what Kurth said to me?"

Lisa looked at Seamus and paused a few seconds before answering. "Of course not. We don't know what he was talking about. We didn't kill Ernst Milch."

"I didn't ask if you were innocent. I asked if anyone else would come forward."

"No. Why would they?" Seamus asked.

"So, as far as you know, the matter died with Kurth?"

"Yes," Lisa said.

"Good. I'll come into the factory and speak to the workers who heard what Kurth was shouting as he left if you like. I can assert that he was delusional, and bent on revenge against you for firing him."

"I think I'd rather let it rest—not draw any more attention to it," Seamus said. "I have the loyalties of the workers."

"As you wish, but this needs to end here and now."

"There's nothing to end. We have no idea what that man was shouting about," Lisa said.

Her father sat back in his seat and took a generous sip of his Irish coffee. "Then we've nothing to worry about, do we?"

An awkward silence descended on the room. Lisa couldn't help the feeling of unease that was spreading through her body.

Her father reached over and put his hand on hers. "It's over now, Lisa. You can put all this nonsense behind you and get on with your lives."

He smiled and brought the mug to his lips once more.

18

Wednesday, May 10

Maureen's nerves, which had been dormant, flared as the taxi pulled up outside Thomas's parents' house. Her father passed two large umbrellas to the children to counter the rain. Thomas was already waiting at the door, looking so handsome in his suit. His parents joined him. They were no strangers to her, and greeted her with a handshake. Seamus, Lisa, and the rest of the children followed behind them.

Maureen had been to Thomas's parents' rented home before, but this was her parents' first time. It was smaller than the colossal home Helmut left them, but it was neat and delicately furnished. The lack of family portraits, or even photographs, on the wall rendered their past a mystery.

"Welcome," Herr Reus said.

"Come in, come in," Frau Reus said. "Dinner's almost ready."

"Mother's an excellent cook," Thomas said as they walked into the living room.

"Thank you for inviting us to your home," Maureen's father said and introduced himself.

"I'm Joachim Reus," their host said. "And this is my wife, Franka."

The two sets of parents shook hands. Herr Reus was a tall, fit-looking man in his late forties, with a tight brown beard. He wore glasses and spoke with an accent Maureen couldn't place. His wife was perhaps ten years younger, with black curly hair and a pale complexion. Maureen's father was in his best suit, and Lisa wore a beautiful navy dress.

"I'm so pleased to meet you at last," Lisa said and took Frau Reus's hand. "Dinner smells wonderful."

Seamus introduced the children to Thomas's parents.

"Such a beautiful family," Frau Reus said. "Would you like to join us in the garden for a pre-dinner drink?"

"Of course," Seamus answered.

"Dinner will be ready in about ten minutes," Frau Reus said.

Herr Reus and his wife led their guests out to a covered porch, and they sat watching the rain come down outside.

"Thank you so much for visiting us on a school night. I'm sorry I had to rearrange from Friday. My business trip came up at the last moment," Herr Reus said.

"Not a problem at all. What business are you in exactly?"

"Commercial real estate," he said. "Franka is a translator."

"Really?" Lisa asked. "What languages?"

"Polish, Russian, Czech, Slovak, and even a little English."

"Could you teach my wife?" Seamus asked, switching to English.

"She can't speak it?" Frau Reus asked.

"I know you're talking about me," Lisa said.

"She knows enough to know when I'm talking about her," Seamus said in German. "What brought you to Berlin?"

"Business. We're both originally from Königsberg, but moved to Cologne a few years after Thomas was born."

"So, you're from all the way out east. Is that where the Polish and Russian came from?" Seamus asked.

"Yes. I was surrounded by language as I grew up," Frau Reus said.

Maureen sat beside Thomas at the table. The smile on his face implied what she was feeling—this was all going well.

The roast pork and potatoes they had for dinner were delicious, and the conversation remained brisk. The little kids didn't do too much to spoil it. Lisa had the good sense to send them into the drawing room to listen to music on the radio as soon as they finished eating.

Herr Reus proposed a toast after the children were gone. "To new friends, and especially Maureen, who Thomas hasn't stopped talking about these last few weeks."

They raised their wineglasses.

Another hour passed before Lisa announced she had to get Hannah home to bed.

"Can I stay a little while longer?" Maureen asked. "I left my bike here the other day. I can cycle it home."

"It's raining," Lisa said.

"I can drive her," Thomas said.

"All right, then," Maureen's father said. "Be home by eleven."

The conversation continued as the Ritters waited for the taxi. Maureen finished her glass of wine.

"Better lay off that," Seamus said. "It's a school night."

"Of course," Maureen said and put the glass down.

"Thomas, how are you settling in?" Seamus asked.

"I love the city. I've moved around all my life—was never anywhere for more than a year or two. So, I'd like to call it home and go to university here next year."

"What do you want to study?"

"Business," he said. "Maureen and I have discussed going to Humboldt together next year."

"I'm glad to hear it. You like sports?"

"Oh, don't mention his obsession," Maureen said. "He'll talk about football—or soccer, or whatever they call it here—all night long if you let him."

Her father laughed. "I'm no expert on football. My mother taught me the Irish variety when I was a kid."

The three men spent the next twenty minutes discussing the finer points of their favorite sports. Maureen was glad to have Lisa and Frau Reus to talk to.

A knock at the front door interrupted the conversation. It was the taxi, and Seamus and Lisa said their goodbyes.

"It was a real pleasure meeting you," Seamus said as they put on their coats.

"You did well, Father," Maureen whispered.

"I don't know how much of a compliment that is," he said with a smile.

"The whole evening was great," she said.

"I look forward to meeting again soon," Frau Reus said.

"That would be wonderful," Lisa answered. "We'll have you at our home next time." She picked up Hannah and ran out through the rain.

Maureen stayed at the door as her family got into the taxi and waved at Thomas and his parents as it drove off.

She walked back into the house. "Can I help with the dishes?"

"No, you're our guest," Frau Reus said. "I'll tend to them. You go and sit in the living room with Thomas and Joachim."

Maureen agreed and took a seat by the radio. Thomas sat beside her, with his father opposite.

"I'll turn on the radio and let you two be," Herr Reus said.

He flicked on the wireless. The sound of Wagner's *Ride of the Valkyries* filled the air.

"One of my favorites," Herr Reus said. Then the music was cut short by a news flash.

Students of the Reich have risen up in Berlin tonight to reject the un-German spirit that has led to widespread decadence and moral corruption in our nation since the Great War. These young patriots are marching to promote clean, Aryan values and reject the filth pervading our society. Students are marching from Monbijou Palace via Karlstrasse to the seat of the corrupt Weimar government—the Reichstag. From there, they will proceed along Unter den Linden to the university, where Reich Minister for Propaganda Joseph Goebbels will address them.

Herr Reus turned the radio off. No one spoke for a few seconds.

"Book burners," Herr Reus said. "The Nazis have corralled the Brownshirts at the university to represent the student union." He reached into his pocket for a packet of cigarettes.

"This is something we both should see. Will you come and have a look with me?" Thomas asked.

Maureen looked at Herr Reus, expecting him to bar them from going, but he didn't say a word.

"Do you want to do that?" Thomas asked again.

An avalanche of fear slid through her, but she'd never let anything like that stop her before. "I'll go."

"Just be careful. Stay back from the crowds, and keep your mouths shut."

Frau Reus came into the room. Thomas got up and hugged his mother. "You're going in to see the protests?" He nodded. "Just make sure you get this girl home safely."

Maureen thanked her hosts for dinner. They both shook her hand in turn and told her how much they enjoyed meeting her family.

"I'm sure it won't be long until we see you again," Herr Reus said.

Thomas's parents walked them to the door and watched as they pulled out of the driveway.

"My parents are committed to the anti-Nazi cause."

"Were they affiliated with any particular party?"

"No. They flitted around from one to the other, but they recognize the danger Hitler and his cronies pose to our country."

"My father is the same. Lisa was a social democrat when the party still existed."

"They seem happy together."

"They have their ups and downs, like anyone else. Are your parents happy?"

"Their definition of happiness has probably changed over time. They're focused on their goals."

"Where do you fit in?"

"I'm their number one goal."

Maureen expected him to smile or laugh, but he didn't.

They crossed the Weidendammer Bridge on Friedrich-strasse and drove on toward Unter den Linden. Thomas rolled down the windows to let the night air in. The rain had stopped a few minutes before. They heard the procession long before they saw it—the distant blare of brass instruments and the chants of the crowd: *Germany awake! Jew die!*

"Are you sure you want to do this?" Thomas asked. "I can take you home."

"Find a place to park."

They left the car a few blocks from Unter den Linden and joined the stream of people meandering toward the procession. A visible minority were dressed in the brown uniform of the SA. The atmosphere among the people was jovial. It was as if they were going to a public festival. Street merchant stands sold hot drinks, cigarettes, and chocolate. Some peddled trench mirrors, relics from the war used to look over the heads of people in front. Everyone seemed eager not to miss what was about to happen.

They joined the crowd of thousands spilling down the wide avenue of Unter den Linden. A sea of hats, torches, and flags was escorted by mounted police on both sides. Maureen gripped Thomas's hand so hard that it must have hurt, but he didn't say a word. The mass of students and onlookers reached all the way back to the Brandenburg Gate, marching forward toward the Opera House at the other end. Trucks loaded with books rolled up the central promenade, usually reserved for pedestrians. Maureen couldn't make out their titles in the half-light.

They saw what at first appeared to be a human body being carried on a pike in front of them. Second inspection revealed it to be a scarecrow.

"See what the sign around its neck says?" Thomas whispered. "Magnus Hirschfeld, the sex researcher whose offices were ransacked a few days ago."

Maureen stayed silent and kept walking.

They reached the square outside the Opera House where the police and fire brigade were beside a massive pyre. Firemen were pouring gas over a gigantic pile of books, still wet from the rain. A lectern draped in Nazi flags sat behind it. Bright lights from portable generators pierced the darkness, illuminating the faces of the students dressed in SA uniforms that ringed the pyre. Newsreel cameras were in place, ready to capture the scene for posterity. All that was needed now was the spark to light the flame.

Corps of students marched in formation in their SA and SS uniforms. A brass band in the corner provided the rousing music.

"Such a disciplined procession," Thomas said.

"An orderly revolution," Maureen replied.

The crowd opened up and the torchbearers were let

through to the left of where Maureen and Thomas stood. Each threw their torches onto the pyre and, accompanied by a mighty roar from the mob, the books burst into flames with a loud *whoosh*.

Students formed human chains, passing the books along to be thrown into the fire.

"Wait a minute," Maureen said and let go of Thomas's hand. She pushed through the crowd and made her way into one of the chains. A student in SA uniform handed her *Amok* by Stefan Zweig, *The Magic Mountain* by Thomas Mann, and a translation of *Sons and Lovers* by DH Lawrence. She passed them on and watched as the last person tossed them into the fire. Having seen enough, she stepped out of line to rejoin Thomas. The morose look he could no longer hide was in stark contrast to the delight painted across almost everyone else's faces.

The mob moved back as the flames grew hotter. Another gleeful roar erupted as Joseph Goebbels, one of the architects of the night's events, appeared at the lectern. He began to speak, lulling the noise of the crowd to a whisper. He was a pathetic little man with sunken eyes and a hairline pushed back so far it was almost to his ears.

"No to decadence and moral corruption," he shouted. "Yes to decency and morality in family and state. The books burned tonight are intellectual, liberal filth. The era of Jewish intellectualism is now at an end. The future German man will not only be a man of books, he will be a man of character. It is to this end that we want to educate you."

The flickering light of the flames reflected back from the windows of the Opera House and the university assembly hall. Maureen let her gaze drift across the people in the crowd. Shadows danced across their faces, lending them a surreal, ghostly look. Old and young watched with the students in their SA and SS uniforms. Every segment of society seemed represented. The majority watched with glee, cheering the Reich minister's words. She wasn't listening to the speech now, just soaking everything in as if it were a movie in her own mind.

"Let's get out of here," she said to Thomas.

They pushed through the crowd, back down toward the Brandenburg Gate. It was only when they left the crush of people behind that she felt safe to speak her mind.

"I read some of those works burned tonight. Those books have power beyond what the Nazis could ever steal. The words gave me insights I could never gain on my own, and made me see the world in ways I never believed I could."

"Why do you think the Nazis don't want people to see them?"

He retook her hand and they kept on down toward the Brandenburg Gate. It was almost deserted now, and illuminated gold against the dark of the Berlin night.

"It's so beautiful," Maureen said. "A contrast to the grotesque ugliness at the other end of the boulevard."

"There's still so much beauty and wonder in this world, but we have to fight to protect it," Thomas answered.

Maureen clenched his hand. "Yes," she said. "This is only the beginning. The Nazis were right about one thing—everything is changed. Everything except us."

What she saw that night would stay with her always. The pyre inside her heart was ablaze.

The End

The next book in the Lion's Den Series—The Golden Age, is coming in April.

ACKNOWLEDGMENTS

I'm incredibly grateful to my regular crew, my sister, Orla, my brother Brian, my mother, and especially to my brother Conor who went above and beyond. Thanks to my fantastic editors. Massive thanks to my beta readers, Cynthia Sand, Cindy Bonner, AJ Ventresca, Maria Reed, Michelle Schulten, Chelsie Stanford, Nicola Hogan, Frank Callahan, and so many others I don't have space to thank here. And as always, thanks to my beautiful wife, Jill and our three crazy little boys, Robbie, Sam and Jack.

ALSO BY EOIN DEMPSEY

Finding Rebecca

The Bogside Boys

White Rose, Black Forest

Toward the Midnight Sun

The Longest Echo

The Hidden Soldier

The Lion's Den (The Lion's Den Series, Book 1)

Printed in Great Britain
by Amazon